D0041346

NO LONGER PROPERTY OF
SEATTLE PUBLIC LIBRARY

Recent titles by Jack Fredrickson

A Milo Rigg mystery

THE BLACK CAGE *

The Dek Elstrom mysteries

A SAFE PLACE FOR DYING
HONESTLY DEAREST, YOU'RE DEAD
HUNTING SWEETIE ROSE
THE DEAD CALLER FROM CHICAGO
THE CONFESSORS' CLUB *
HIDDEN GRAVES *
TAGGED FOR MURDER *

Other titles

SILENCE THE DEAD *

* *available from Severn House*

THE BLACK CAGE

Jack Fredrickson

Many thanks to Mary Anne Bigane, Eric Frisch, Ted Gregory, and Terry Riley for helping to smooth this story. Special thanks to Sara Porter and Penelope Price for their superb editing of this project.

This first world edition published 2019
in Great Britain and 2020 in the USA by
SEVERN HOUSE PUBLISHERS LTD of
Eardley House, 4 Uxbridge Street, London W8 7SY.
Trade paperback edition first published
in Great Britain and the USA 2020 by
SEVERN HOUSE PUBLISHERS LTD.

Copyright © 2019 by Jack Fredrickson.

All rights reserved including the right of
reproduction in whole or in part in any form.
The right of Jack Fredrickson to be
identified as the author of this work has been
asserted in accordance with the Copyright,
Designs & Patents Act 1988.

British Library Cataloguing in Publication Data
A CIP catalogue record for this title is available from the British Library.

ISBN-13: 978-0-7278-8916-4 (cased)
ISBN-13: 978-1-78029-657-9 (trade paper)
ISBN-13: 978-1-4483-0355-7 (e-book)

This is a work of fiction. Names, characters, places and incidents
are either the product of the author's imagination or are used fictitiously.
Except where actual historical events and characters are being described
for the storyline of this novel, all situations in this publication are
fictitious and any resemblance to actual persons, living or dead,
business establishments, events or locales is purely coincidental.

All Severn House titles are printed on acid-free paper.

Severn House Publishers support the Forest Stewardship Council™ [FSC™],
the leading international forest certification organisation.
All our titles that are printed on FSC certified paper carry the FSC logo.

Typeset by Palimpsest Book Production Ltd.,
Falkirk, Stirlingshire, Scotland.
Printed and bound in Great Britain by
TJ International, Padstow, Cornwall.

ONE

The color had been sucked from everything, not just the dead. The sky, about to drop new snow, had clouded into charcoal, rubbing away the horizon. Both ends of the two-lane country road, narrowed into a ragged ribbon by the jumble of dark official vehicles, had disappeared into the gauze of gray mist rising from the sudden melt, unusual for late January. It was what the melt had revealed.

A mud-spattered red ambulance idled low in the center of the rough stone bridge that crossed the Devil's Creek. Fifty people milled about: cops in blue uniforms and ball caps, others in suits and dark trenches; television cuties in clingy coats and cameramen in cargo jackets and big-pocket pants; and a few print reporters. They crowded the north side of the bridge, kept back by a steel guard rail scraped bare by the bumpers of beer-buzzed teenagers and factory workers drifting home late from the taverns in Joliet. Most looked away, but some kept staring directly down into the ravine, transfixed by the horror.

They lay nude, like contorted marble mannequins, whiter than the melting snow. Beatrice Graves – at fifteen, the oldest – was on her right side, her knees drawn up as though against the cold. Priscilla – three years younger, but already taller – lay on her back, across her sister's head, as if slung to form a rough cross. No obvious signs of trauma were visible.

Milo Rigg made notes of none of it. After a quick glance down into the ravine, he moved back along the edge of the woods. He knew most of the uniforms and the detectives and the reporters, and they knew him. He wasn't there to report. He wasn't supposed to be there at all.

A fat hand shot out to squeeze his upper arm from behind. 'What the hell, Milo, back on the beat?'

Even under the overcast sky, the fake diamond on the man's pinky sparkled cheap – a fraud, like the sheriff's most senior deputy himself. He'd come up like a panther, silent behind the cars parked along the road.

Rigg shrugged himself free. 'Glet,' he said.

The deputy made a show of studying him. 'You've dropped what, twenty pounds?'

It was closer to thirty, the last time he'd owned a scale. And that was months ago, right before he'd given away most of his and Judith's things, hoping to rid what was left of his life of some pain.

'Just clean, honest living, Jerome,' Rigg said, stepping back from the foul cigar that smoldered in the man's other fat hand. 'You need to try it.'

There was need for that. Jerome Glet was pushing sixty. His dirty black trench tugged at the buttons like he'd gained Rigg's thirty lost pounds. The deputy had been heavy before, but now he was a mess, and not just from the weight he'd piled on. New furrows cut into his cheeks, his hair was grayer, and, despite the cutting wind, sweat was beading on his pasty pallor. Glet was dragging demons, too.

'So, what gives, you being here?' Glet said.

'I was in the neighborhood.'

Glet smiled at the lie and gave his cigar a wet suck. 'Still living on some damned dune in Indiana, drifting into town half-time to write non-news, uncredited, for the *Examiner*'s daily suburban stuffer?'

'You can relax, Jerome. I'm not reporting this,' Rigg said, without adding that, soon, he might not be working at all. The *Examiner*'s next round of cost cuts was rumored to include its suburban outpost, known at the Bastion downtown as 'the Pink'.

'You'll always be Milo Rigg, conscience of the unavenged.' Glet's anger still festered, like that of most of the cops milling about this newest discovery site. Most had turned away when Rigg walked up, though a few had given him the acknowledgment of a frown.

Rigg gestured at Joe Lehman, Cook County sheriff, keeping back the throng stomping their feet against the cold, like tethered mules. 'Your boss is not letting them trample the crime scene?'

'Not like last time?' Glet wheezed. 'Live and learn, Milo. Live and learn.'

'What, exactly, is not like last time?'

'This ain't a repeat,' Glet said.

'Naked kids found by water is new?'

'These girls ain't bruised. Not a mark on them. Bobby Stemec and the Hendersons, they were battered.'

'Nice you still remember, Jerome.'

'We're still chasing leads on them, but, for now, I'm seeing only two dead girls. So should you queens.'

Glet was dreaming if he thought the three queens of Chicago's newspaper trade – the *Tribune*, the *Sun-Times* and Rigg's own *Examiner* – wouldn't touch back to the still-unsolved killings of three boys, the October before last. The memory of those murders still grated raw in the minds of every praying parent in Chicagoland. Pressure to solve these two new kid murders, related or not, was going to howl at the county's sheriff's and medical examiner's departments fiercer than the winds icing Lake Michigan.

At the bridge, Sheriff Lehman began waving people back so the two EMTs could lift a gurney over the guard rail to get down the shallow embankment. Lehman made sure to face the television cameras as he did so, every bit a posturing showboat.

'The girls were found *exactly* like that?' Rigg asked, trying to keep his old fury out of the words.

'Up yours,' Glet said, his face flushing with fresh sweat.

Rigg had nicked one of the deputy's big nerves. Fifteen months earlier, a television cameraman had recorded Glet repositioning Bobby Stemec and the two Henderson boys, supposedly for a better look before the sheriff's forensics team arrived. Glet had needed to do no such thing; he was preening for the lens.

The video went viral. All six of Chicago's local television news shows broadcast it later that evening. Hell rained down on Glet and his boss, Lehman, for ruining the crime scene. It was merely the beginning of their bungling.

The ambulance men lifted Priscilla Graves from across her sister's head, set her on her back on the gurney and started up the embankment. Her legs remained frozen together, but her rigid, wide-flung arms began flexing gently up and down from her shoulder joints, as though they were wings and she was attempting to fly away. A young blond man in a camel-colored wool topcoat noticed the grotesque movement. He grabbed a blanket from the ambulance, jumped the rail and held the blanket down to cover the girl's arms as the attendants lifted her over the rail. It helped. Priscilla's arms continued to beat, but less noticeably, as the blond man and the two attendants made their way to the ambulance.

'Johnny-on-the-spot,' Glet said of the young man. After the girl was loaded into the ambulance, Glet gave the young man a wave, motioning for him to come over.

'Milo, have you met Mr Feldott?' Glet asked, a small smile forming around the wet cigar.

In stark contrast to Glet's greasy appearance, Feldott was dressed more for an Ivy League alumni dinner than a death scene. He was slender and no more than five foot eight. Visible beneath his camel overcoat were sharply creased black pinstriped trousers, a spread-collared white shirt and a narrow, bright red necktie that centered the whole ensemble like a flaming exclamation point.

The young man offered up a wide grin and stuck out his hand. 'We've not had the pleasure,' he said.

Rigg shook the hand. He knew of the Cook County assistant medical examiner from several long, laudatory features in the *Examiner*. A product of a working-class suburb and scholarship private schooling, Corky Feldott had attracted notice when those that moved and shook Chicago jammed him down the throat of the hack that ran the county medical examiner's office just days before the Stemec Henderson murders. Rumor was, he was being prepped to ultimately become governor.

'He was lucky,' Glet said, placing a paw on Feldott's shoulder. 'He wasn't here long enough to get slapped around when you were beating on the rest of us during Stemec Henderson.'

Feldott shrugged Glet's hand from his shoulder.

'You'll autopsy today?' Rigg asked.

'Tomorrow, if they thaw,' Feldott said, 'but please don't report that they're frozen. Too gruesome.' He turned then and saw that the EMTs had descended back into the ravine. He hurried to join them.

'Not much younger than you, Milo,' Glet said, 'but so much prettier.'

It was true enough. Rigg was thirty-five, only several years older than the impeccable Corky Feldott, but, since Judith, he felt like he was pushing eighty.

'He'll make sure things are done right?' Rigg asked.

'Bet your ass. All by the book.' Glet reinserted his cigar and headed up the center of the road, decades ahead of, and miles behind, a young medical examiner dressed in better clothes than anyone should wear to a discovery site.

Snow began to fall in big wet flakes, like tiny shrouds descending to cover the horror of what had been found there. The two EMTs knelt down to lift Beatrice, frozen fetal from rigor and cold, on to the gurney. Feldott grabbed the blanket from the ambulance, went down and covered her. Keeping her on her side, for it would be nightmarish to roll her on her back with her knees frozen up in the air, the three men carried her up the ravine to the ambulance and slammed the rear door.

Glet made his way down the embankment and helped the forensics team unfurl a yellow plastic tarp over the site where the bodies had lain. Other cops and sheriff's men came over the guard rail to fan out into the woods and down to the creek, trampling another crime scene. Unlike the Stemec Henderson fiasco, this time the trampling could not be helped. The melt was about to be covered with fresh snow.

It was pointless, Rigg thought. The girls had most likely been tossed nude from an idling car by people who knew not to leave even clothing behind.

He watched for a while more, until the air turned colder and the snow came down harder, brittle and cutting like little daggers. He began to shiver, maybe from the cold, maybe from the mess of the last investigation, most probably from the sight of the two girls who'd just been discovered. And he supposed he shivered from Judith because he always shivered from Judith. He tugged his coat to his chest and headed back to his car.

TWO

It was four o'clock when Rigg got to Elm Grove, a blue-collar suburb two towns west of Chicago. The *Examiner*'s branch office was in a windowless concrete tower above a windowless ten-lane bowling alley, which was itself above a bank on the ground floor, which did have windows but rarely any customers. The building was made of concrete, poured gray in the late 1920s but darkened almost black over the next ninety years by diesel soot from the bus yard next door. Rent for the walk-up, third-floor tower space – formerly a beauty salon until the elevator blew its bearings and was deemed too expensive to fix – was cheap.

The Pink's entire staff, such as it was, was in the preposterously pink-walled and pink-floored newsroom. There were two other reporters, both part-time, kindly women past retirement age who

kept track of bridge scores, weddings and the like; the receptionist
who doubled as the copy editor for the terse paragraphs jammed
online and in print between advertisements, also elderly; and the
supplement's relentlessly smiling advertising salesman, dressed as
always in a conflict of plaids – and they were all huddled in front
of the old television. The discovery at Devil's Creek was being
broadcast on the early evening news.

Harold Benten was not quite among them. The supplement's
editor, 140 emaciated pounds of leathered skin, limp white hair and
rheumy eyes, sat in his usual cloud of cigarette smoke behind the
filmy glass wall that separated him from his small staff. As always,
his office thrummed. Once a place for shampooing and toxic hair
dying, the room now pulsed from an exhaust fan laboring irregularly
on worn bearings, now to rid the air of Benten's carcinogenic cigarette smoke. Nothing could be done about the two black, curved
sinks plumbed into his side wall, but Benten had moved the leaned-
back red vinyl shampoo chairs to the front of his battered, black
metal desk to serve as guest seating. Money had not been spent to
enliven the *Examiner*'s satellite operation.

Benten raised a nicotine-yellowed finger to motion Rigg into
his fog.

For once, the editor's desk was barren of anything except the
cigarette smoldering in the huge, overflowing yellow ashtray that
sat atop a burn-pocked linoleum desk pad advertising a heating-oil
company. Like Benten himself, the desk pad was a throwback to
the time when most people needed heating oil, desk pads and newspapers. Benten's empty desktop signaled he'd lost his appetite for
work, likely sitting, smoking and staring at nothing since word came
that the Graves girls had been found cast off a bridge. He carried
the demons of the unsolved Stemec Henderson murders, too.

'Dumped nude, like the boys?' Benten asked, not pretending to
wonder why Rigg had showed up for work on a Monday, a day
early, or where he'd been.

'In a ravine next to a dribble called Devil's Creek, if you can
believe the name.' Rigg sat on the front edge of one of the red
shampoo chairs, careful not to set the tired chairback into an almost
inescapable full recline.

'Younger across the head of the older, forming a cross?' Benten
spoke in a tense staccato, clipping his words as if each one cost
him a dollar he didn't have.

'Like it was somehow satanic?' Rigg shook his head. 'I think they just got pitched that way.'

Benten lit a Camel, oblivious to the smoke curling from the one already burning in the ashtray. 'Trauma?'

'Glet said there were no obvious signs,' Rigg said.

'Glet? What the hell? Glet was there?'

'It's Lehman's jurisdiction, and Glet's his most senior man.'

'Glet's a pig. Not only was he front and center on the Stemec Henderson botch, he's got that assault pay-off.'

Rather than risk trial, Cook County had paid out 900,000 dollars to a seventeen-year-old girl who'd claimed Glet sexually assaulted her during questioning for drug possession.

'Alleged assault,' Rigg said. The girl's family had dropped the matter once they'd received the payout.

'Glet's a pig,' Benten said again. 'He shouldn't have been there.'

'Besides Glet, the other same clowns were there, too, except for McGarry. He sent the new kid, Feldott.'

'CIB,' Benten said, of Feldott's mentors. The Citizens' Investigation Bureau, a supposedly advisory-only group, had been formed by the city's elite following the sharp increase in street violence two years before.

'A miracle child, if the pieces in our own paper are to be believed,' Rigg said.

'Luther Donovan,' Benten said. The *Examiner*'s owner and publisher was a man most solicitous of the moneyed elite, especially those that had formed the CIB.

'Glet's scared we'll use our Graves coverage to remind people of the Stemec Henderson fiasco,' Rigg said.

'Then we should make the link,' Benten said, a sly smile crossing the deep creases of his face.

'*We?*' Rigg had been bereft of a byline for months. And hard news, especially crime, was for Rigg's old haunt downtown, the Bastion, not for the Pink.

'You were noticed.'

'I saw Wolfe, too,' Rigg said. Though he'd stayed back from the news herd at the bridge, turf insecurities sharpened the antennae of every reporter. Wolfe, a nervous, twitchy little man, had become the Bastion's chief crime reporter when Rigg got banished to the Pink. 'He called?'

'Afraid for his job, unlike you.'

'I already lost my job.' Working three days a week at the Pink without a byline was not real reporting.

'Then why were you by that bridge?'

'I was just watching.'

Benten waved the lie away. 'If it's the same killer . . .'

Rigg nodded. 'A perverse part of me is hoping it's the same killer,' he said, 'if it forces another look at Stemec Henderson. But I made sure to tell Glet I was off crime. Car dealership openings, PTA meetings, new sewers – that's me now.'

'And he said . . .?'

'That I'd always be the conscience of the unavenged.'

'You wore the robes; you were the judge last time. Unsatisfied, forever demanding.'

'They messed it. Lehman, Glet, the other deputies, local cops, forest-preserve security, even the state's attorney – they all messed it. And us, the queens, we messed it by egging them on for progress they didn't know how to make, forcing them to chase leads they knew would never pan out. Covering ass got more important than looking for truth.'

'And you? You messed it?' Benten said.

'Me most of all, and I'm still messing it.'

'Still searching your wall of files?'

Rigg nodded. He'd told Benten long ago about his twenty-six boxes of notes on the Stemec Henderson investigation. He pored over them during every one of the three nights he spent in his suburban apartment every week, looking for some clue he'd missed.

'You still talk to her?' Benten asked.

'Who?' Rigg asked. He talked to two. One was dead. One was alive, wishing she were dead.

'Carlotta Henderson, damn it.'

'You mean the mother of two of the dead boys and the widow of the man that keeled over at the Dead House?' Rigg said, suddenly furious. The woman hadn't only lost her kids. She'd lost her husband, and then she'd gotten trashed in the press.

'Easy, easy,' Benten said. 'I wasn't referring to . . .' He let the thought trail away. Carlotta Henderson had become scandalous along with Rigg.

'She doesn't call much anymore,' Rigg said. Not much meant no more than two or three times a week, but only on the landline in his apartment. He'd refused to give Carlotta his cell phone number because he didn't want her to get at him in the dunes. The dunes were Judith's place.

'I just meant it would be natural to stay in touch,' Benten went on, probing a little more now. He'd been known as a newsman with a renowned sniffer before he got old and booted to the Pink.

'Carlotta's never given up hoping for good leads,' Rigg said. She'd begun getting crank stuff – false leads, rants, judgments of those who spoke directly to God – beginning the day after her husband collapsed over the body of one of his two murdered sons. She began calling Rigg to report all of them, usually in the middle of the night, when she was most vulnerable. And he listened, every time, for by then he was vulnerable, too, trapped by his nightmares of a black cage that kept him from touching the arms of the woman who'd been shot beside him.

Benten cleared his throat. 'Perhaps you could write a short piece?'

'To poke a stick in the Bastion? Crime is for downtown, not for us at the Pink.'

'Something to let them know we've still got game.'

'Even under your byline, they'll suspect it's me, and that will stop it from getting past any copy editor downtown.'

'All is chaos at the Bastion, fearing more lay-offs,' Benten said, getting up to put on his topcoat, and forgetting for once to make a comic show of dropping his brown fedora at what he always took for a jaunty angle, but which only made his head look like it was on crooked. Today he just tugged the hat on like a helmet. 'Around a thousand words, recap and update, digestible for the limited attention spans of our website readers,' he said. 'No need to research.'

He walked out fast then, maybe because he was in a hurry to get a space in a bar. The gin mills would be crowded that day.

Rigg stubbed out both of the Camels Benten had left burning in the ashtray and went out to the desk jammed against the back wall. It was tiny and it was red and it was all that was available for a part-time reporter.

The television coverage had ended. The two lady reporters and the advertising peddler were gone. Only Eleanor, the copy editor, remained, to tend to Rigg.

He pushed aside the clutter of notes on the middle-school expansion he still hadn't written up, sat down and opened his laptop.

A hand touched his shoulder from behind, making him jump. He hadn't heard her get up. 'Not like before, Milo,' Eleanor said softly, meaning he should not get caught in the teeth of the old gears.

He nodded without turning around. Not like before? Two more children had been found. Disappeared after going to the movies, like before. Naked, like before. Lying atop one another, jumbled like pick-up sticks, like before. Left just a few feet off a road, like before. In Cook County, to suffer its incompetent sheriff's jurisdiction, like before.

His fingers began to tremble above the keyboard. He dropped his hands to his lap before Eleanor could see and kept them there until she turned and walked away. Sweat stung into his eye. He wiped at it. There was no 'before' to it, no past. It was still all so damned present. Kids dead again.

Just like before.

THREE

GRAVES SISTERS FOUND DEAD
Harold Benten, *Chicago Examiner*

The nude bodies of Beatrice and Priscilla Graves were found yesterday, January 21, beside a low bridge along German Church Road in suburban Willow Springs. The discovery ends the largest missing persons search in Cook County history. Sheriff Joseph Lehman and Cook County Medical Examiner Charles McGarry were tight-lipped, saying that no further information would be released until after McGarry's office conducted autopsies on the two sisters.

As reported at the time, the girls left their home on South Damen Avenue in Chicago at 7:15 Friday evening, December 28. They were headed for the local premier of the latest *Star Wars* movie, playing at the Brighton Theater on Archer Avenue, a mile and a half away. Fifteen-year-old Beatrice had planned on going alone that evening, but her mother, Leona Graves, 48, insisted she take along Priscilla, 12, thinking both girls would be safer if together. She gave her daughters fifteen dollars to add to the Christmas money they planned to use for bus fare, tickets to see the movie, popcorn and candy.

At the concession stand, the sisters ran into a young girl friend from the neighborhood, who was there with her 6-year-old sister. The four girls sat together for the movie's first showing, then the girl left to take her sister home. The Graves girls stayed for the second showing, and were seen leaving the theater at 11:30 p.m.

Nothing is known for certain about their whereabouts after that.

Once news of the girls' disappearance was reported on Sunday, December 30, leads came seemingly from everywhere. A Chicago bus driver thought they got off his bus at Archer and Western Avenues, along the correct route to their home, though several exits prior to their usual stop.

A young male acquaintance of Beatrice's, seeing them leave the theater, is certain they did not take a bus, but rather began walking home, several yards behind him. Hearing a screech of brakes, he turned to see a late-model green Buick slow beside the two walking girls. He reported that the girls hesitated, as though they knew the occupants of the car, but then the car pulled away and the girls kept on walking. When he stopped to look in the window of a men's clothing store, they passed him by. Several blocks later, he saw another vehicle, a black Ford Explorer with two teenaged boys inside, pull alongside the girls. The passenger rolled down the window and said something to the girls. Beatrice's acquaintance reported that the girls laughed and kept walking.

Two other young men, ages 17 and 15, were driving around close to midnight and claimed they saw the sisters four blocks from their Damen Avenue home. The boys knew the sisters from the neighborhood and observed them giggling and jumping out of doorways at each other, playing what appeared to be a sort of hide-and-seek.

A pizza delivery driver reported he'd seen both girls that night getting into a dark-colored car with three men inside when it was stopped in front of him at a red light on Western Avenue.

The loud voices of occupants of a Ford Escort parked on Archer Avenue and well beyond the route the sisters would have taken if they'd headed directly home drew a car salesman to his upstairs apartment window after midnight. He went down to the sidewalk and saw two girls wearing bright scarves, like those worn by the Graves sisters that night, talking to two men inside the car. The car salesman could not describe the men other than to report that the one sitting in the passenger's seat was blond. He also noted that one of the girls was wearing a dark cloth coat similar to that of Beatrice Graves.

Farther afield, a cashier reported seeing the sisters leaving her theater on Clark Street in Chicago at 12:45 a.m. on Saturday, 75 minutes after they were known to have left the Brighton Theater. A clerk at the 24-hour Walgreens at 63rd and Halsted was certain the two girls bought sodas there, early Sunday morning. That same day, a junk dealer in downstate Gilman is certain he saw the sisters riding with two men in a dirty maroon car bearing Tennessee license plates and a Chicago vehicle sticker.

Readers following this case know that Captain R.J. Hudson of the Brighton Park Police District, in charge of the local search for the Graves sisters, gave the greatest emphasis to this last report, and to two reports placing the girls in Nashville, Tennessee. An employment agent there identified photographs of the girls and said they'd applied for work on Wednesday, January 9. A week later, a woman reported encountering the sisters in a Nashville bus station. Captain Hudson believed the accuracy of both Nashville sightings and thought it likely the pair was headed to Elvis Presley's home in Memphis, Tennessee.

Mrs Leona Graves gave no credence to the distant sightings, steadfastly maintaining that her girls had suffered harm, or were being held against their will, close to home. Tragically, she has now been proven correct.

Throughout the 25 days the girls were missing, as many as 150 local Chicago police officers at one time conducted searches of the Brighton Park Theater neighborhood and the area surrounding the girls' Damen Avenue home. Garages, schools, vacant lots and railroad yards were searched.

Among the hundreds of leads pursued, the cruelest may have been the telephone tip received by Angeline, the Graves girls' older sister, instructing Mrs Graves to bring $1,000 to a church in Milwaukee. The caller promised that Beatrice would come to collect the money from her mother and, once it was turned over to the kidnappers, Priscilla would then be freed and both girls could join their mother. Mrs Graves journeyed to Milwaukee, but no one showed up at the designated church. Like many of the calls received by the Graves family, it was a horrid hoax, this one perpetrated, it was later learned, by an inmate of a Milwaukee mental hospital.

On January 15, an anonymous caller dialed the police, saying that the sisters could be found in Santa Fe Park in the village of Tiedtville, about a mile and a half south of where the girls were found a week later. Stock car and motorcycle races are held there, and the park is frequented by local gang members. Police converged to search the grounds, but no trace of the Graves girls was found.

The anonymous call was traced to a tavern on South Halsted Street, where it was learned that Klaus Lanz, an unemployed pipe fitter, had used the phone booth at the time the anonymous call was placed. Lanz admitted placing the call, explaining that he was descended from generations of psychics, and that it came to him in a dream that the girls were being held in Santa Fe Park. Lanz was arrested and subjected to a lie-detector test. The results were inconclusive, and he was released.

Since the girls were found in unincorporated Cook County, investigation into the homicides falls under the jurisdiction of Sheriff Joseph Lehman.

Rigg eased back in his chair, mulling the last sentence. It was direct, truthful and, he hoped, horrifying. Sheriff Joe Lehman, a rough, streetwise and crooked cop, was going to be in charge, like when the Stemec Henderson boys were found. Like when nothing more had ever been found.

Behind him, Eleanor drummed her fingers on her desk. The print deadline for the next morning's *Examiner* loomed, though the piece would be posted shortly after midnight on the paper's online site.

He typed one more sentence: *Sheriff's police are steadfastly stressing that, so far, there is nothing to link the deaths of the Graves sisters to the murders of Bobby Stemec and John and Anthony Henderson, the three boys found in Robinson Woods, fifteen months ago.*

He sent his words to the editor, grabbed his coat and ran down the stairs to the street before he could dwell on what he hadn't written.

FOUR

Since Judith was killed, the Rail-Vu Diner in Lisle had become his one-night-a-week custom, but only a one-night-a-week custom. He wasn't going to become one of those newly single men who huddle over a plate, eating noodles on the cheap, in the same restaurant every night. So it was that, on one of his three nights in Chicago from Indiana, he ate dinner – though sure as hell, never noodles – in Lisle, across from the train station.

That night, it was as if something nuclear had exploded, vaporizing all life. Lisle was a ghost town. The flakes that had started to fall on German Church Road that afternoon had thickened, blanketing the empty streets and sidewalks with three inches of new snow, with more forecast. He parked directly in front of the diner. His footfalls made the night's only noises, hushed soft crunchings, the few feet to the door.

The Rail-Vu was as empty as the town. There were no customers. Blanchie, one of the diner's two veteran waitresses, got up from the table where she'd been reading a newspaper. 'A Monday?' she asked, crossing the empty diner with a pitcher of water. 'You're here on a Monday?'

But her face belied her pretense at surprise. She knew why he was in town earlier than usual.

He slipped into the middle yellow plastic and green vinyl booth along the wall. Blanchie's hand shook, spilling a little water as she filled his glass.

He pulled a paper napkin from the chrome dispenser and blotted up the few drops.

'The usual?' she asked.

'I have no usual,' he said.

'Mushroom burger, fries and coleslaw?'

He tried to summon up memories of his other nights there. They came with tastes of mushroom burgers and fries and slaw. He couldn't remember ordering anything else. Maybe he'd avoided the noodles of a solitary man, but he'd been just as stuck in routine, only with something else.

'Sure,' he said, because a mushroom burger really didn't matter.

'You ought to try something different.' Though she stood right next to his booth, her voice echoed across the empty, throwback diner, unchanged decor-wise for fifty years.

'Like McDonald's, up the street? I can eat big there for five bucks and still get change,' he said, trying for a grin.

'Yellow damn arches? Hamburgers thin as a dime?' She snorted as she wrote up his order, though the ticket, like his banter, was for show. The grill cook behind the window had heard them just fine. There was no clatter that night at the Rail-Vu.

'So, top my burger with olives this time,' he said.

'Wild man, Tarzan,' she said, changing the order on the pad as she walked back to slide it through the grill window.

Five minutes later, she came back with the water pitcher, though he hadn't taken a sip. 'No one's out,' she said.

'The snow,' he said, like he believed it.

'This is Chicago. We get customers when it snows.'

Tonight, there was no answering that.

Blanchie knew he was a reporter and knew his history. Even in the darkest days of his notoriety following the Stemec Henderson murders, she'd always managed to offer up something to laugh at. But she didn't try that evening. 'Those poor girls,' she said, walking away.

'And poor boys,' he amended, but only as a whisper inside his head.

He opened up his laptop and went to the *Sun-Times*' latest online postings. GIRLS FOUND NUDE IN WOODS, the headline read in big type, followed by the inevitable hot words, *forming a cross on top of her sister*, and *frozen*. And then, at the end, the words most responsible for keeping the usual diners of Lisle locked tight inside their own homes that evening – *many similarities to the murders of the Stemec Henderson boys* – summoning up the fear that a serial killer had been reawakened, and was out there stalking, ready to strike again.

He scrolled down to the next *Sun-Times* headline: $150,000 REWARD OFFERED IN SLAYING OF THREE BOYS. Young Assistant Medical Examiner Feldott's mentoring group of well-heeled Chicagoans had announced a new reward in the Stemec Henderson killings. Some would see the timing of the offer, coming on the same day that the Graves girls were discovered, as coincidence. Rigg did not. The Citizens' Investigation Bureau was putting Sheriff Lehman's department on notice: they weren't going to let the Graves murders, or any kid killings, new or old, be forgotten.

He closed his eyes. Most everyone would see the reward as good news, a big-buck goading for a renewed investigation into the Stemec Henderson case. But Rigg, as desperate as he'd been to find the boys' killer, had always seen the Citizens' Investigation Bureau as erosion. The organization that several industrialists, two judges and others had formed was a pronouncement that Chicago's leading players had lost faith in law enforcement and had the means to form their own force. Private cops and vigilantes taking the law into their own hands might be next.

'Want me to wrap it?' Blanchie asked from nowhere.

He glanced down at the table and then at his watch. He hadn't been aware she'd brought his burger. Almost an hour had passed.

He shook his head. His appetite wasn't going to get any better.

'Then go home, Milo, find comedies on TV and turn the volume up loud,' she said. 'Shut out the world for an hour or two.'

Judith had said the same thing a thousand times. 'Look at the TV,' she used to say, turning on the television. 'Not at your notes about the horrible killings you have to think about every day. Watch *Seinfeld* or *Lucy* or *Jack Benny* re-runs. Laughing's like riding a bike. You can learn again.'

He'd tried. He'd stared at the TV. But it was never Seinfeld or Lucille Ball or Jack Benny he was seeing. It was victims, usually kids, that seemed to be forever strewn about Chicago like spillage from a garbage truck.

It was that moroseness that made Judith insist they buy the ludicrous railroad caboose that some eccentric had tugged on to the top of an Indiana dune. If television wasn't going to work, if nothing was going to get his head away from Chicago crime, then, by golly, she'd said, she'd get his head out of Chicago and on to a dune. He'd so loved her for that.

And, for precious months, it worked. They labored on the old rail car, scraping and scrubbing and painting. And they'd walked – walked into the dunes and down to the shore of Lake Michigan to listen to the waves. She loved the waves, and he loved her for that and for the caboose and for getting him away from the gloom that followed him in Chicago.

And then she was gone, slammed dead by a random gang-banger's bullet as they drove south along the Dan Ryan Expressway, the two of them laughing about something he could no longer remember as they headed for their special place of refuge in the dunes.

He drove east along Ogden Avenue. The snowfall had lessened into a thin, gentle tumble and the road was freshly plowed. Even so, Ogden Avenue was as empty as when he'd set out for the Rail-Vu. No one was driving; no one was out.

In Westmont, he turned right on to Cass Avenue, headed south and crossed the tracks that split the old railroad town. Two blocks down, past the last of the small storefronts – some empty, some still struggling – unfamiliar faint lights appeared ahead on the right. For an instant, he thought his mind had wandered and he'd taken a wrong turn south. But glances to the right and left showed he was on the right street.

It was his building that had changed. Always dark at night, too dark even for shadows to be cast by the single street lamp at the corner, Judith had made a rhyme to mock their penurious landlord: he was too tight for light. It was true enough. Every exterior fixture, save for the ones in front of the first-floor barber shop and dry cleaners, had burned out, likely long before Rigg had moved in, four years before.

Not this night. This evening, the central, open staircase glowed. Not from major kilowatts, to be sure, but from what he guessed were the smallest available energy-efficient light bulbs. They lit the stairs rising up to the open-air hallways on the second and third floors like the softly phosphorescent spine of some prehistoric dinosaur. The building was still dim, but, compared to before, it was blinding, its mix of beige, brown and blackened bricks now lit in harsh relief against one other. It was a building hunkered, afraid, lighted against the night.

He parked on the gravel lot behind the alley and climbed the stairs to the third floor, surprised to realize he was actually looking down at his keys instead of fumbling for the right one by feel in the dark.

Something scraped softly down in the alley behind him. He paused, clutching his keys, sure that any strange sound could frighten in the night after a day that had been so filled with death. Still, he crossed back through the open hall to look down, well aware that he was backlit to anyone looking up.

Nothing shifted in the strange new pools of light below. It could have been a cat or a rat, but, more surely, it had been his nerves. The night was so still, so lulled by the falling snow, that any sound would be magnified.

He went back to his door, unlocked it, went in and kicked off his shoes.

Removing his shoes was one of his necessary post-Judith protocols. The apartment had been his bachelor place for a year before he met her, at the time a newly hired researcher at the Field Museum of Natural History. They'd married just months later, and she'd quickly made his apartment theirs. She covered the dark wood floors with a large, orange and yellow rug with a thick pad beneath. They'd bought sofas, one large and one small, to replace the single La-Z-Boy chair he'd bought used, right after his graduation from Chicago's Columbia College. And she brought plants, two dozen plants, to add even more new life to his spartan digs.

They'd lived together in that apartment for less than two years. And then she was gone, for forever. She was only thirty-one.

In his despair, in the distortion of the first days following her death, he'd sought to rid his life of everything that reminded him of her. He wouldn't yet dare go to the caboose on the dune to find a realtor to sell that place she loved above anything else, but he could strip the Westmont apartment. He jettisoned almost everything, save for the mattress, one dresser and the small black sofa the furniture salesman had called a love seat. They'd laughed at the sly challenge in the name, for the thing was too short for anything approximating routine physical love.

The jettisoning hardened the apartment. There were no soft furnishings, no padded rug left to absorb any of his sounds. Each of his footfalls fell loud and seemed to echo the hollowness of his new, widower's life. Padding around in his socks quieted the apartment some, though never did it quiet his pain.

He went to the kitchen, took down the quart of Johnny Walker Red from a cabinet that held nothing else, and poured half an inch into a tall glass to make the mildest of sedatives. He'd just filled it the rest of the way with water when the landline phone rang.

'Milo?' The voice was hushed, a woman's.

'Who . . .?' he asked, like he always did, but he knew who it was. Today was a big news day: girls had been found in a jumble, like her boys had been found in a jumble, the October before last. Normally she called in the darkest of the night hours, when she was deep in the vodka and perhaps clutching the latest crank note or the memory of the most recent, whispered, sick call, when she was most defenseless and he was trapped hardest in the black cage. But today she'd not waited for the darkest hours. Today was not like the others.

'Is it him, Milo?' she asked, her voice barely a murmur.

'It's too soon to know.'

'The papers, the television – they said they were naked.' Like her boys, but she didn't need to whisper that.

'Yes . . .' He pressed the phone closer to his ear.

'You'd tell me, wouldn't you, Milo? You'd tell me if it was him?'

He wanted to remind her – like he'd tried to remind Glet and like he'd so wanted to remind himself – that he'd been reassigned to meaningless, suburban, safe little stories, that the story of her boys was no longer his burden. But she, of all people, wouldn't believe. She knew it would always be his story, as surely as it would always be hers. And so he said nothing, and, after a moment, she hung up when the strain of hearing him say nothing was too much to endure.

He held the glass up to the light. The whiskey had barely colored the water. He spilled out an inch of the watery mix, replaced it with Scotch and went to the front window.

Someone was standing across the street, in the falling snow, next to one of the old thick trees, making no move to disguise that he was looking up at Rigg's window. He was the first person Rigg had seen out on a sidewalk that snowy night.

He remembered the unsettling sound from the alley when he'd come home. Nerves, that had been. And nerves it surely was now. No one was out on such a night, simply to stare at his window. The person was waiting for a ride, or walking a dog that Rigg could not see.

He took the Scotch to the small sofa, sat, and stared at the boxes stacked nearly to the ceiling against the opposite wall. Files and notes on the murders of Bobby Stemec and Johnny and Anthony Henderson, they defined the life that had begun for him just weeks after Judith was killed. He'd put his fury into untangling the mess Lehman, Glet and the others had made of the investigation, chasing down every lead he could wheedle out of any cop that took his call or that he badgered in a hallway, and making notes of everything. None of it led anywhere.

He never took the Stemec Henderson files to the caboose – unlike the apartment, it had become a comfort how close Judith felt to him there – but he pored through his boxes every evening he was in town, Tuesdays through Thursdays. Still, worries over what he'd overlooked in the files followed him to his dune, though the incessant nightmares of being trapped in a black cage, unable to reach through the thick, flat bars to grasp Judith's beckoning arms, never found him there.

He sipped the Scotch and thought of what he hadn't said to Carlotta Henderson. There were similarities between the boys' and girls' cases and there were not. The kids were all roughly the same age. All had been found naked, stripped by a killer, or killers, perhaps to leave no usable evidence behind, though Cook County Medical Examiner Charles McGarry had found foreign DNA, still unidentified, on two of the boys. It was too soon, yet, to know what, if anything, was left on the girls.

There'd been no sign of sexual trauma on any of the boys – though, unlike the Graves girls, their bodies bore strong signs of violence. Bobby Stemec's fingernails had been torn ragged; he'd fought back, ferociously. Johnny Henderson had been killed by several blows to the abdomen. His brother, Anthony, had been garroted.

As with the Graves girls, the boys' bodies appeared to have been dumped hurriedly, mere feet from a winding road in a forest preserve. A psychologist Rigg had interviewed offered the theory that certain kinds of degenerate sex murderers do little to hide their victims, as if leaving them to be discovered quickly was a sort of last kindness, a gesture of redeeming tenderness.

The boys had been discovered soon after they'd been dropped, having been missing for only two days. Not so the girls. They'd gone missing on December 28, a night that had been rainy, turning into snow as it got colder. Depending on how much snow had fallen that night, they might have been lying where they were discovered, concealed by snow, for almost a month.

Or, more horribly, not. They might have been kept alive somewhere for that missing month.

Both the boys and the girls had gone to the movies right before they disappeared: the boys to a theater in downtown Chicago, the girls to a neighborhood movie theater.

Rigg stared at the boxes stacked against the wall. They contained similarities to the Graves case, and things that were vastly different.

The only thing he was sure of was that he was too tired to do what he always did on his nights in that apartment – to take a box at random and pore through notes he'd already read a hundred times.

He finished his Scotch and headed off to try to sleep. And, almost surely, to face the black cage that came for him in the hours before dawn.

FIVE

AUTOPSY ONLY DEEPENS MYSTERY
Harold Benten, *Chicago Examiner*

Despite bringing in a team of three renowned forensic pathologists, Drs Kemp of St Francis Hospital, Hennessy of St Michael's Hospital and Robards of Stroger Hospital, Cook County Medical Examiner Charles McGarry announced inconclusive results in the autopsies of Beatrice Graves, 15, and her sister, Priscilla Graves, 12.

The sisters had not been sexually molested, the statement released by McGarry's office stated. They were not strangled or poisoned, nor were there any signs of violence on their bodies. They appeared to have been subjected to cold temperatures for a number of days, though neither the doctors nor McGarry would hazard a guess as to how long that was without studying the weather records for the 25 days since the two sisters disappeared.

Three puncture wounds were found on Priscilla's chest. They are of unknown origin, but were only one quarter of an inch deep, and thus too superficial to have caused death. The doctors believe they were inflicted post-mortem.

Beatrice's stomach contained particles of food that indicated she'd eaten four to five hours before she died.

The doctors concluded that, because the bodies showed insignificant deterioration, they had been kept in some previous cold place between the hour of death and the time they were dumped where German Church Road crosses Devil's Creek in unincorporated Cook County. Since that road is well traveled, the doctors theorized that the girls were dropped or placed there not much earlier than the night of January 2, when a foot of snow fell over parts of northern Illinois and drifts accumulated to two feet or more, covering their bodies. Last weekend's thaw melted the snow and revealed the bodies.

Cook County Medical Examiner Charles McGarry postponed plans to open an inquest today, citing a need to spare the parents the strain of testifying so soon after the girls were discovered. His statement reads: 'After all they have been through, they need time to be left alone. They have a tough enough cross to bear as it is.'

Cook County Sheriff Joseph Lehman announced he'd invited eight law enforcement agencies to plan a unified and integrated investigation into the murders, to be directed by his office. Lehman said this will forestall any inefficiencies between Cook County's Lehman and McGarry and the heads of other agencies during the investigation into the murders of the Graves sisters. State's Attorney Benjamin Bronkowski offered his support for Lehman's move, stating that a lack of cooperation between law enforcement units had helped bring a dead end to the investigation of the Stemec Henderson murders, and cautioned that a repetition of such a lack of cooperation could bring a similar result to the Graves case.

Benten finished reading Rigg's piece and turned away from his screen. 'It's two o'clock. When can we post to our site?'

'Four o'clock. Glet made me promise when he called with the heads-up that I'd hold back until both Lehman's and McGarry's statements are released.'

'He's currying favor.'

'Yes.'

Glet had called at eight o'clock that morning. Judith's arms had already awakened him three hours before, beckoning from beyond the thick grid of black, flat iron bars. Every night, before he drifted off to sleep, Rigg begged the darkness to make her show him what she wanted. But, every night, she showed him nothing but her arms, gently beckoning.

'No formal presser?' Benten asked now.

'They're just releasing the written statements. They don't want to answer questions.'

'You contact these other agencies Lehman's invited to join his investigation?'

Rigg laughed. 'I spent the morning calling around. Nobody's interested in being dragged into another mess of Lehman's. They see it as a phony ploy, a way for Lehman to pass off blame in case his investigation collapses into another Stemec Henderson. They're relieved it's Lehman's jurisdiction. They're going to let him rise or fall alone with it.'

'McGarry?'

'He's weak. Lehman will make him get on board,' Rigg said. 'Even worse for McGarry, he's got young Corky breathing down his neck and reporting his every move back to the CIB. One false step and they'll find a way to replace him with the kid.'

'You think McGarry will run for re-election?'

'Maybe if his ego demands it, but this case could threaten that. It's a bomb, set to explode. That's why he pulled in those three other doctors, to cover every inch of his ass. But that failed. The three wise men came up with zero, and that's going to come down on McGarry. Too many false steps and the county Dems will boot him out of office, no matter how much money he gives to the party.'

'You mean how much of his father's money he contributes to the party.'

'Inheritance buys its privileges,' Rigg said.

'CIB just upped the Stemec Henderson reward,' Benten said.

'They're taking law enforcement into their own hands. Next step? Hiring private cops.'

Benten turned to his keyboard, typed *Hold until four o'clock*, and sent Rigg's piece down to the Bastion.

And then Rigg's cell phone rang.

Rigg's headlights swept across the freshly plowed forest-preserve parking lot. It was empty.

He came to the Robinson Woods one of the three nights he was in from the dunes each week. He'd started right after the boys were discovered, hoping to jog a thought about something everyone had missed – and hoping that focusing on Stemec Henderson later in an evening might help banish the nightmares of Judith beckoning to him from beyond the black cage.

After the first few visits, when clarity didn't come and the black cage still did, he began bringing a pint of any drug store's cheapest whiskey. And, in no time at all, he found himself begging the dark to show him what he could not see.

He managed to quit the drinking, but still he came, one night in every short week, hoping for a nudge to what he knew, and didn't know, about the murders of the boys who were found just yards from where he parked. There seemed so little else he could do.

He shut off the engine and cut his headlamps. Almost instantly, a fist beat hard on the passenger-side window. He jerked forward, banging his knee on the steering column. 'Jesus, Glet!'

'I hid my car a quarter mile in,' the sheriff's most senior deputy said, sliding his bulk on to the passenger seat. 'I heard you chugging in nice and loud. This Taurus ain't your regular heap. A ninety?'

'Ninety-one.' His insurance company had sold the Camry in which Judith was killed to someone who wouldn't know its history. 'What's so urgent, Jerome?'

'I haven't forgotten the boys.' He pulled out one of his foul cigars and raised it to his mouth.

'Don't dare to light that rope,' Rigg said. Already the car stunk from Glet's clothes and the man's corruption, rumored though never proved. Like that of his boss, Lehman.

Glet lowered the unlit cigar amiably enough. 'Your editor like the advance tip I gave you?'

'He said it belongs at the Bastion,' Rigg lied. He wasn't in this yet, he wanted to tell himself. At least not all the way in, like last time.

'Bullshit. People are getting laid off down there, like at the *Trib* and the *Sun-Times*. You're all scrambling to save your jobs. Good tips on the hottest case in town can save your ass.'

'I told you earlier: I've got no byline. I'm school boards, now – road improvements, local elections.'

'You can do better than hiding out at the Pink or playing in the sand in the dunes.'

'I just bought a new pail and plastic shovel, for when the beach thaws.'

'And you were just in the neighborhood, back at that bridge.' Glet turned to lean his foul breath closer. 'I'm senior man at the sheriff's. You can't get deeper inside this Graves case than through me.'

'Find another boy,' Rigg said, but it was for show.

'You're the son of a bitch people remember.'

That might have been true, but only because they remembered more bad than good – his righteous near-hysteria, the shrillness he used to mask the grief he felt over Judith. And they'd remember the photos that drove Rigg – Chicago's premier crime reporter, with a twice-a-week column of his own – out of the Bastion and into semi-seclusion at the Pink.

'You think Lehman's going to fumble again, like last time?' Rigg asked.

'Abbott and Costello – you remember their baseball routine, "Who's On First?"'

'No.' Rigg reached to start his engine. Glet was trotting out riddles.

'You got a TV, don't you?' Glet said.

Rigg relaxed his hand around the ignition key. 'Abbott and Costello were before my time – like, decades.'

Glet chuckled. 'Abbott and Costello are talking nonsense about a baseball game, see? Abbott's asking who's on base. "Which base?" Costello asks. "Any base," Abbott says. Costello's not getting it. Back and forth, back and forth, they're talking past each other. Neither of them can agree who's on what base. It's hilarious.' He turned to face Rigg. 'It's not funny when coppers do it. And, instead of just two comedians, we had all kinds on Stemec Henderson – us at the sheriff's, of course, but also Chicago cops, locals, forest-preserve rangers, state police, not to mention that putz McGarry. They all talked nonsense to each other, nobody was calling the shots, saying who was on first. And we all got clobbered for that in the press, mostly by you, Milo. This time, nobody wants to play. They're giving Lehman a pass to do it all on his own. And that's dangerous, because Lehman's the most crooked guy in town.'

'What have you got that's new, Jerome?'

'Remember the guy Lehman picked up – Lanz?' the deputy said.

'The psychic dreamer who said the Graves girls were being held in the construction near the old Santa Fe Park? Lehman gave him a lie-detector test. He passed. He was let go.'

'He didn't pass, he didn't fail,' Glet said. 'The results were inconclusive. Lehman was in a panic to show progress in searching for the missing girls. He knew Lanz was a moonbeam, but he was better than nothing. He was showboating to impress you queens, showing that he was doing something.'

'You're still not telling me anything new, Jerome.'

'It's desperation time, Milo. He's got all of us chasing our tails. The latest? I got sent to talk to a goofy broad at a Starbucks who swears both girls were in her place, sipping five-dollar lattes while the whole town is looking for—'

'Damn it, Glet!'

'Moon dancers – cops, witnesses, all of them. Lehman's petrified. McGarry's worse, dodging his own shadow.'

'It's Lehman who's leading the charge, not the medical examiner.'

'They're both watching Corky Feldott. Straight up righteous, he'd kill for the CIB. We all got to watch out for him.' He shifted his bulk on the seat to stare out the windshield. 'Look, Milo, I know you had a rough time that last go-round, what with your wife, then the killings, then those photos and having to take a leave because of that Mrs—'

'I was only helping sort the leads she was getting in the mail.' He stopped, realizing he sounded defensive. 'I got set up with those pictures, Jerome.'

'She's a fox, ain't she, Milo? Gorgeous face, boobs like twin torpedoes.'

'Her sons were murdered. Her husband dropped dead viewing one of the bodies.'

'I need you on this. Tell your editor your source will deal only with you.'

'Because you need Mr Integrity to spruce your career?'

'Beatrice might have been penetrated,' Glet said, staring out into the darkness.

'What the hell, Glet? McGarry's release said just the opposite. No sexual molestation.'

'And nobody's going to say nothing about it for the time being, including you. Besides, maybe the results were inconclusive. It's just something McGarry passed on to Lehman.'

'Who knows this?'

'About Beatrice? The three pathologists, McGarry, Corky Feldott, likely the whole Citizens' Investigation Bureau, Lehman, me – and now you. And your editor, if you need to use it to get assigned to the story. But, so far, nobody's leaking. Nobody wants the extra uproar. So, you don't write it now. It's for later, if ever.'

'I don't write it at all; I'm suburban.' Rigg started his car, but it was just to spur the man along. The deputy's foul cigar smell was giving him a headache.

Glet didn't budge. He lit his cigar fast, blowing noxious smoke at the windshield. 'I got something maybe you can use tonight, something hush-hush that I wasn't supposed to come across. A cabbie named Rocco Enrice. Called in a tip. He works Midway Airport from that cab lot south of the terminal.'

Rigg powered down his window and Glet's. 'What's the deal with him?'

'Maybe nothing, like I said. It was a name on a piece of paper Lehman's secretary seemed too quick to cover up.'

'Why not chase him down yourself?'

'I don't need to be accused of grabbing stuff meant for Lehman. Plus, I got something else working.'

'Something better?'

'I'll let you know.' Glet got out and disappeared into the night.

SIX

Checking out Glet's cryptic tip needn't be more than waltzing his reporter's nose out for a new whiff of old times. And it wasn't like he didn't have the time to waste. He had nothing planned except a sandwich before heading home to a weak Scotch, a new stare at his wall of old file boxes, and whatever sleep he could snatch before the black cage came for him.

He drove east, but turned south well before Midway Airport and the cab lot beyond it. Pictures of the Graves house had run online and in the papers, and it was easy to recognize. It was in the middle of the block, a narrow two-story frame cottage, three windows up, two windows and the front door down, rectangular and ordinary and no different than its poor neighbors. Every window was lit, that night. He didn't imagine any of those still surviving in the house – the divorced mother, a daughter in her late teens and two sons younger than the murdered girls – had gotten much sleep since the sisters went missing on December 28, and perhaps for months before that. Another daughter, the family's firstborn child, had died of illness just the year before.

He parked across the street. The Brighton Theater was west of there. He'd walk that same route, beginning at the Graves block.

It was an old Chicago neighborhood, looking as it must have for fifty years. The sidewalks were wide and cracked and fronted a mix of stubbornly surviving retail – a dry cleaner, a shoe and leather repair shop, a small fruit and vegetable peddler, a bicycle shop – all places that Amazon had not yet figured out how to annihilate. All were closed for the evening, but most had left their display-window lights on against crime and maybe against the future. Combined with the brighter street lamps at the corners, there was enough light to make a night-time walk home safe for two girls, even at 11:30 p.m., when the second showing of the movie let out.

The night the girls disappeared, December 28, had been cold, faint rain turning to faint snow. He moved at the fast pace he thought two shivering, giggling *Star Wars* fans would have used on such a slushy night. It took less than fifteen minutes, which fit with what Mrs Graves had told police. Her daughters left at 7:15 to attend a 7:30 show. Leaving the theater at 11:30, they should have been home at 11:45 or midnight at the latest.

Just past Pulaski, the Brighton Theater loomed bright in the night. It was one of the fine old movie houses, built a decade before the Great Depression of the 1930s slammed the lid on grand architectural ornamentation. The bulk of the Brighton was stolid, red-brown brick, but its facade was dominated by a tall, two-story, white terracotta arch, framed by rectangular pillars of more ornate terracotta. A men's clothier was on the near side. A large furniture store was on the other.

The marquee looked to be lit with a thousand bulbs, bright enough for the several witnesses who claimed to have seen the Graves girls being approached by at least two carloads of young men as they left the theater. The news reports made the encounters sound ominous, but that could have been overly aggressive newsmongering. It had been a Christmas vacation night for school kids. The approaches could have been the innocent, normal jabberings of cruising teenaged boys.

He turned around and walked back to his car. The impression he'd formed heading to the theater held on the way back. The side-walks were wide and the lights were bright. Beatrice and Priscilla Graves should have been safe all the way home.

He drove to Cicero Avenue, turned past the airport and pulled into the cab lot, four blocks south. Two drivers were leaning against one of the hacks, smoking.

'I'm looking for Rocco Enrice,' Rigg said.

'I'm just as good, just as cheap and better looking,' the taller of them said. The other cabbie laughed.

Rigg offered a laugh, too. 'Sorry, it's got to be Rocco this trip.'

'Rocco ain't here,' the taller man said. 'I'll call dispatch.' He reached into his cab for his radio handset, spoke into it, listened and said to Rigg, 'You're in luck. Rocco's on his way. He'll be here in five minutes.'

Right at five minutes, a cab cruised up and a grizzled, unshaven face leaned to look out of the front passenger window. 'You looking for Enrice?' he asked.

'For a little conversation.' Rigg passed through a ten-dollar bill.

The driver's eyes got narrower and he didn't grab the bill. 'About what?'

'A tip you phoned in about the Graves girls.'

'You with the sheriff's?'

'Reporter,' Rigg said.

'I tipped the sheriff's, yeah,' Enrice said, taking the ten. 'They said they'd look into it, but ain't nobody been calling me.'

'When?'

'When did I see them girls, or when did I tip the sheriff?'

'Both.'

'I saw them girls early this month. I tipped the sheriff's later.'

'How much later?'

'Last week. You packing more than the ten, pal?'

'Depends.'

'Get in.'

Rigg got in the back seat and they headed out of the lot.

'Where we going?' Rigg asked.

'Forty more will tell you,' Enrice said, reaching back with one hand, palm up.

Fifty total was too much to bet on a lark. Rigg handed forward another ten. 'Twenty more if you impress me.'

The ten disappeared into the cabbie's shirt pocket. 'I picked up them two sisters, early January.'

'From where?'

'From someplace, but the location comes only with the twenty you're holding back.'

'You recognized their pictures from the newspapers, right?' Rigg slumped back in the seat. By now, a thousand supposed sightings of the Graves girls must have been reported by people chasing bucks like Enrice. What Rigg couldn't figure was why Glet had fluttered this one at him.

'They was drunk, the both of them girls.'

'They were twelve and fifteen.'

'Don't matter; drunk is drunk. They was with two guys.'

The cabbie kept driving, heading north on Cicero Avenue, and then turned east, then north, and then east again, into the city. 'You're gonna be impressed.'

'Where are we going?' Rigg asked.

'You're thinking I'm taking you for a ride?' Enrice, a wit, asked into his rear-view mirror.

'In every sense of the word.'

'People where I picked up them girls will vouch for my story.'

'You're sure they saw the girls?'

'They called the sheriff's, too. Plus, somebody where I dropped them girls might vouch, too.'

'All sorts of people are saying they saw the girls.'

'This is straight dope. I drove them girls.'

They turned on to Madison Street, the old Skid Row. The neighborhood was gentrifying, buildings were being razed. But it was slow-going. Plenty of the decrepitude of the old blocks remained. Street drinkers – some wobbling upright; some sitting, despite the snow on the sidewalks – were braced against the wire-gated pawnshops, gin mills and flops that lined the remnant of Chicago's sleaziest street. Madison Street was still clinging to its past as a portal to hell.

Enrice pulled to the curb, turned around and offered a grin, spotted here and there with teeth. 'Time to part with that double sawbuck.'

'What's to keep you from pulling away when I get out?'

'You want the whole shebang, right? Beginning with where I picked them up?'

'The twenty comes when your stop checks out.'

Enrice shrugged and gave it up. He drove up two more blocks and stopped in front of a diner. 'Gus is behind the grill window. He does the hash. Lucille's the wife. She waits the tables, collects the cash.'

The diner had no name, just a narrow door to the right of a

grease-clouded window that reminded Rigg of Benten's nicotine-fogged office window.

'Your twenty buys you exactly ten minutes of me waiting,' Enrice said, looking straight ahead. 'If you're not out by then, I'm gone.'

Rigg handed up the twenty and got out. 'I'll find you if you take off.'

'Ten minutes,' Enrice said.

SEVEN

Only one table inside was occupied. Three men, unshaven, sat staring into chipped porcelain mugs of black coffee, not speaking. There were no plates on their table. Homeless men, they were roosting cheap, in from the cold.

The woman behind the cash register looked up. She was in her sixties, squeezed into a faded pink waitress uniform that looked like it had been tight for years.

'How can I help you for?' she asked after Rigg didn't head for a table.

'Lucille?'

The woman nodded.

'I heard you saw those two girls who went missing.'

The frown lines around her mouth deepened. 'You from the cops, too?'

Rigg took out his press card. 'Reporter. Cops were here?'

'We called. They came by. We told them what we knew.'

'Which was what?'

'Them two girls, the missing ones, was here some weeks back.'

'Do you remember exactly when?'

'Of course. Last week.'

He'd been asking about the girls, but she'd misunderstood his question, thinking he was asking about the detectives.

'I recognized one of them from TV,' she said. 'Sheriff, I think.'

Rigg pulled out his phone, dialed up an Internet picture of Joe Lehman. 'Him?'

'Bingo.'

'And the other guy?'

'Same age.'

'Not a fat guy, bald, smoking a cigar?' Rigg asked, to rule him out. Glet lied plenty, but steering Rigg to a lead he'd already chased made no sense.

'Fat, not so much. Didn't say anything. No cigar.'

Rigg found an Internet picture of Glet.

'Nah,' the woman said.

He put his phone away. 'Can you remember exactly when the girls were here?'

'Gus!' she shouted to the bald-headed man behind the grill window. 'When did you tell those cops the girls was here?'

'January 6,' he yelled back.

'January 6,' she repeated, as if Rigg was deaf.

Gus came out from behind the grill window. 'I remember, because the exhaust fan blew out later that day and I had to pay a repairman two hundred damn dollars. The girls was here January 6, five-thirty or six in the morning.' He pointed to one of the four booths along the wall. 'Sat right there, girls on one side, men on the other.'

'Had you ever seen the men before?'

'One was that dipshit, Richie Fernandez. The dark-skinned guy, I never seen.'

'African-American?'

'No, just a dark-skinned white guy. Tasmanian, maybe.'

'I've never seen a Tasmanian,' Rigg said.

'Me neither, but they're different, I heard,' Gus said.

'You're sure it was the Graves girls?'

'Their pictures been in the papers and on TV a hundred times,' Gus said.

'Recognized them right away,' his wife added.

'You know this Richie Fernandez?' Rigg asked.

'Washes dishes here sometimes when he needs extra for wine,' Gus said.

'He's got another job?'

'Runs a machine, swing shift, somewhere. Fill-in, cash work. He don't do regular; says he's got a weak heart. Weak tongue is what he's got, for the grape. Sometimes he's there mornings, sometimes afternoons, sometimes nights. Mostly, he's not there at all.'

'Tell me about the morning they came in.'

Lucille spoke. 'They came in, eyes all messed up, wanting coffee. Like I said, I recognized the girls right off, and thought, oh, Jesus,

Richie, you're stepping in it for sure this time. The older girl, that Beatrice, looked sick or doped up. The younger one, Priscilla, was just plain drunk. They finished their coffee, none of them saying nothing, and then the four of them went out the door. Then that Beatrice came back, saying, "They're trying to put me in a cab, and I won't go." She sat in the same booth and put her head in her arms. The other one, the younger drunk girl, came in and tried to roust Beatrice. I asked her, that Priscilla, "Why don't you just leave her alone?" And she says, "This is my sister." The two men come back, Richie and the dark one, and walked that Beatrice out of the restaurant, holding her up by her arms.'

'That was it?'

'No,' Gus said. 'The four of them came back again, about ten-thirty that same morning, only this time they was paired up. That Beatrice sat next to Richie, Priscilla with the other one, only having coffee. I wanted nothing to do with any girls the cops was looking for. I told them to leave. Richie the big shot left a fin for the coffees, like five bucks covered tax and tip, and that was the last I seen of him until he came back the next day, or maybe the day after, this time by himself. "What did you do with the girls?" I asked him, since I didn't see nothing in the papers about them being found. "Nothing," Richie says. I told him, "You better turn those girls loose and tell them to go home. The police is looking for them. Their pictures are in the newspapers and on television. They're underage, and it will be your neck if they catch you with them." Richie said nothing to that, just hung his head and walked out into the street.'

'At the time you say the girls were here, there'd been nothing in the papers about a reward?' Rigg asked.

Gus shook his head too quickly. No reward meant there'd been no point in calling the cops when they'd first encountered the girls.

'So, why'd you finally call?' Rigg asked.

Gus looked at the cab outside the greasy window. 'It was right.'

It was baloney. The cook and his wife had gotten the jitters, perhaps from Enrice telling them there'd be trouble if it became known they knew about Fernandez and the girls and hadn't reported it.

'Do you know where Richie lives?' Rigg asked.

'No place special. Flops. He moves around,' Gus said.

Rigg started for the door, and then stopped. 'This is an all-night place?' he asked Lucille.

'Sometimes,' she said. 'Depending.'

Depending on what crawled in with cash, Rigg supposed. He went outside. 'You picked up the girls here?' he asked Enrice, sliding into the back seat.

'Them and the two clowns they was with, about six-thirty in the morning.' Enrice started the engine.

'The girls had to be muscled into your cab?'

'I only remember the four of them jamming in the back seat, then the one girl jumping out to go back in the diner, then the other going in after her.'

'Like one of them was trying to get away?'

'Nothing like that. They was just under the weather. The one jumped out, came back without a peep.'

'Cops never talked to you?'

'Not yet.'

'Where'd you drop them?'

Enrice grinned into the mirror as best he could, being so shy of teeth. 'Cost you another twenty.'

'Cost you your cab medallion if I tell the cops you've been chauffeuring underage girls for immoral purposes – girls that later got found dead.'

Enrice's grin disappeared, and he pulled away from the curb.

The Kellington Arms was less than a mile away, six stories of bricks missing so much mortar it looked as though one good wind would drop it to rubble. The buzzing red neon sign above the door had gaps, too, flashing only, *The Kell*, into its gin-drunk world.

'I'm giving you only ten minutes here, too,' Enrice said, cutting the engine. 'This ain't the fanciest neighborhood.'

'Remember that medallion,' Rigg said, getting out.

Something glistened in a small melted patch on the unshoveled walk. It was fresh, and it was urine. Rigg stepped around it and went into a scuffed linoleum lobby, big enough for only two pushed-together armless wood chairs. 'Richie Fernandez,' he said to the bristle-headed, bearded man behind the marble counter. A speck of pink was stuck to the side of the man's beard. Gum or a speck of cupcake.

'Nope,' the man said.

'I'll pay.'

'What for?'

'His room number.'

'Mr Fernandez ain't in,' the desk clerk said, but he'd arched his eyebrows, anticipating.

'I'm an old friend. I want to drop off some flowers.'

The desk clerk didn't bat an eye at Rigg's empty hands. 'How much?'

'Ten.' That late in the evening, it might have been enough for a night's stay in the flop.

The desk clerk presented his palm for the grease.

'Two-oh-two,' the clerk said, once his fingers had closed around the bill.

'I'll need the key.'

'It's unlocked.'

'How come?'

'Up the stairs, to the right.'

Rigg hustled up the stairs, avoiding a patch on the frayed carpet that had been dampened like the sidewalk. Room 202 was to the right and unlocked, as the desk clerk had said.

And it had been trashed.

The room stunk of whiskey and cheap perfume. The stained mattress had been pulled off its frame and leaned against a wall. A tattered tan canvas shaving kit was tipped on top of the bureau, scattering a can of Barbasol shaving cream, a disposable razor, a toothbrush and a tube of Colgate that was down to its last squeeze. The three drawers below had been emptied hurriedly, spilling a half-dozen pairs of patterned boxers, three yellowed sleeveless undershirts and some loose black socks, most dangling threads at the heels, on to the stained brown rug. A pair of blue work pants and two long-sleeved blue work shirts had been jerked off their hangers and lay on the closet floor, a few feet away.

A picture of the American flag hung in an unpainted frame on the wall, next to a thumb-tacked photo of a blonde wearing only work boots and a smile.

He went downstairs. 'The room's been tossed,' he said to the desk clerk.

The man nodded. 'Two coppers hauled Richie's ass away last week.'

Likely it was Lehman and a deputy, come directly from the diner,

who'd tossed Richie's room. No doubt the night desk man and some
of the other denizens of the Kell had taken their own turns around
the room after the cops left, looking for anything of value. It was
forage, the way of the world in a flop when someone got hauled
away by the police.

'Did the cops give you names?'

'I don't brace badges for names. They flashed tin, I pointed them
up the stairs.' He paused, draping his open palm like a wet rag on
the counter, except his fingers were twitching. 'Maybe I recognized
one of them from the papers.'

Rigg took out his phone, summoned up the photo of Lehman
to be sure.

The night clerk shrugged.

Rigg fanned open his billfold, exposing the last of it. Two
singles.

The clerk's fingertips danced on the marble counter, impatient.
Rigg passed over the two bucks.

'It was himself,' the clerk said, tapping Rigg's phone with a
filthy forefinger.

'The other one, same age as the sheriff?' Rigg asked.

The clerk nodded. 'They both went up. There was a ruckus.
They came down with only Richie, fifteen minutes later. They had
him cuffed.'

'What do you mean, "only" Richie?'

'Richie was alone by then. He has broads up there sometimes,
sometimes him alone, sometimes with another guy. Damned near
break the floor with their . . .' He paused. 'Well, you know, some
of our residents are still able. Cops wanted to know about any young
girls Richie might have brought around. Told them I didn't know
about any broads being young.'

'You didn't recognize the girls from the news?'

'The cops was yelling at Richie about some two girls. They
braced me, too, on their way down. I told them we don't allow no
underage – no, sir. This is a moral place,' he finished, with a straight
face.

A horn tapped twice outside. Rocco Enrice was getting nervous.

'Where'd they take Fernandez?'

The desk clerk cocked his head as though he was inspecting a
dullard. 'What's it matter?'

EIGHT

R igg started calling around for Jerome Glet at seven-thirty. It was another morning that had come too early, after a night that had ended too late, staying up thinking of a cabbie, a diner and a flop.

And then the cage came at five o'clock.

It never varied – just a wall of thick bars, like prison bars, but thicker and flatter, too close together for him to reach the slender arms that beckoned to him in the mist just beyond. Judith's arms, though he could never see her hands, her wedding ring.

Her beckoning was clear. Her killer had never been caught. She wanted him to find who'd shot her; she wanted justice. But, in Chicago, that was impossible. Fewer than a third of the city's murderous shooters were ever identified. And her killing had been unintended – a shot fired by a punk firing at someone else, or maybe just up in the air, in anger at the world. Almost certainly, the shooter never knew his bullet had found Judith's neck.

The cage brought his only dream of Judith, though he went to sleep every night praying she'd come to him – young, dark-haired, beautiful – to touch, to kiss, to whisper or laugh or murmur or yell or anything at all. But, in the interminable months since she was killed, only her pale, slender arms came, unreachable beyond flat, black bars.

Glet's cell phone gave him only voicemail. He called the sheriff's headquarters, but was told Deputy Glet was not expected in for some time. He called the Dead House, thinking Glet might have drifted over there, but the woman who answered the main number said it was too early for anyone important to be in, except the dead, ha ha.

He gave up on Glet, decided to look for Richie Fernandez directly. The Cook County Jail had no normal hours, since booking killers and cons, pervs and peepers was a twenty-four-hour-a-day proposition. It was where Lehman would have brought Fernandez. Rigg knew plenty of people to call there, from when he reported real news.

He asked first for Lehman, but, no surprise, was told the sheriff was not there. Then, those who didn't hang up when they recognized his voice gave him the same three responses: 'You working crime again, Rigg?' and, 'Nope, ain't seen Lehman,' and, 'Never heard of Richie Fernandez.'

Several times, there were additional responses. 'You still banging that Henderson woman, Rigg?' two asked. And four others stayed on the line long enough to express their delight at having heard he'd been bounced from reporting crime and out to the Pink. They remembered the drubbings he'd given law enforcement at their failure to solve the Stemec Henderson killings.

But one, a night officer just getting off his shift, was polite.

'I heard the sheriff personally made an arrest in the Graves case,' Rigg said.

'What?' The officer's surprise sounded genuine.

'A guy, Richie Fernandez. Lehman himself made the grab.'

'You got a bum tip. Klaus Lanz was the only real arrest, the only booking, and he was released. Lanz is a bobble-head, damaged upstairs,' the night man said.

Rigg supposed that word might have gone out to keep mum, for whatever reason, about the Fernandez bust, but he doubted the lid on the arrest could have been kept on for a whole week.

And something else nagged. Lehman knew the value of good publicity. He'd trumpeted his grab of Lanz. A personal bust of a solid prospect in the Graves case would have been golden publicity. He should have made sure news of Richie Fernandez's arrest got out.

But he hadn't.

Rigg called the sheriff's office again. The same secretary he'd spoken to earlier said the sheriff was still out.

'Out to me, or out to everyone?' Rigg asked.

She hung up.

He took a chance. He called back one of Lehman's senior deputies who'd hung up on him just moments earlier.

'Lehman's gone underground – why?' Rigg said fast, before the man could hang up on him again.

'Where the hell did you hear that?'

'Everywhere. Lehman's gone underground.'

'No attribution on this, Rigg?' the cop whispered, lowering his voice.

'Fine, fine,' Rigg said.

The cop laughed, loud, and hung up.

*   *   *

The Dead House was on the south side of Chicago, in a block just past a tattoo parlor, a bar and a hock shop. During the worst of Stemec Henderson, Rigg had gone there so often to pester Medical Examiner McGarry for updates that driving there became an unthinking routine.

This day, like those days, he drove the distances and took the turns like he was on rails. But, after he parked at the curb, his hand froze on the car door handle. Images from inside the building across the street came flashing back in a staccato-like slide show: the frantic echoing footfalls of the families pounding down the beige-tiled corridor; the steel doors banging open; the dank chill and gloom of the morgue; the almost gentle sagging of Anthony Henderson Senior, collapsing over the beaten body of his youngest son, Anthony Junior.

He pulled hard on the door handle, pushed out and hurried across the street.

The same receptionist sat at the rounded, black laminate desk. Her name was Jane, and her skin and her hair were the same beige as the glazed tiles lining the floor and the walls of the hallway, as if the colors of her life had been leeched away by the dead being refrigerated down the hall.

'Long time no see, Milo,' she said in a monotone voice. The morgue leeched away inflection, too.

'Happier stuff, now. School boards, pet parades, zoning battles.'

She nodded. Like everyone on his old beat, she knew he'd been bounced from the Bastion.

'I'm looking for Glet,' he said.

'Here?' She shook her head. 'He hasn't been by.'

'Is McGarry in?'

'Him, neither.'

'I'll go up and talk to Doris, then.' Doris was the medical examiner's secretary.

'No press, Milo.'

'What's going on?' Never had the press been shut out of the morgue by McGarry.

'Ask McGarry at the next press brief.'

'When's that?'

'Days, weeks, months. Who knows?'

Or never, Rigg thought. Everybody seemed to be going clam. Except maybe the CIB's most favorite young man. 'How about Corky Feldott?'

'*Cornelius* Feldott,' she corrected, with just the barest twitch of a smile. 'Our assistant M.E. thinks "Corky" lacks respect.'

'How about him, whatever his name is?'

She gave him an exaggerated sigh, pushed a phone button and cupped her free hand around the mouthpiece to make sure no unauthorized word escaped. A moment later, she waved a liver-spotted hand toward the tiled stairwell.

Doris was at her desk. Like Jane, downstairs, she was another grim veteran of the cold halls of the dead. He gave her a smile, which she didn't return. She remembered the thrashing he gave McGarry.

Feldott's office door was open, and Feldott himself adorned the threshold, smiling. Primed for success, he wore natty, chalk-striped charcoal suit pants, a white shirt that likely had never seen a wrinkle, and, in an attempt to show he was as common and careless about color as most men, a loosely-tied, inch-wide purple necktie, which most common men would never wear.

'Mr Rigg,' he said, holding out his hand.

'Cornelius,' Rigg said, holding out his own.

Feldott smiled more broadly. 'I see you've been given the word about my appellation.'

'"Cornelius" does have a certain gravitas.'

Still smiling, Cornelius gestured Rigg inside and they sat at a desk arranged neatly with four small stacks of Manila folders and a yellow legal pad. A laptop computer was on the back credenza, below an antique-looking drawing of Northwestern University.

'How can I help?' Cornelius asked.

'What's being learned about the Graves case?'

'And about Stemec Henderson?' Cornelius gestured toward one of the stacks of folders. 'I've just reread all your pieces in the *Examiner*. Lots and lots of outrage, but well deserved.'

'Always Stemec Henderson,' Rigg said.

'We've not forgotten.'

'You weren't involved.'

'I'd only been here for a couple of months. So, the Graves girls?' Rigg nodded.

'We defer to the sheriff. You should ask him.'

'I can't get through to him. I heard he made a major bust last week.'

Feldott frowned. 'There's been no news of that.'

'The suspect's name is Richie Fernandez.'

'Where did you hear it?'

'Street talk, a name, a mention,' Rigg said.

'A source you can't divulge?'

Rigg shrugged.

'Well, I don't know anything about a Richie Fernandez,' young Feldott said. 'And nothing about anyone else, unfortunately. The sheriff's investigation is still evolving, as they say.'

It could have been a lid, it could have been truth.

'So far, only Klaus Lanz,' Rigg said.

'Everybody knows about him. A quick arrest, a quick release.'

'For show,' Rigg said.

'You must understand, the reporting last time . . .' He let it slip away, that gentle accusation. 'Maybe your Mr Fernandez was simply another catch-and-release, though you're saying he was released without anyone knowing he'd been caught?'

Rigg gave it up. 'When will there be a more conclusive autopsy on the girls?'

'You mean, more than the three wise men?' Feldott said of the three doctors who'd found nothing except that the girls had been frozen. 'Anything more is up to Mr McGarry.'

'He's not around, like Lehman.'

'Off the record again?'

'All of this is,' Rigg said.

'The girls haven't fully thawed, but we don't want that released.'

'Too long frozen?'

'We're being more meticulous than last time. Surely you of all people can understand why.'

'Any chance either of the girls was violated?' Rigg asked, giving Feldott the opportunity to lie.

'No chance I'd tell you something like that until we do complete examinations. Please do not speculate.'

'I'm hearing McGarry wants out,' Rigg said, to keep them talking.

'We'd go on, regardless,' Feldott said. It was interesting. He hadn't denied the possibility of McGarry's bailing out when his term was up.

'You're his assistant. You'd run?'

'Gosh, no. Most, including me, think I'm too young, too new at the job.'

'Who, then?'

'An outsider, I imagine.'

'You're an outsider, sent over by the Civilian Investigation folks.'

Feldott smiled. 'I meant a seasoned man from outside. What else do you know about this Richie Fernandez?'

'Nothing beyond a name,' Rigg said, standing up.

'Maybe that's more than anyone else knows,' Feldott said, walking him to the door.

'Except Lehman,' Rigg said.

NINE

Rigg went looking for Glet's house.

He'd shown up there unannounced a couple of times, months before, late at night, in full fury at the lethargy of the Stemec Henderson investigation, demanding progress, and – he finally had to accept – in full fury at the random slaughter of the woman who'd been the core of his life.

Glet lived on the northwest side of Chicago, in a block of identical brown brick bungalows. Rigg drove slowly until he came to one that had the wispy remains of some summer weeds poking above the snow in a cracked cement urn at the base of the front steps. Either a bachelor lived there, or someone who didn't give a damn about neighborly grace. Glet was both.

Walking up confirmed his guess. Dozens of cigar butts had been stubbed into the weed remains. The cracked urn reeked of Glet.

'He ain't home,' a woman said. Tugging at a thin terry robe, the old woman had stepped out on to the tiny front porch next door. 'Didn't come home last night.'

'Glet's got a girl?'

She barked a laugh at that and slipped back into the warmth of her house.

Rigg went up the steps and banged on the front door anyway. There was no response. He walked back to his car.

'Something stinks,' Rigg said.

Benten lit a Camel, as if to underscore the point. At probably four dollars a pack, they had to be setting him back close to a hundred a week – a big enough dent in any wage, let alone one that must have diminished when Benten, like Rigg, was banished to the Pink.

'So . . .?' Benten asked, after a lungful of smoke.

'I've been incurring expenses. Cab rides, and another twelve to bribe a desk clerk.'

Even nickels mattered to Rigg now. Working part-time at the Pink paid $400 a week, barely enough to cover the Westmont apartment's rent. Everything else came out of Judith's small life-insurance payout from the Field Museum, and that would go dry in about six months.

Benten blew a lungful of smoke at the exhaust fan and laughed. 'Twelve bucks for a bribe? Nobody bribes for twelve dollars.'

'It was all I had left.'

'And cab rides? Why cabs?'

Glet had said he could tip his editor, if it meant that Rigg could work the story. 'I met Glet last night. Very private, very clandestine.'

The editor's eyebrows arched with new interest. 'Where?'

'The site.'

'Sweet shit. You can't stay away from those woods?'

'It was his suggestion. He parked away, came up through the snow on foot. He doesn't want anyone to know he's talking to me.'

'He's reeling you in. He wants Lehman's job, and he wants you to glow about him.'

'Lehman is old Chicago, a bully, too thick with the other crooks that run things. He's not going anywhere.'

Benten shook his head. 'He will, if the Graves case greases his chute. City Hall will have to cut him loose if he screws up like last time.'

'Glet gave me a nugget and a lead.'

'What's the nugget?'

'Beatrice Graves might have been penetrated.'

Benten swiveled around to look at a taped poster of a forest, where a window should have been. 'Sweet shit,' he said to the printed woods.

'Glet swore me to secrecy, except to tell you if you needed convincing to keep me on this.'

'And the lead?' he asked, still with his back to Rigg.

'He pointed me to a cabbie who phoned the sheriff's department last week, saying he'd picked up the Graves girls with two men at a diner on Madison, January 6. The husband and wife who run the diner tipped the sheriff about that last week, too.'

'Trolling for reward dollars?'

'More likely jitters from sitting on information they should have reported earlier. The cabbie picked up the girls and two men from the diner and drove them to a flop nearby.'

Benten swiveled back around and made like he was stifling a yawn. 'Could have been any two girls.'

'Two cops went to the diner last week and then to the flop. They busted one of the men.'

'There's been no news of that. Catch-and-release.'

'The guy they arrested, Richie Fernandez, hasn't been seen since. Never came back to the flop, not even for his stuff.'

Benten leaned across his desk. He knew Rigg was tossing bait. 'And . . .?'

'The husband and wife that run the diner, and the night clerk at the flop, all got good looks at the two cops . . .'

Benten bit. 'Damn it.'

'Lehman was one of them. He made the bust himself.'

'And now this guy, Fernandez, has disappeared?'

'No record of the arrest, no booking. Nobody knows anything about him.'

'Glet didn't know about Fernandez, just the cabbie?' Benten asked.

'So it appears.'

'Why didn't he chase the lead to the cabbie himself?'

'He said he was afraid of getting caught poaching a lead meant for Lehman. And he implied he was working on something better.'

'What's better?' Benten asked.

'I don't know that either.'

'It's you now, Milo.'

'What do you mean?'

Benten gestured at the latest *Examiner* lying on his desk. 'You saw that ours was the only piece running on the Graves case this morning?'

'I noticed.'

'Wolfe got cost-controlled yesterday – fired, along with six copy editors and probably the cleaning lady that vacuums the Bastion at night. You get to continue to write under my byline. The Bastion gets the Graves case covered cheap.'

'And the Richie Fernandez story – that's part of it now.'

Benten started to nod, but then apparently noticed something through the filmy glass wall. 'Eleanor, what the hell is going on?' he shouted through his open door.

'Lehman's on TV!' she yelled, pointing at the television. 'We just got the email five minutes ago. Only WGN is covering it!'

WGN was a local, unaffiliated television station.

Benten followed Rigg out to the general office. Lehman was at a podium surrounded by nobody at all.

'I'm announcing that we've taken into custody the man we allege perpetuated the horrible crimes against Beatrice and Priscilla Graves.'

'Here comes your Richie Fernandez,' Benten said.

'Klaus Lanz is known to most of you. He was . . .'

Rigg lost the words coming through the tinny speaker. He looked over at Benten. Benten stared back at him.

'We had insufficient grounds initially to hold Mr Lanz,' Lehman went on. 'We had to release him. But now, thanks to us never letting go, we believe we've developed enough compelling evidence to request that Mr Lanz be held without bond.'

Rigg stared at the screen as he listened to the lunacy that was being spouted. Lanz was a drifter, a two-bit nobody. He'd been vetted by cops and by reporters, including the *Examiner*'s just-ejected Wolfe, and was found wanting of everything except psychic signals. Nothing solidly incriminating pointed to Lanz.

It was over in the next instant. Lehman, usually a showboat who went on and on, announced that further details would be forthcoming, and strode out of camera range.

Benten turned to Rigg. 'Richie Fernandez, my ass,' he said.

'Klaus Lanz, Lehman's herring,' Rigg said.

'Write without speculation,' Benten said.

And so Rigg did.

REDO?

Harold Benten, *Chicago Examiner*

Klaus Lanz, an unemployed pipe fitter, was arrested again by Cook County sheriff's officers for the murders of Beatrice and Priscilla Graves, Sheriff Joseph Lehman announced today. Lanz had confessed previously to placing an anonymous call to police, explaining that he was descended from generations of psychics, and that it came to him in a dream that the girls were being held in Santa Fe Park, south and west of the location on German Church Road where they were subsequently found last Monday. Lanz was arrested mid-January, before the girls were found, in conjunction with the girls' disappearance, and subjected to a lie-detector test. According to the sheriff's department at the time, the results were inconclusive, and he was released. Today, Lehman announced he'd uncovered sufficient new evidence for Lanz's re-arrest. Lehman took no questions at the press conference, promising that further details would be forthcoming.

Rigg sent Benten the copy and followed it to the threshold of the cigarette fog.

Benten read it, typed a small change and sent the story across the room to Eleanor at the front desk. 'Ah, investigative journalism, gotten straight from television,' he said, grinning.

'He didn't hold a press conference because he didn't want questions,' Rigg said. 'Lanz is a red herring. Lehman's got a different suspect that he doesn't want anyone to know about.'

'You've got no corroboration on Fernandez,' Benten said.

'I've got the desk clerk.'

Benten laughed. 'A wino at a flop who can be bribed for twelve bucks?'

'What did you change on my piece?'

'The byline. It's time to announce you're back.'

Rigg crossed the pink-tile floor to his desk and began calling to find Lehman, Glet, or any of the sheriff's other minions who might open up more about Lehman's news. But nobody was in and nobody knew when anybody was expected back. And so, for the rest of the afternoon, there was only one suspect in the Graves case, and that was Klaus Lanz.

'What the heck, Milo?' Blanchie's voice boomed across the diner when he walked in. The Rail-Vu in Lisle was as deserted as it had been the night after the Graves girls were discovered.

'"What the heck" what?'

'You only come in once a week, remember?' She gave him an elaborate curtsy, adding, 'Not that I'm not flattered.'

'I'm adding days to my weeks.' He slid into a booth and opened his laptop. 'A burger,' he said, logging on to the Internet.

'Mushrooms,' Blanchie said.

The piece he'd written, under his own byline for the first time in months, had been up on the *Examiner*'s site for two hours. The other queens had been just as prompt.

The *Chicago Sun-Times* reporter had written the story as Rigg had, letting the brevity of Lehman's announcement raise its own questions about why the sheriff had offered no specifics about re-arresting Lanz. Likely enough, Rigg figured, the *Sun-Times* reporter suspected Lehman was using the hapless Lanz to show progress when there'd been none – unlike Rigg, who saw Lanz as a herring to disguise sweating a better suspect elsewhere.

Rigg clicked on the *Tribune*'s site. Their crime reporter played it the same way, too. But the *Trib* had a short sidebar, written by their media man, Greg Theodore, who'd picked up on Rigg's byline:

> Milo Rigg has come out of suburban solitude to take over the reins of reporting on crime for the *Examiner*, following the latest round of lay-offs at Chicago's number-three newspaper. First up is covering the explosive case of the murders of the Graves sisters, whose bodies were discovered just three days ago in a ravine in suburban Cook County. Covering the perhaps similar murders of the Stemec and Henderson boys fifteen months ago proved problematic for the *Examiner*'s venerable crime reporter, and resulted, some said, in his banishment from the *Examiner*'s downtown Chicago headquarters.

Blanchie brought him his mushroom burger. Rigg took two bites and a forkful of coleslaw, and held up his credit card.

'Lost your appetite?' Blanchie asked, coming over.

Rigg nodded. Theodore's small sidebar and his own byline had said it all.

He was back.

TEN

Sunlight hitting his face woke him, and it felt later than usual, and warmer. Eyes still shut, half asleep, he felt for his phone on the floor to check the time. He had to reach too far. He opened his eyes. He wasn't in his Westmont apartment. He was in the dunes.

He'd left the Rail-Vu unnerved by a certainty that the resurrection of his byline was going to resurrect the tawdriness of his past. He hadn't wanted to go back to his hollowed-out apartment, where his every move echoed with the absence of what he'd lost. He'd wanted to drive. And so he'd driven, despite the late hour, to the refuge of the dunes.

He swung out to put his feet on the floor. He slept on the bottom bunk, now. Judith's bunk. His had been on top, up the short, narrow metal ladder. She'd laughed every time he climbed up, for there was no graceful way to ascend. He'd gotten somewhat good at it, but still she laughed. He'd laughed, too. They'd laughed a lot in that caboose.

She'd seen it advertised for sale in a local shopping rag – a quirky, odd thing that an eccentric retiree had tugged to the top of a small dune and that his heirs wanted gone. 'A place in the dunes,' she'd said.

'An old railroad car, stinking of creosote and oil,' he said. But they'd gone to look, and they bought it because it was cheap and because she wanted it so very badly.

They'd labored on that relic, scrubbing and sanding the old wood of the sides, painting it the original vibrant red, its interior clapboards a glossy white. They installed the bunk beds and had custom cabinetry fitted to make tiny closets and a kitchen. It was cramped and narrow and exactly what they wanted to enjoy for fifty years. And then she was dead.

He'd intended to gut the caboose of their things and put it up for sale. But, when he finally summoned the courage to drive back to the dune for the first time after she was killed, he was surprised to find calm inside the tiny rail car. He didn't know whether that was from the dunes' almost preternatural quiet, now that field ecologists had scraped away almost all of the surrounding old cottages to restore the area to its natural state; whether dreams of the black cage never found him there; or whether he felt Judith's presence much stronger there than in the apartment. Whatever it was, the caboose became his refuge, and he quickly abandoned any thought of eliminating it from his life.

Even months later, when his life descended even further into chaos following the Stemec Henderson murders, the botched investigations and the trashing of his reputation, calm always welcomed him in Indiana. It was how he had survived.

He walked the five steps to the galley kitchen, made coffee and sat at the two-person banquette to look down from the dune. The hard-crusted ice on the small lake below sparkled like a million diamonds in the sun. It was completely frozen over, like always by late January.

Out for a walk their first summer there, he and Judith had stopped to talk to one of the field ecologists supervising the removal of one of the old cottages on the other side of that small lake. 'This thing freezes three, four inches thick every winter,' the bearded man had said. 'So thick, young bucks back in the day used to race in circles on the ice – race, that is, until they hit a soft spot and went in.'

'My God!' Judith had said.

The man had held up a hand. 'I never heard that anyone got killed, but the cars were sunk for forever. They're sinking still, I expect.'

'What's that mean?' Judith asked.

'The lake's got a bottom a million times softer than a baby's,' the man said, with a wink.

'Softer?' Judith asked, confused.

The man laughed. 'Soft, meaning layers and layers of silt,' he said. 'Tree limbs and leaves and all sorts of things fall on to the ice over the winter. Come spring, the ice melts and all that sinks into the water, to be welcomed as nourishment. That's why the lake bottom never hardens. It just keeps decomposing, getting softer and softer as the old keeps sinking, making way for the new. Hell, those old racing cars ought to be coming out of the other side of the world any day.' He looked up then, at the caboose they'd been painting. 'Your little caboose there is just beyond our reach,' he said, the expression on his face leaving no doubt that he would have loved

to have scraped away their rail car along with everything else that
was man-made.

That snippet of conversation seemed decades old, words even
from another lifetime, but they'd been spoken just little more than
two years before.

He rinsed his coffee cup, locked up and went down the railroad-
tie steps to his car.

Benten was right. Rigg needed a second witness to Fernandez's
arrest.

In daylight, the Kellington Arms looked to be missing more
mortar than it had the night before last. And, inside, the counter
looked to be missing a clerk, though perhaps there was no need for
one in the painfully bright hours before noon. There was no bell to
summon anyone, so he improvised with his fist on the wood below
the counter.

'What the damned hell?' a grizzled veteran grunted behind him,
pulling himself upright to sitting from behind the two chairs in the
lobby.

'Richie Fernandez,' Rigg said. 'I heard he got arrested. I want
to know who saw it.'

'Never heard of him,' the man said, clinging to one of the chairbacks
as if it were the deck rail on a ship tilting to sink.

'He lives in room 202. I heard he got busted.'

'A lady and a gentleman just rented that room,' the morning clerk
mumbled, teetering behind chairbacks. His ship had hit fifty-foot
swells. 'They just went up for the night.'

Rigg headed for the stairs. Behind him, the grizzled veteran
dropped with a soft thud.

The doors upstairs were not thick. By their sounds, there was no
doubt that the lady and the gentleman in room 202 had not yet
arrived at their most urgent of destinations. Rigg stood a respectful
few feet away, to wait for the sounds to diminish.

'Peeper, are you?' a man's voice creaked.

Rigg turned, surprised by yet another someone up and about in
the halls that early. 'I'm looking for Richie Fernandez.'

'That ain't Richie in there,' the man said. He was in his fifties
and had only one arm. 'Richie was moved out.'

'What do you mean, "moved out"?'

'Meaning his stuff was tossed a few days ago.'

'I heard he got arrested.'

'Heard that, too, but can't say for sure,' the man said.

'Who saw it?'

The man shrugged. 'Nobody sees anything here.'

'He does factory work. Any idea where?'

'Screw machine place, three blocks over.' He pointed south with his one arm.

Apex Screw Products was in a brown cinder-block building with impenetrable glass blocks for windows.

'Can't say for sure who's here and who ain't,' the woman behind the desk said, not bothering to glance behind her. The building was one long room, twenty-five feet wide and maybe a hundred feet long. A dozen people, Mexican men and women, toiled at slender, tall machines, easily visible from the front.

Rigg showed her his card. 'Off the record, deep background, I heard Richie Fernandez got picked up and I'm trying to get his side of the story.'

'What story?'

'Witness to a drive-by,' Rigg lied.

'Gang-bangers?' she asked, because gang-bang shootings happened every day in Chicago.

'My editor wants me to check him out.'

'Richie ain't here. He ain't often here. He's one of our irregulars.'

'Mean guy?'

'Harmless,' she said.

'But a highly skilled machine operator?' he asked.

She laughed. 'Part-time man, sweeps for grape.'

'When did you last see him?'

'A week, maybe two, maybe more,' she said. 'Like I said, irregular.'

'You got a human-resources person, someone who knows next of kin?'

The woman stared at him, saying nothing, because hers was a shop run with undocumented workers. She didn't keep records.

'Which of your other workers knew him well?' Rigg asked, anyway.

She kept staring, saying nothing.

He checked his phone out on the sidewalk. He'd gotten a text from the county medical examiner's office. McGarry was holding a press briefing at two o'clock.

There was no press room at the Dead House. A dozen folding chairs had been set in two rows in the lunchroom – inadequate for the twenty men and women attending. Four of them lugged video cameras for television. The room was hot from so many people cramming the small space.

Three greeted Rigg with seeming pleasure, but most had a hint of feral in their eyes. Law enforcement had slapped back hard at all reporters after the lashing Rigg had handed out during the Stemec Henderson investigation. Like the cops, the reporters hadn't forgotten Rigg.

At precisely two o'clock, Medical Examiner Charles McGarry attempted to stride into the lunchroom, but he didn't stride with the cool assurance of a man in charge. His normal ruddy complexion had lost its red, and he was sweating. Profusely.

Three men in business suits followed him. Rigg guessed they were the doctors McGarry mentioned in his earlier, preliminary statement, when he announced that nothing of value had been learned from the initial examination of the Graves girls.

'Good afternoon,' McGarry began, jamming a shaking hand into his pants pocket. 'Let me first introduce the three most notable physicians who assisted in our examination of Beatrice and Priscilla Graves.' McGarry identified the doctors from St Francis, St Michael's and Stroger.

'It is their unanimous, and I mean unanimous, conclusion,' he said, 'that both girls died of hypothermia.'

The room erupted. 'They froze to death?' a reporter shouted. 'That's it? They froze to death?'

McGarry bit his lower lip, probably to keep it from trembling, but said nothing.

'Like they'd just gone out to play, naked, in the cold?' It was a wise-ass question from the wise-ass Primer, who wrote and blogged for the *Curious Chicagoan*, Chicago's gamiest scandal rag. And ruined lives, like Rigg's, by spinning words into untruths.

'Or were they deliberately frozen to death?' Rigg asked.

'My God,' another reporter murmured.

'I know that, to some,' McGarry said, 'this finding might be unsatisfactory—'

A dozen reporters shouted. 'Come on, McGarry,' one of the louder ones yelled, 'you can't brush this off as exposure to cold. They didn't just wander into that ravine! They were tossed.'

'What about those punctures?' someone else screamed.

'There were three, yes, on Beatrice,' McGarry said, his voice quivering. 'But, as we said in our previous announcement, they were shallow, less than a quarter-inch in depth, and could not have caused death.' All three of the doctors nodded like bobble-heads, perhaps to encourage McGarry to keep taking the arrows that could have been shot at them.

Their relief was short-lived. More questions were shouted, and McGarry turned, pleading, to the three doctors. Kemp, from St Francis, stepped forward. 'We understand that hypothermia is an unsatisfactory finding in cause of death,' he said. 'But we have very carefully examined the two young ladies, and I mean extremely carefully, and we simply cannot determine any cause of death except hypothermia.'

'How long were the girls lying in the ravine?'

Kemp didn't retreat. 'No telling, because of the extreme conditions that existed between December 28, when they went missing, and January 21, when they were found. The cold and the snowfall insulated the bodies from deterioration, making a conclusive analysis impossible.'

'Your findings are no findings at all?' a reporter from WGN shouted.

'Essentially, yes,' Dr Kemp said.

Rigg then asked, 'Is there any evidence of sexual assault?'

Kemp hesitated just long enough for Rigg to believe Glet's tip was accurate. Beatrice may have been penetrated. Finally, Kemp shook his head and looked away to take another question.

Each of the three medical men took turns facing the same incredulity, answering the same questions over and over. Murder by freezing was not unheard of but there might never be a final accounting for the deaths of Beatrice and Priscilla Graves.

The press finally gave it up. Rigg turned to file out with them and spotted Greg Theodore leaning against the back wall, smiling at him. The *Trib*'s media reporter had always been a scrupulous associate, and his short, factual sidebar about Rigg's return was more evidence of that, but Rigg didn't want to get buttonholed for a comment that might make him newsworthy for a second day in a row. He hurried to his car and sped away.

He spotted a McDonald's a mile later and realized he'd not eaten since before he'd ignored the hamburger at the Rail-Vu the previous evening. He pulled in and took his laptop inside. It was three-thirty, mid-afternoon, and the McDonald's was deserted enough to work. He got two Quarter Pounders and a coffee, and took them to the table farthest from the counter.

He wrote the McGarry presser straight, reporting every smart question and every wooden non-reply exactly as it had played out. He made no mention of McGarry's trembling hands, waxen face, or the obvious discomfort of the three forensic physicians. There was plenty wrong with the stilted, tentative question-and-answer performance he'd just witnessed, but that was for analysis, not factual reporting. He hesitated a bit, then inserted his byline and sent the piece off to Benten.

He'd just finished the first Quarter Pounder when his computer dinged with an incoming email: *Got it, thanks. Aria.*

The response came from Aria Gamble, someone he'd never met, but whose name he recognized as the features reporter who'd written the *Examiner*'s laudatory pieces about Corky Feldott. Every day seemed to be a shuffle at the Bastion, an ever-fragmenting puzzle of shifting jobs and lay-offs, and now it seemed the scramble had come to the Pink. Aria Gamble had come to replace someone, likely Eleanor, the supplement's copy editor.

He finished his coffee, tossed the second burger in the trash, and had just gotten outside when his cell phone rang.

It was Glet.

ELEVEN

'You heard?' Glet asked.

'Hypothermia.'

'The only things frozen are the brains of McGarry and the three wise men he paraded out to take the heat,' Glet said. 'McGarry's a nervous fool. He should have insisted they keep examining, instead of trotting out those doctors to say they couldn't find shit other than murder by freezing.'

'And Lehman's Klaus Lanz pinch?'

'Everybody knows Lehman's just buying time, using Lanz to show he's hot on the case.'

'What are you hot on, these days?'

'Chasing a lead.'

'Working the girls though, right?' Rigg asked.

'I don't know yet.'

'You don't know if you're working the biggest heater case in town?'

'It's a fragile thread I'm pulling.'

'Cut the poetic, Jerome. Why the subterfuge?'

'I heard you came by the house,' Glet said, dodging.

'Something came from that cabbie you tipped me to.'

'What?' Glet asked.

'He had a story. Does the name "Richie Fernandez" mean anything to you?'

'Who?' Glet's confusion sounded genuine.

It was Glet's tip, so Rigg gave it all to him.

'No shit?' Glet said when Rigg was done. 'Lehman actually arrested the guy?'

'But never charged him with anything, and now the guy's disappeared. He didn't even go back to his flop for his things.'

'It was a catch-and-release, then,' Glet said. 'Guy was probably so scared, he ran all the way out of town.'

'Or Lehman's still got him.'

'Unbooked for a whole week?' Glet paused to think, and then spoke slowly. 'It's possible. He could have stashed him in some motel where Lehman scares the owner, but that's risky, even for Lehman. He can't just book a suspect after holding him for a week. Unless . . . No, Jeez, it's got to be another catch-and-release.'

'Why didn't you chase the cabbie yourself, Jerome?'

Glet named Lehman's secretary. 'I told you: I was near her desk when the tip came in. "You're sure it was the girls?" she's saying to the caller, writing, *Rocco Enrice, cabbie*, on a pink message pad. I called downtown, got the licensing bureau, found out he drove a Checker south of Midway. I gave it to you as a gesture of goodwill.'

'You copped a lead meant for Lehman—'

'Which, as it turned out, was a damned good lead,' Glet interrupted.

'What's got you more interested than the girls?'

'Like I said, I don't know yet.'

'You're sounding odd, Jerome.'

'Maybe I'm looking back further.'

'The boys?'

'Not now, Milo.'

'Lehman knows what you're chasing?'

'He thinks I'm assisting on a weapons distribution thing, which ain't all untrue.'

'Tip me, Jerome.'

'Later,' Glet said, and hung up.

From the doorway, the Pink was the same, and it wasn't.

Eleanor and one of the bridge hens were there. The pink-tile floor was just as scuffed, the pink walls just as faded. The five metal desks were arranged as always: Eleanor's gray one in front, the two gold ones used by the part-time hens right behind it, and, farther back still, the black one that had once been used by the cuttery's owner and was now reserved for the relentlessly plaid advertising salesman. Rigg's red desk, too, was where it should be – jammed against the back wall, as if to isolate a recalcitrant child.

It was the sound of the place that had changed. The Pink never had been energized by the clatter of a real working newsroom. It was a former beauty salon, a place that still smelled of dyes and shampoos intermixed with Benten's cigarette smoke, peopled now by folks who chuckled softly to entice eighth-of-a-page advertisers. But, overarching it all, there'd always been the irregular thrum of Benten's exhaust fan vibrating the glass of his office wall and the metal of the desks, and even the plaster of the old walls.

That thrum was gone; the fan had been silenced. Now, the Pink squeaked.

Eleanor gave him a half-smile as he walked past her desk.

A woman stood making great brownish swirls on the inside of Benten's glass wall. She was quite beautiful, quite tall, quite dark-haired, quite slim, and she wore a quite black sheath of a dress and pearls – pearls, for damned sake. She was spraying Windex on to the glass with her right hand, wiping away great gobs of dark brown nicotine goo with the bunched paper towels in her left. Benten was being cleansed away.

Rigg went to his red desk, sat down and turned to watch the woman behind the smeared glass. She seemed to give him no notice and continued scrubbing, though the glass seemed to give her scrubbing no notice as well. Benten had been exhaling tar and nicotine on to it for several years and, despite the efforts of the rickety fan, much of it had stuck like glue, apparently. All she was accomplishing was to smear the brown film into wide swirls before tossing each bunch of toweling into one of three open black garbage bags and reaching for more. After a couple of moments, Rigg got up and walked to her doorway.

'It's going to be really nice when you get it done,' he said. 'You'll have a clear view of all of us, or at least those who are left.'

'You're Rigg,' she said, dropping another bunch of soiled paper towels into a bag.

'You're Aria, the person who intercepted my copy.'

'Not intercepted. Accepted.'

'You're Features at the Bastion.'

'I'm no longer necessary at the Bastion,' she said, reaching for more towels and misting more Windex on to the glass. 'I'm here to help boost ad revenue.'

'Where's Benten?'

'At home, I presume.'

'Whacked?'

'Leave of absence, I heard. I don't know.'

'Why are you wearing pearls?' The woman's vagueness was irritating.

'Don't you like pearls?' she asked, swirling.

'I do, so long as they're not sported by someone who got a good editor like Harold Benten bounced from his job.'

'I told you: I don't know what precipitated the change. Call Donovan,' she said, naming the real-estate developer bastard who'd bought the *Examiner* two years earlier and was hastening its descent into oblivion.

'Are they real, or are they plastic?'

With the briefest glance down toward her chest, she smiled. 'You're referring to the pearls?'

He felt his face flush, which hadn't happened in years. 'Yes . . . yes, of—'

'Why don't you call Donovan – or Benten at home?' she said, grinning even more broadly now, from making him stammer.

'He knows pearls?'

'I'm here to help bring in advertising, like I said.'

'But Benten's not coming back?'

'Call him at home,' she said again.

'And the rest?' he asked, pointing out to the almost empty newsroom.

'They scattered when I came in this morning.' She dropped more soiled towels, grabbed more clean ones.

'Should I scatter, too?'

'Meaning, should you back off the Graves case?' She stepped back from the glass, frowned at the swirled film and went to sit behind the desk.

'I'd like to pursue things,' he said, sitting at the edge of one of the shampoo chairs.

'By "things", do you mean the Graves girls or Stemec Henderson?'

'At the moment, it's something else. Richie Fernandez, mystery man,' he said.

'What's that supposed to mean?'

'Are you my boss?' he asked.

'As I keep saying, call Donovan or Benten.'

Trusting her was preferable to calling Donovan about anything. He told her what he suspected.

'You don't have corroboration on the arrest?' she asked, when he was done.

'So far, only the night clerk at the Kellington Arms has Lehman and another cop arresting Fernandez. Nobody at the sheriff's knows anything about him being charged.'

'And you're sure Glet knew nothing of the Fernandez bust when he tipped you to the cabbie?'

'Meaning, was he setting me up somehow? I don't think so – though, with Glet, you never know when he's lying. He said he's got a better lead to chase.'

'Better than a good lead in the Graves girls?'

'He implied it might go back to the boys, or it might be something else entirely. As for Fernandez, Glet thinks Lehman turned him loose right away, scared the guy so badly he left his stuff behind and took off for parts unknown.'

'Fernandez is here illegally or he's dodging a warrant,' she said.

'Either would explain why he ran.' He paused, then said, 'Benten picked a hell of a time to leave.'

She gestured toward the still-filthy glass. 'He should have quit smoking,' she said.

He hung around until she, the bridge hen, and Eleanor were gone, and then he Googled. Aria Gamble's byline had begun appearing in a suburban weekly four years earlier, reporting the same sort of inconsequential bits he was doing now for the supplement. She came to the *Examiner* two years later, to cover society goings-on along the North Shore, city fundraising events, marriages of prominent Chicagoans and, occasionally, in-depth profiles of people in the news. He found two of the long and admiring pieces she'd done on Corky Feldott, citing his Northwestern education, his joining the Citizens' Investigation Bureau after two years at an insurance company following graduation, and then his advancement to become the assistant to the Cook County medical examiner.

He also found a piece written about a party held to celebrate her graduation from Northwestern University. She'd been Aria Fall then, and the party had been hosted by her uncle, Benjamin Fall. He was one of the Lake Forest and Chicago Falls, who were among the richest families on the North Shore. Luther Donovan was a North Shore multimillionaire, and, likely, the families knew each other.

He searched further, but could find no mention of a husband named Gamble. Rigg figured him for irrelevant. What mattered, even if it was only for help dropping into a losing outpost such as the Pink, was how well one's family knew their neighbors.

He called Benten's landline on his way home. A woman answered, presumably Mrs Benten.

'Hi,' Rigg said. 'I work for Harold.'

'He's out.'

'I'm calling to find out if everything is OK.'

'Just peachy,' the woman said, and hung up.

TWELVE

T he cage came again, well before dawn. Again, he was trapped behind the flat black bars, helplessly watching Judith's bare arms beckon for what he could not do.

He got up. Sleep never came after the cage.

He'd just gone into the kitchen to make coffee from instant granules when Carlotta Henderson called.

'I got something,' she said.

She'd gotten so many letters and whispered phone calls – tips, threats and fanciful revelations from the heavens – that Rigg often thought a normal person would give up and flee, but there was nothing normal about losing sons to murder and a husband to grief. Carlotta stayed, resolute, praying that one letter, card or phone call would point to whoever killed her boys.

'Milo?' she asked. 'Did you hear me?'

'Another letter, Carlotta. Yes, I heard.'

'This is different – not a letter. This is real.'

'Just tell me.' He'd raced over to her place so many times, so many dawns. Even after the photos.

'No. You've got to see for yourself.'

'What came, Carlotta?'

'Somebody was here, Milo. Someone came up to my house.'

'When?'

'This night, last evening; I don't know. You've got to come.'

'I work in the morning.'

'Those girls?' she said.

'Of course, those girls.'

'What about the boys?'

'Always the boys, Carlotta. You know that.'

'Come.'

'Later, after work.'

'Later?' Her voice rose an octave. 'Like, really, really after dark, when you think you won't be seen?' She tried to force a laugh. 'Nobody's taking pictures anymore, Milo. Nobody gives a damn. I want them to watch my house. I want them to care, but they don't, not anymore.' She began crying softly.

'Give me an hour,' he said.

He showered to get the stupor out of his head, gulped down half a cup of the coffee and got to her street while the dawn was still an hour away.

Even in a night lit only grudgingly by a sliver of the moon and veiled further by sparsely falling snow, there was no missing the morbidity of her place. Once an immaculate, happy suburban home on a cul-de-sac five miles north of O'Hare International Airport, a gutter now hung down loose above the front door, and a pushed-through window screen lay against the side of the garage. The unshoveled snow on the driveway and front walk was boot-pitted by peddlers and mail people. A red Toyota RAV4, the battlewagon of so many middle-class moms, sagged on a flat rear tire in the driveway.

He sat in his car for a moment, remembering how she'd tried to keep up appearances at first, refusing to accept the horrors that had come to her. In the first weeks after her boys were found and her husband had collapsed dead on the body of the youngest of them, she'd left the boys' bicycles lying on the front lawn where they'd last dropped them, ready to be picked up again when their lives resumed. Right up until they'd been stolen.

And she'd tried to keep up her dark Latin beauty. The frowners made much of the pictures of her in the first weeks. Even numbed with grief, she looked spectacular. Sickos said she was keeping up her looks for any male that might stop by; she was Latin, after all, with hot Latin needs.

Letters and phone calls came. She read and listened to them all. For a time, the cops and the other reporters did, too, but they dropped away as new horrors and new victims demanded their attention. Except for Milo Rigg, Chicago's most prominent crime reporter. He came to the house on the cul-de-sac, daytimes, night-times, it didn't matter. He read the letters, he listened to her recount the whispered phone calls. He chased down every new lead and passed the more credible of them to whoever in law enforcement would listen. He bought Carlotta's pain because, some said, it tugged him from his own fresh grief.

And he raged. By God, he raged. He raged at the cops and the medical examiners, in print and on the web and on the phone, for doing nothing, until nobody in law enforcement would pick up the phone if they knew it was Rigg on the line.

For months and months, he kept coming to that once-happy house on the cul-de-sac, until at last he'd come too many times in the middle of too many nights. Primer, of the rag, the *Curious Chicagoan*, got tipped, falsely, that more linked Carlotta Henderson and the *Examiner*'s respected crime reporter than a hunt for justice. He had Carlotta's house staked out, published photos of Rigg leaving the home in the wee hours of a couple of those too-many mornings – proof, he said, that Rigg had been spending his nights doing something more than sifting through information that might lead to killers. The city's other queens, the *Trib* and the *Sun-Times*, reluctant at first, finally had to report the rumors, though both refused to run Primer's photos.

Primer offered up another bonanza. He published other, older photos. Carlotta Henderson, a beautiful woman seemingly mismatched to the portly building contractor who'd collapsed over the gurney of his youngest son, had been an exotic dancer in New Orleans, and had once been arrested in an escort sting. No matter that she'd quit that life when she'd taken up with Mr Henderson and come north to bear and raise two sons in what appeared to be a loving home. The past is never past, wags write, and Carlotta Henderson's past became her present and her future. She became white-hot, untouchable, a hussy who deserved no sympathy.

Rigg kept on raging, but his readers began looking at his columns with changed eyes, until finally they looked away. Rigg's credibility was shot.

Luther Donovan wearied of it all. The publisher of the *Examiner* was besieged by declining circulation and plummeting revenues – problems more immediate than Carlotta Henderson's tawdry history and Milo Rigg's relentless hammering of seemingly every law-enforcement officer in Chicagoland. He sent his crime columnist to the Pink to work part-time, writing suburban stories under Harold Benten's byline.

By then, Rigg had wearied of himself as well and wanted only to retreat to the dunes. He welcomed the part-time assignment as much as he could welcome anything in the wake of Judith's death. He could stretch her life-insurance proceeds for a couple of years by writing innocuous piffle for the Pink three days a week and spend the rest of his time hunkering down in the dunes.

Except, now, he was no longer writing piffle. He was back on Carlotta's cul-de-sac, chasing murderers. He got out of the car and walked up.

She opened the door before Rigg got to the threshold, as had become her custom after the first of the photos had been published in the *Curious Chicagoan*.

'I thought you said nobody was watching,' he said, trying for a joke as he stepped into the stifling heat of her home. He remembered how she kept her thermostat set at eighty degrees. The murders that had taken her children and husband still chilled Carlotta Henderson.

She looked at him with dead eyes and nodded.

She'd lost weight, more even than him. Deep furrows bracketed her mouth and a dozen new wrinkles ribbed her forehead. No one would ever think of her as having being voluptuous or the object of any man's desire.

They walked to the dining room, which was where they always sat when he came over. Cardboard file boxes, identical to those Rigg had stacked against the long wall in his living room, still surrounded her table in a ragged sort of semicircle. No doubt she knew the contents of each box as well as he knew his own.

A box of purple hospital latex gloves was placed at one end of the table, next to two Ziploc plastic bags. One contained a plain white envelope without any postage or other marking. The other held a single, pale yellow index card, printed in what looked like computer-generated lettering.

He sat down in front of the bags and put on the gloves. 'That's why you called?' Rigg asked, pointing to the index card.

'First, the envelope,' she said. 'As you can see, it has no address or postage. The card was inside. It had to be dropped off here sometime between last evening and two hours ago, when I noticed it. Do you understand?'

'You'll probably never be rid of the cranks, Carlotta. Even after all this time, they still come – now, right up to your door.'

He leaned over the table to read the computer-printed yellow index card in the second bag. 'Tiny purplish birthmark, below right ear . . . crossed toes, right foot . . . one large freckle, actually three, behind her knee . . . one-inch scar, left ankle.'

'There's nothing on the other side,' Carlotta said.

Rigg leaned back. 'Any idea what these body identification marks mean?'

'The first one is Anthony's. He had a tiny purplish birthmark below his right ear. No one would have noticed except family. Only a mother and a father would see.'

'And the killer,' he said.

'Obviously.'

'The other three – the toes, the freckles and the ankle scar?'

'Not on my boys.'

'Perhaps on other victims,' he said.

She took a larger plastic Ziploc bag from behind her and placed the bags containing the plain envelope and the yellow index card into it.

'Keep me out of it, Milo,' she said, handing him the bag.

THIRTEEN

The Dead House was the only place answers about body marks would be. He got there at seven fifteen that morning.

He didn't know the woman at the front desk. She was overnight staff. Her skin was even paler than Jane's, the beige, daytime receptionist.

'McGarry?' he asked.

She shook her head. He was relieved. The M.E. would just blather, and there was no time for that.

'Cornelius, then.'

That drew a shrug, a touch of her phone and the murmur of Rigg's name. And then she pointed to the stairwell. Rigg wasn't surprised. He'd figured Corky for a regular eager beaver, first among the staff to arrive.

Feldott was waiting in his office doorway, smiling and precise in a white shirt, green ribbon of a necktie and – perhaps in defiance of the snow falling outside – summer khaki trousers. For a guy who spent his days among the dead, Rigg thought it remarkable that young Feldott always seemed to be smiling.

'What a pleasant surprise,' Feldott said, ushering Rigg into his office and pointing to a chair.

'Is McGarry going to dodge the press after that sham of a news conference yesterday?'

'He's a smart, seasoned veteran.'

'He looked a little under the weather yesterday.'

'Wouldn't you, if you had nothing to report?' Feldott asked, sitting behind his desk. 'This is off the record?'

'OK,' Rigg said, like he had a choice.

'The girls' killer was smart. As horrible as were the Stemec Henderson murders, at least the brutality they suffered gave us causes of death, and DNA.'

'DNA on two of the boys, right?'

'Bobby Stemec and Johnny Henderson,' Feldott said. 'We don't have that this time.'

'The weather obliterated everything?'

'It wasn't just the weather. The girls' bodies were scrubbed with bleach.'

'Any evidence of sexual assault?'

'You asked Dr Kemp that yesterday.'

'He didn't answer.'

'I wasn't part of the autopsy team,' Feldott said, 'but no one's talking sexual assault.'

'You're sure Beatrice wasn't penetrated?'

'Why do you keep asking?'

'She was the oldest. I thought, maybe—'

'No,' Feldott said. 'And, please, don't spread that around as rumor.'

'Fair enough,' Rigg said. 'So, Lehman's got Klaus Lanz again?'

'A dodge,' Feldott said. 'What about your Richie Fernandez?'

'Just a name I heard.'

'Have it your way. What brings you around so early?'

'Crossed toes, tightly clustered freckles and an ankle scar.'

'Huh?' Feldott asked, but his eyes had narrowed. He'd recognized something.

'What do they mean to you?' Rigg asked.

'What do they mean to you?' Feldott countered.

'I'm wondering if any of them were noticed during the girls' autopsies.'

'Where did you hear of these . . . things?'

'A tip.'

'I'm not a doctor. I don't do the autopsies,' Feldott said, evading.

'You attend, right?'

'The M.D. that does the work is front and center. If I'm in the room, I'm back, away from the table.'

'So, crossed toes, clustered freckles and an ankle scar mean nothing?'

Feldott stood up. 'I'm late for a meeting, Mr Rigg,' he said, which Rigg supposed was as good a way as any to throw him out before the questioning progressed.

In the car, Rigg used his phone to summon up the office numbers of the three doctors who'd attended McGarry's presser and called each. He didn't get through to any of them and was referred to McGarry's office each time.

He drove to the diner, asked Gus and Lucille if Richie Fernandez had turned up, but that was for show.

'Sometimes we don't see him for weeks,' Lucille said. 'He pops up in all sorts of places, scrounging for work.'

'You're sure this was the cop who came looking for him?' Rigg took out his phone, showed them Lehman's picture again.

Both Gus and Lucille nodded.

'And the other guy?'

Gus shrugged. 'Same age, like I said before.'

'No uniform, right?'

'Plain clothes, but a better-looking overcoat than most cops wear.'

Lucille cleared her throat. 'We wondered if there might be a reward . . .'

For withholding information that might have been useful in keeping them alive? Rigg wanted to ask, but he didn't. He needed them for corroboration of Lehman's bust, so he shook his head and left.

The Kellington Arms went even faster.

'Richie Fernandez got arrested, I heard,' Rigg said to the guy dozing on one of the chairs across from the counter.

'Lots of people leave, one way or another,' the man mumbled.

'Who saw the bust?'

The man shrugged.

Rigg had expected nothing and got it. He hoofed it to the screw machine shop. The woman who didn't want to talk to him the last time didn't want to talk to him that morning, either.

Three stops, thirty minutes. As wastes of time went, they hadn't been much.

The Graves house was guarded by a Chicago cop out front.

The cop recognized him. 'No press.'

'Just a quick question, no interview.'

'No press.'

'Can you take a note inside?'

'For you?'

'For me.'

'No.'

The front door opened and a young woman, about nineteen, came down the steps and walked out to the sidewalk. 'You're that reporter, right? The one that pushed so hard about those boys?'

'Bobby Stemec and the Henderson brothers,' Rigg said.

'You took up with one of the mothers?' No doubt she was the oldest Graves daughter.

'That never happened,' Rigg said.

'Why are you here?'

'Do crossed toes, a small cluster of three freckles or an ankle scar mean anything to you?'

The woman flinched a little, like Feldott's eyes had narrowed. Not much, in either case, but enough to show Rigg had scored something. 'Which of them means something to you?'

The cop stepped between the reporter and the young woman and breathed on Rigg. 'Leave these poor people alone.' The cop's breath was hot and stunk of kielbasa.

The young woman hesitated, obviously wrestling with something.

'Beat it,' the cop said to Rigg.

The young woman turned and began going up the front walk.

Rigg went to his car, sure that the young woman recognized one of the marks printed on the yellow card, but more worried about the ones she didn't know about.

Aria called, fifteen minutes later. 'Where are you, Milo?'

'Is Donovan looking to lay me off? He can do it over the phone.'

She laughed. It was a good laugh, deep, hearty. 'Economics has cleansed your toxicity. I'm sure he loves you working full-time for part-time wages.' Then, 'I'm asking because I'd like you here.'

'It's still rush hour,' he said.

'Don't dawdle. I'm expecting visitors in an hour,' she said, and hung up.

He wanted to dislike her, but the woman always seemed to intrigue.

FOURTEEN

The Pink still smelled strongly of Windex when he stepped in that morning, though garbage bags and paper towels were nowhere in sight. Eleanor was where she should have been, at her front desk, but not so the two hens and the advertising salesman. They were gone.

Aria Gamble was supremely visible through the sparkling glass. So, too, was Benten's poster of the woods. It had to be just as coated with nicotine film as had been the glass wall, but she'd not removed it. She had respect, and that was good.

Aria had company. Sheriff Lehman and Medical Examiner McGarry sat with their backs to the glass, facing her across the desk. Lehman was upright, wisely balanced at the front edge of his shampoo chair. Not so McGarry. He'd made the mistake of sitting too far back, setting his tired chair into the beginnings of a slow recline. The veins on the backs of his hands bulged. He was struggling to pull himself more upright without being noticed.

'Join us,' Aria said, when Rigg came to her doorway.

'That won't be necessary, Miss Gamble,' Lehman said, standing up.

'It's Mrs,' she corrected.

'I apologize; I didn't know you were married.'

'I'm not,' she said.

Her gamesmanship stopped Lehman. 'We only need to speak with Rigg,' he managed, but it was after a pause.

'My digs, my Rigg,' she said, smiling at the rhyme.

Rigg's mind flashed back to Judith's 'too tight for light' rhyme about their landlord. He pushed the comparison away.

Sweat had broken out on McGarry's brow. He'd reclined past the point of no return. Without help, the only way out now was to roll on his side and get up as one would from a bed.

Rigg stepped over and extended his hand to pull the man forward. 'All first-time visitors have the same problem.'

McGarry stood up and gave Rigg a grateful smile.

'We'd really prefer to talk to Rigg alone,' Lehman said.

'Then arrest him,' Aria said. 'Haul him downtown for questioning. I'd actually prefer that, because it would give us a hell of a lead – the arrest of a reporter for unspecified charges, perhaps in response to doing his job. That would kick our scheduled front-page bowling championship story out on its ass.'

Rigg laughed. No one else did.

Lehman turned to Rigg. 'We understand you paid a visit to the Graves family.'

'Actually, I visited one of your officers, about an hour ago. He just happened to be standing outside the Graves house.'

'Don't get cute. You harassed a member of the Graves family.'

'The young woman? She came out, we exchanged pleasantries and she went back inside. Nice young woman.'

'You asked her about crossed toes, freckles and ankle scars.'

'She didn't answer.'

'Why did you ask her that?'

'Do crossed toes, freckles and ankle scars mean something to you?'

Lehman began to shake his head.

'We could run the question on our front page,' Aria said.

'In your supplement?' Lehman asked, not quite disguising his contempt.

'The Bastion's front page,' she said, smiling.

Lehman sighed. 'Off the record?'

Rigg nodded. Lehman looked to Aria. She shrugged and nodded, too.

'We're holding it back,' Lehman said, 'but Beatrice's second and third toes on her right foot were crossed, second on top of the third. She was self-conscious about it, as you can imagine. Only her family knew.'

'And her killer,' Rigg said.

'That's why we're holding it back.'

'How about the other marks – freckles and an ankle scar?'

Lehman turned to McGarry.

'I'm not an M.D.,' McGarry said. 'The three doctors did the autopsy.'

'And Corky?' Rigg asked. 'Was he there?'

'He's not a doctor, either. I don't recall any mention of odd freckles or an ankle scar, but I can double-check,' McGarry said.

'How did you find out about the crossed toes, Rigg?' Lehman said.

'An anonymous tip, with no mention of how they related to anything,' Rigg said. 'What about Klaus Lanz?'

'Anonymous, how?' Lehman said, not to be deterred. 'Did you get a phone call, or was it a letter?'

'A phone call,' Rigg lied. He wasn't ready to turn over the envelope and index card. 'Lanz?'

'Admittedly, a cheap shot, but Lanz was willing to go along for a few nights' free lodging and three meals a day,' Lehman said. 'I was hoping the real killer would stick his nose out by now, wanting recognition, but, so far, nothing's happened. We'll have to let Lanz go.' He stepped an inch closer to Rigg. 'Who tipped you about the toes?'

'And the freckles and the ankle scar?' Rigg added, taunting just a little.

Lehman again looked to McGarry.

'Like I said, I'll check it out,' McGarry said.

Rigg turned back to Lehman. 'You have no good suspect?'

'No.'

'You're sure? No other suspects?'

Lehman stared at Rigg but said nothing.

'I got a tip about that, too,' Rigg said.

'Richie Fernandez,' McGarry blurted. 'You asked Corky about Richie Fernandez, but we don't know anything about that.' The sweat had returned to the medical examiner's brow.

'I don't remember a Richie Fernandez, but he could have been a catch-and-release; I've been bracing plenty of people to get the girls' killings solved.' Lehman grabbed McGarry's elbow and steered him toward the door. 'And keep that damned crossed-toes business to yourselves,' he called back as they went down the stairs.

'What the hell?' Aria asked.

Rigg put his index finger to his mouth. The door hadn't quite closed and the sound of angry voices drifted up as their footsteps pounded down the stairs. Rigg grabbed his coat and hustled out on to the landing, but by then the hallway below had gone silent.

He hurried down to the outside door, peeked out and saw them walking quickly away. Lehman was still angry, jabbing his forefinger into McGarry's upper arm.

They stopped at a white Cadillac Escalade. McGarry got in behind the wheel, Lehman climbed in the passenger's side. It was odd that they were not using Lehman's official car and driver. Lehman hunted for stature wherever he could find it, and nothing screamed stature like an official car and driver.

Rigg ran for his Taurus. With luck, driving McGarry's car meant that they were intent on some sort of anonymity.

McGarry headed west, the opposite direction to either of their offices. Rigg was no expert at tailing a car, but there was enough traffic for him to stay four cars back and still keep McGarry's white Escalade comfortably in view. Three miles up, McGarry entered the east–west tollway.

They sped west. Ten miles passed, then twenty, and then the Escalade exited on to a two-lane blacktop, running through farmland. There was no traffic there and Rigg stayed a mile back to avoid being seen.

Two miles later, McGarry swung into the parking lot of a local bar that sat by itself at an otherwise barren intersection. There was nothing but flat farmland around, covered with snow. Rigg's only option was to pull off alongside the road.

It could have been that Lehman and McGarry had stopped simply because they were hungry and wanted an early lunch. More likely, Lehman, an old-line cop, had kept an eye on the rear-view and spotted a car tailing them out into the county, and that car had pulled in, stark against the landscape, once they'd stopped, becoming even more conspicuous.

Rigg's phone rang.

'They found another girl,' Aria Gamble said. 'Montrose Harbor. The Bastion wants you on it, since you're the paper's only crime reporter now.'

'I'm tailing Lehman and McGarry,' he said, which was a laugh.

'Back to their offices downtown?'

'Out in the boonies, the two of them together, arguing.'

'Montrose Harbor,' she said. 'Go there, and God help us all.'

FIFTEEN

REMAINS OF GIRL FOUND IN LAKE
Milo Rigg, *Chicago Examiner*

Chicago Police discovered the partial remains of a girl or young woman in a 55-gallon barrel yesterday on Chicago's lakefront. The barrel, probably trapped in the ice out in Lake Michigan until it began to melt, washed up to the shore along Montrose Harbor. Chicago Park District personnel, thinking it had fallen off one of the cargo ships that ply Lake Michigan, opened it and discovered a mutilated body. Chicago Police released it to the county medical examiner, who has scheduled a news conference for this afternoon at two o'clock.

It was the next day, a Saturday, at noon. The office was deserted except for Rigg and Aria. Though she'd dressed down a fraction by wearing tailored black slacks and a black cashmere sweater, she still wore her pearls. Rigg didn't know her well enough to inquire whether she wore them to bed.

'We can't do more than a bulletin,' he said. 'A damned waste of time.' He'd been up half the night, fuming over his missed opportunity to tail Lehman and McGarry.

'Another dead girl is a waste of time?'

'No, but racing to the lake just to watch a sealed barrel being loaded into an ambulance is.' He took a breath. 'They'd only hint that she's not all there. If that's true, they might never identify her.'

'What's your guess? Is it the Graves guy?'

'It's a different modus operandi. The Graves girls were unmarked. The barrel girl was mutilated, dismembered.'

'And both sets of girl killings are different from Stemec Henderson,' she said.

'Maybe the killer is being clever by varying his attacks.' It was another of the things that had kept him up all night.

'The Montrose Harbor girl, she was frozen, like the Graves girls?'

'That's something else I didn't get from being pulled off that tail.'

'You're angry.'

'Somebody from the Bastion could have run over to Montrose Harbor in ten minutes to report that nothing's known yet about the barrel girl. On the other hand, Lehman left here furious with McGarry. We should focus on that, for now.'

'Not that business about crossed toes; he answered that calmly enough. And both of them seemed genuinely confused about the other marks you mentioned.'

'McGarry blurting about Richie Fernandez is what set Lehman off,' he said. 'Lehman hustled McGarry out of here right after that, and they headed out of town. Fernandez is a story.'

'Route 39, Ogle County,' she said.

'Route 39?'

'That's where McGarry and Lehman were headed – or they were until, by your own admission, they spotted you tailing them and pulled into that bar.' She smiled.

'How do you know where they were headed?'

'Lousy grilled cheese.' Her smile broadened. She was enjoying the taunt.

'What the hell are you talking about?'

'Nobody eats at that dump of a bar. They offer cheese, ham and baloney sandwiches in sealed plastic bags that they heat in a microwave until the bag balloons up enough to kill whatever is growing inside. Horrible.'

'I'm not following this,' he said.

'McGarry has an estate just off Route 39 with an in-house chef, wine cellar and cold imported beer on tap. They wouldn't eat at that bar when they could avail themselves of that. No, they stopped there so they could have a look back at whoever was so obviously tailing them, and wait you out, if necessary. Your tail was blown.'

'You've been to McGarry's estate,' Rigg said.

'Several times, in a previous life. It's secluded. Lots of pines and bushes surrounding the perimeter, though you can see in easily enough.'

'Good place to sweat a suspect,' Rigg said.

'Richie Fernandez?'

'Why not?' he asked.

'Maybe. So, how did you know about those toes and the other marks?'

'I got tipped, the same way I got tipped about a fourth physical marker that I didn't mention – a tiny purplish birth mark.'

'Why hold that back from Lehman and McGarry?'

'That tiny purple mark was behind Anthony Henderson's ear.'

'My God!' she said, understanding instantly.

'A blank white envelope was dropped in Carlotta Henderson's mailbox by hand – no postmark. Inside was a yellow index card, computer printed, listing those crossed toes, a tight cluster of three freckles that appear as one, a small ankle scar and that tiny purple birth mark, which Carlotta confirmed was Anthony. Whoever left the yellow card knew about minor marks not only on the Graves girls, but also on one of the Stemec Henderson boys,' he said.

'The killer,' she said.

'The same killer,' Rigg said.

'You've got to tell Lehman where you got the card.'

'Carlotta made me promise to keep her out of it . . .'

'Because she got so trashed in the press?'

'Yes.'

'Could you be holding back because you also got so trashed—?'

'I've already lost what I had to lose.'

'The ankle scar and the freckles?' she asked, but knew the answer to that question. She was changing the subject. 'Waiting for two more girls?'

'We'll know whether it's two, or maybe only one, when they find the rest of the barrel girl,' he said. He went to his desk to make a call.

'How did you know I'd be in on a Saturday?' Corky Feldott asked.

'Everybody's working this Saturday.'

'Montrose Harbor girl,' Feldott said. 'We've got nothing yet for release.'

'What's missing?'

'Her head, right hand, left arm and left ankle are missing, but you can't report that.'

'Where's the sense in that?'

'We're thinking the killer couldn't fit all of her inside one barrel. We've got people with binoculars along the shoreline, looking for another one.'

'No reported missing girls fit her description?'

'None that jump out, but we need . . .' Feldott let the implication dangle.

'The rest of the parts. I understand,' Rigg finished for him. 'Could the Montrose Harbor girl have been killed at the same time as the Graves sisters?'

'No telling. Like the Graves girls, she was frozen.' Then Feldott asked, 'What's Jerome Glet doing at Alcohol, Tobacco and Firearms?'

'Glet's with Feds at ATF? I didn't know.'

'Strange, isn't it, when all hands are supposed to be working the Graves case?'

'And now the girl in the barrel,' Rigg said. 'He should be all over that.'

'Strange,' Feldott said.

Rigg went back to Aria's doorway. 'I've got to run into the city, check something out.'

'What's up?'

'Something that might explain McGarry and Lehman beating it out of here.'

The tables were empty. Lucille was behind the cash register. Gus, presumably, was behind the grill window, invisible.

'Seen Richie?' Rigg asked her, but it was not why he'd come.

'Not since the sheriff came, asking about him. Or you, afterwards.'

'Is this the guy that was with the sheriff?' Rigg showed her the picture he'd summoned up on his phone.

'That's him,' Lucille said.

'You're sure?'

'Gus!' she shouted.

Gus came through the swinging door, nodded at Rigg in recognition.

Rigg held up his phone.

'That's the guy came with the sheriff, looking for Richie,' Gus said. 'Who is he?'

'I'm not sure yet,' Rigg said, putting his phone into his pocket. But he was. He'd shown them McGarry.

'Learn anything?' Aria asked when he got back.

He paused outside her office. 'More than I'd hoped.'

'What did you learn?'

'First, a phone call,' Rigg said, and walked to his desk to call Glet's cell phone.

'Glet here,' the deputy said, picking up for the first time in days.

'Glet where?' Rigg asked.

'What the hell are you doing, calling me on a Saturday?'

'Trying to figure out what the hell you're doing at ATF. You haven't been home.'

'Who told you that?'

'Woman next door.'

'Well, I'm home now, not that it's an invitation for you to stop by. I been working late nights and leaving early in the morning. That old bat goes to bed right after nine, regular as clockwork, and doesn't wake up until ten the next morning. She's into the vodka, five minutes later.'

'What are you doing at ATF, Jerome?'

'It's no secret. Officially, I'm assisting our federal friends in an illegal weapons distribution case.'

'And unofficially?'

'Something more.'

'Something about the boys, as you implied last time we spoke?'

'It's always the boys, Milo. I told you I never forgot. Not for publication yet, but ATF picked up someone who might know something.'

'Like what?'

'That's all for now.'

Glet was playing cagey. Rigg would hold back, too, like he'd held back with Lehman and McGarry, and not say anything about the yellow card that linked the boys to the girls. 'I've got something new on Richie Fernandez,' Rigg said instead. 'Remember I told you it was two cops that pinched him?'

'One of them was Lehman, you said, and that the guy was never booked, that he never returned to his flop. Catch-and-release, I said it was probably, and Lehman scared him so bad the guy left town.'

'The other guy along for the bust wasn't a cop. It was McGarry.'

For a moment, there was only silence, and then Glet said, 'That doesn't need to be no big deal, Milo. The M.E.'s a real interested party this time around. You hammered him for not helping on Stemec Henderson. Maybe he pushed Lehman to get him involved so he could look good. We all want to look better, this time.'

'Lehman came to the Pink yesterday. He brought McGarry.'

'What for?'

'They wanted to brace me about going to the Graves place about a tip I got.'

'McGarry doesn't brace anybody; he's too soft. What tip?'

'Just a tip, for now, Jerome, unless you want to tell me more about ATF.'

'I can wait.'

'What if Lehman's got Fernandez somewhere?' Rigg asked. 'Stashed without being booked, like we talked last time?'

'I called around. Nobody knows anything about Fernandez and, when I asked Lehman about him, he acted as confused as everybody else. But McGarry? He got real nervous. Cracked a sweat. Lehman had to hustle him away.'

'You're saying McGarry helped Lehman do a nasty on Fernandez?'

'I don't think Fernandez was a catch-and-release,' Rigg said.

'McGarry? McGarry's not a doer; he's a . . . he's a keeper,' Glet said, but he said it softly, as if he was trying out the idea on himself. And then he hung up before Rigg could ask what he meant.

Rigg walked back to Aria's office. 'I just told Glet how nervous I made McGarry when I asked about Fernandez.'

'And?'

'I think I might have agitated Glet a little, too.'

She looked at her watch. 'Do you have dinner plans?'

'I never have dinner plans.'

'Let's go for grilled cheese,' she said.

SIXTEEN

'It looked huge on the Internet, but, up close, it looks endless,' Rigg said, looking through the pines on the other side of the road. Night was coming fast, but there was still enough light to see.

Aria had pulled off on to the shoulder of the side road and cut the engine. It was a relief. She'd insisted on driving her MINI Cooper because she said Rigg's Taurus was compromised from his too-obvious attempt to tail McGarry and Lehman. No doubt she was right, Rigg allowed, but there was nothing compromised about the way she drove. Her Cooper was red, fitted with a loud, high-performance exhaust system, and she drove it like she was fleeing the hounds of hell, thirty miles an hour over the posted limit, dodging recklessly in and out of traffic, all the way out to Winthrop County.

'Twenty million dollars' worth of endless, in fact, according to his wife's divorce filing,' Aria said. 'Why a man with all that would want to be medical examiner in a crooked county is beyond me.'

'Word was, he wanted stature of his own, instead of coasting on his father's business success. There was talk he was going to run for president of the county board after the M.E.'s office.'

'And from there, governor?' She turned to give him a smile. 'Your reporting on Stemec Henderson trashed that.'

'This is Illinois, remember? Our last two governors had enough millions to buy the office. McGarry has enough, too, starting with television commercials to make voters forget his incompetence.' He leaned forward. 'Definitely someone's home.' Several lights were on inside McGarry's mansion.

'Could be just the staff. Housekeeping, the chef and a maintenance manager, I imagine.'

'The wife is gone?'

'She's at their penthouse condo on Longboat Key, probably communicating hourly with her divorce attorney and perusing chalets for sale in Switzerland. And McGarry spends most of his time at their mansion on Astor Street. He doesn't come here much.'

'Except for yesterday, with Lehman, in a hurry,' Rigg said.

She turned to look at him. 'You really think they're keeping Fernandez, a suspected murderer, among the staff in the main house?'

'None of the other buildings look heated,' Rigg said, of the several unlit outbuildings.

'My God,' she said. 'You're not thinking . . .?' She let the thought trail off. The idea that Fernandez was being kept freezing, or frozen, in an unheated, unlit outbuilding was too heinous for words.

She twisted the ignition key. 'It's getting too dark to see,' she said.

She swung the car around, spinning her tires on the snow-slicked road until they bit into the asphalt. Three miles later, she pulled into the parking lot of the bar where McGarry and Lehman had stopped the day before. Three pickup trucks and one dirt-encrusted sedan were parked on the gravel.

'Do you ever drive rationally?' Rigg asked.

She laughed. 'I took a performance driving course, out in California. It's added controlled risk to life.' She reached for the door handle. 'Shall we dispel all doubt that they stopped here to eat?'

The place was the dump she'd described – paneled in knotty pine, faintly crunchy underfoot from grit dragged in from the parking lot, and lit by ancient neon freebie signs for Old Style and Bud Lite, and a strand of multi-colored Christmas lights draped across two stuffed deer heads on a side wall.

'My treat,' she said.

The three bearded men in flannel shirts and worn jeans perched on stools there grinned as she walked up to the bar. Stunning in tailored slacks, a short black wool jacket and the hint of pearls beneath, she was obviously a quantum leap in visuals from the deer heads, even ones so festively draped with Christmas lights. She ordered two grilled cheese sandwiches, but it was when she added two regular Budweisers – no Lites – to chase the cheese that their grins stretched into worshipful smiles. No doubt, this was a creature of discernment rarely, if ever, encountered in their pine-paneled midst.

The bartender, a bearded man of flannel as well, but also of efficiency, put both bagged sandwiches into the microwave behind the bar. They ballooned in an instant, presumably rendering them bacteria free. Aria laid a twenty on the bar and they took their cans, their bloated sandwich bags and the admiring eyes of all four males to the scuffed plastic laminate table in the farthest corner.

'Not your usual dining experience?' she asked, as they sat down. The light from the neon beer signs danced colors in her eyes.

'I'm comfortable in places like this,' he said.

'Even now that you're alone?'

He shrugged at her directness. He didn't want to talk about Judith.

'There are so many stories about you,' she said, taking a sip of beer. 'Joined the *Examiner* fresh out of city college, quickly rose to be a crusader reporter with his own column, loner, except devoted to his wife, became a traumatized widower, and finally, and most unkindly, exposed lover.'

'I was never anything to Carlotta Henderson except an ear.'

'As you wish,' she said.

'There are so very few stories about you,' he said.

'You scrubbed me?' she asked, using the newspapermen's term for deep background checking.

'I Googled, was all,' he said. 'Northwestern grad, reporter for a local suburban rag, society writer at the *Examiner*, and now advertising peddler at the Pink. No mention of a marriage.'

'Three months to a boy during college. Annulled. Kept his last name because it sounded better than my maiden name, which is "Fall".' She took another sip of her beer.

'Feldott's a Northwestern grad, too. Did you know him?'

'When he got named assistant M.E. I recognized his picture in the paper as someone from school, but we never spoke or anything.'

'Aren't you going to open your sandwich?'

'I like things to harden,' she said, arching her eyebrows just a little.

Rigg looked down to concentrate on unwrapping his sandwich rather than chase thoughts he hadn't had since before Judith was killed. Besides, the woman – the very attractive woman – was his boss.

The escaping steam smelled old, like something from a rusted pipe. 'I think you're right about Lehman and McGarry not coming here to eat,' he said.

She laughed. 'So, rich bitch is right, not just getting by on her looks?'

He smiled. She was so very direct. 'About the grilled cheese, certainly. Then again, you are North Shore.'

'My immediate family is not incredibly rich like Luther Donovan.'

'Just a modest number of millions?'

'Not even close,' she said.

'One more question about you?'

'Shoot,' she said.

'Are those pearls real?'

She laughed her good laugh again. 'You asked that when we first met.'

'You didn't answer.'

'I'll say this,' she said. 'If they're real, their size would make them worth a lot of money, and that would be risky, wearing a fortune around my neck.'

'You said you like risk. Your driving proves that.'

'Most people assume they're fake.' She raised her beer in a toast. 'I like that you're tenacious, Milo. I like that you're loyal to Carlotta Henderson.'

'She's the one left to shoulder it all, after everyone else has forgotten.'

'Except you.'

'She calls in the middle of the night when she gets something, and she keeps getting things. Lots of wackos, lots of nut jobs are out there. But she treats every one as if it was the real thing, the final clue, and now comes a yellow card that might tie the girls' killer to Stemec Henderson.'

'Can it be he's started up again, after a fifteen-month lull?' she asked.

'We might know soon enough. Glet implied he's working a new angle to Stemec Henderson, someone ATF picked up who might know something about the boys. It might lead to the girls.'

'So, who has the card now?' she asked.

He said nothing, which said it all.

She reached across the table to touch the back of his hand. Her fingers were light and warm. 'This could blow back past you and on to the *Examiner*, like those pictures did. It's a delicate time, financially, for Donovan.'

'I know,' he said.

She took her hand away, peeled open the plastic bag containing the sandwich and took a bite. 'Just as I remembered.' She reached quickly for her beer.

He tasted his sandwich. It was like paste.

They finished their beers, dropped their uneaten sandwiches in the trash barrel by the door and left.

Neither of them spoke as she raced them through a night spotted only here and there by houselights, but when she downshifted to speed up the ramp to the east–west tollway, she said, 'I heard you gave away all your furniture.'

'Where did you hear that?'

'From somebody who heard it from somebody who doesn't know anything about it at all.'

'I needed to declutter the apartment.'

'You didn't want reminders,' she said.

'I kept our place in the dunes intact,' he said.

'So, does your apartment have furniture, or not?' she asked.

'A love seat.'

'You kept a love seat?'

'Yes.'

'Is that metaphorical?'

'I'm not sure.'

'I heard you also have a wall of boxes filled with Stemec Henderson files.'

'Answers might be in them.'

'Don't file that index card away,' she said, swerving around a tank truck. 'You have to turn that over to Lehman, if only for your own safety.'

He turned to look at her. Her beauty and her pearls glittered in the glow of the instrument panel. She was right.

'You know, too,' she went on, 'that the Henderson woman was only a messenger, right? You were the intended recipient.'

'Yes,' he said.

The loud exhaust from her Cooper masked the sounds of the cars they passed, and again they didn't talk. After another ten miles, they exited the tollway. Five minutes later, she swung into the parking lot behind the Pink. She switched off the engine, but still they did not speak. The night was not late.

He got out.

'You have to turn over that card,' she said, but she said it to the windshield, not facing him.

'I know,' he said.

'And I want to see your wall of boxes,' she said, still looking straight ahead.

He knew that, too. He closed her door, she sped away and he walked to his car.

SEVENTEEN

Glet called at 8:30 that Sunday morning. Rigg was sitting on his love seat with an open file box on his lap. In the four hours since he'd been rousted by the cage, he'd rearranged his wall of boxes so that the bottom ones were now on top, and he'd begun looking through notes he hadn't gone over in some time. But the search for clues he'd missed would still be scattershot, because there was nothing else left for it to be.

'Lehman is issuing a statement, no press conference, in thirty minutes,' Glet said. 'Two boys, both age ten, found a sealed, five-gallon drum along the beach two days ago. It was heavy, wrapped with waterproof duct tape. Thinking it was valuable, they snuck the drum into one of the kids' garages and opened it last night after hockey practice. They freaked. The garage boy's old man called the Chicago cops. They called us.'

'Parts?'

'All that were missing. McGarry brought in his three fancy doctors to sort of reassemble her. Five foot six, 150 pounds, mid-teens. Lehman thinks her face matches a photo of a missing girl.'

'You're working this?'

'We got people on it.'

'But not you?'

'I'm working other angles, like I told you.'

'Remember when I told you it was McGarry who was along for the Fernandez bust?'

'So?' Glet asked.

'You said McGarry was a keeper, or the keeper. What did you mean?'

'Nothing I can remember,' Glet said, and hung up.

The beige receptionist at the Dead House shook her head. 'No press right now.'

'Call Corky.'

'*Cornelius*,' she corrected, not moving a finger toward her phone, 'but Mr Feldott is busy.'

'Call him anyway.'

'No,' she said.

'I'll wait for Corky,' he said, motioning to the row of plastic chairs against one wall.

'This isn't a bus station,' she said.

He sat on one of the chairs and smiled back at her glare.

Forty minutes later, two men emerged from the hall that led back to the morgue. One man was trembling, supported under one elbow by the second man. Corky Feldott followed close behind. He wasn't sporting his perpetual grin that morning; the look on his face was stricken. Even his narrow necktie that day was black, funereal. With the barest of frowns at Rigg, he put his hand on the trembling man's shoulder and then the two visitors walked out on to the sidewalk.

Feldott nodded to Rigg and motioned him over. 'Poor people,' Feldott said. 'They've been sitting on a ransom card that never got followed by a money demand for a month, hoping their girl was alive.'

'Card?' Rigg asked, trying to sound casual.

'Not for publication, but it wasn't even a letter, just a little yellow thing,' Feldott said.

'Where's McGarry?' Rigg asked.

'I'm handling this part of it,' Feldott said.

Rigg asked about freckles and a faint, slight scar. Feldott nodded, remembering when Rigg had asked about them earlier, but said nothing further now. Feldott gave him details about the Montrose Harbor girl, asked him to wait until noon to file, so that the men who'd just left could notify their other family members, and sent Rigg on his way.

Noon was still two hours away and Rigg's story on Fernandez was still single-sourced and flimsy. He had time to drive back to the Kellington Arms and try again. Not surprisingly, a different man was behind the counter.

'Richie Fernandez,' Rigg said.

'Don't know him.'

'Busted here.'

'Don't know him.'

'The night clerk saw it.'

'Talk to him, then.'

'Where is he?'

'No telling which night clerk you're talking about. A lot of us take turns at the desk. Get free nights that way.'

Rigg took out a ten. 'Who else might have seen the bust?'

The man's face came alive at the sight of the green. 'I heard Wally was down the hall when the cops came.'

'Is he here now?'

The clerk nodded, his eyes on the ten. Rigg handed it over.

'Two fourteen,' the counter clerk said.

Rigg went up and knocked.

'Yeah?' a voice slurred through the door.

'Ten bucks for two minutes of conversation.'

The door opened ten dollars' worth, which was more than a crack, less than a welcome. One red eye, part of a second and a face full of whiskers appeared behind the crack, in a mist of muscatel.

'You saw Richie Fernandez get cuffed?' Rigg asked.

Wally beckoned the money with a rub with his thumb and forefinger. Rigg folded the bill lengthwise and pushed it through the opening.

'I was down the hall and saw it, sure.'

'Was this one of the cops?' Rigg held his phone to the gap so Wally could see Lehman's picture.

'Another ten,' Wally said.

'Five, after you look at a second picture.'

'Up front.'

Rigg passed through the five.

'Yeah, that's him,' Wally said.

Rigg then summoned up the digital McGarry.

'The other, yeah.'

'Your full name?'

'Just Wally.'

And so it would be Just Wally, but it was enough.

He called Aria's cell phone and asked her to meet him at the Pink. She said she was already there, working. He got there at 11:30.

'You said you've got more than Lehman's statement about the girl,' she called from inside her office.

'Write first, to release at noon,' he said, and headed for his desk.

He'd worked it in his mind driving back, so it only took a few minutes. He forwarded it to Aria and followed it into her office.

HARBOR GIRL IDENTIFIED. SECRET SUSPECT?
Milo Rigg, *Chicago Examiner*

According to a statement by the Cook County Sheriff's Department, the girl whose body washed up in a barrel in Montrose Harbor has been identified as Jennifer Ann Day, 16, of northwest suburban Des Plaines. She disappeared December 30, after leaving her home to go to the public library. Her parents received a ransom note the next day demanding that they not inform the police and await further instructions that never came. Miss Day was a junior at Maine Township High School West. Funeral arrangements are pending. Cook County Sheriff Joseph Lehman is working alongside the Chicago and Des Plaines police departments in the investigation.

Perhaps related to the murder of Miss Day is the troubling disappearance of a person of interest in the Graves sisters' killings, Richie Fernandez, of Chicago. According to witnesses at the Kellington Arms, Sheriff Lehman, accompanied by Cook County Medical Examiner Charles McGarry, arrested him at the hotel a week before the Graves girls' bodies were discovered on German Church Road in suburban Cook County. Information about the arrest, including whether and where Fernandez is being held, has not been forthcoming. Both Sheriff Lehman and Medical Examiner McGarry have denied any knowledge of the arrest of Mr Fernandez.

'Feldott wants some things held back,' Rigg said. 'Everything else was off the record.'

'The yellow card the Day family received and that faint scar on their Jennifer Ann's ankle?' she said.

'Most especially, Feldott won't let me use those yet.'

'Good, because you haven't yet given Lehman your card,' she said. 'Turning it over might speed things up when one more victim is discovered.'

'The one with the tight cluster of three freckles,' he said.

'And now you want to report Fernandez. Your two sources to the bust: they're both winos?'

'Maybe just the fellow down the hall from Fernandez's room. I didn't smell grape on the night clerk.'

'And where is Lanz, these days?'

'Perhaps still dining and sleeping free at the county's expense, or quietly released. I can't get any confirmation about him, either.'

She pursed her lips, glancing again at Rigg's piece on her screen. 'I don't know. It seems extreme, you making such a show of Fernandez. Lehman would have to know there'd be hell to pay if he brought forth a suspect he's been holding illegally. Unless . . .'

'Unless Fernandez is no longer capable of being brought forth,' Rigg finished for her. 'Or, maybe Fernandez is fine and healthy, and they think nobody will care, so long as Fernandez is the guy.'

'"They"?'

'McGarry's in on it, Aria.'

'That's problematic,' she said.

'Why?'

'He's rich,' she said, 'and Donovan likes rich people.'

He looked past her, drawn to the woodland picture Benten had taped to the wall. It looked to be the safest place on earth.

'Milo?'

He turned back to her.

'This is going to hit the fan. You're accusing important people of suppressing information.'

'Like I'm suppressing information by not reporting the card?'

'We're agreed that it's time, right now?' she said.

He nodded.

She managed a small smile, reaching for her phone. 'Bombs away, babies.'

She'd insisted that Lehman come to them, and so they sat in Aria's office.

'Where the hell did you get this?' Lehman asked, reading the pale yellow card through the Ziploc plastic bag. Rigg had replaced both of Carlotta's Ziplocs with ones he'd run out to buy, to make sure no stray fingerprint of hers would be discovered. Aria agreed to keep her out of it.

'Left inside my car,' Rigg said. 'I heard the Day family received a ransom demand on an identical card.'

Lehman set the bag on Aria's desk. 'This was how you knew to ask the Graves daughter about the crossed toes?'

'And to ask you and McGarry about freckles and ankle scars. Jennifer Ann Day has a scar on her ankle.'

'This card lists a fourth thing, a purplish birth mark. You didn't ask about that.'

'I didn't,' Rigg said.

Lehman stared at him for a few seconds. 'What's it link to?'

'Anthony Henderson had such a mark behind his right ear,' Rigg said.

'Damn it,' Lehman said.

'The Stemec Henderson killer knows about that purplish birthmark, like he knows about the crossed toes on Beatrice Graves—'

'And the ankle scar on Jennifer Ann Day,' Lehman interrupted. 'Same damn killer?'

'Have you pressed Richie Fernandez about the Stemec Henderson boys?' Rigg asked.

'Who the hell is this Richie Fernandez you keep mentioning?' Lehman asked, but his face showed no curiosity. He was lying.

'Somebody you arrested. Remember how the name upset McGarry?'

'Where exactly did you hear about this Fernandez?'

'Tipped.'

'We've been leaning on dozens of people,' Lehman said. 'Your Mr Fernandez could have been one of the hundreds we braced.'

'This one you actually took away, you and McGarry. I'd like your comment on him.'

Lehman grabbed the Ziplocs off Aria's desk and stood up. 'In exchange for not charging you with withholding evidence in a murder investigation, I'll count on you not to report this?'

Aria looked at Rigg, then at Lehman, and nodded.

'Mum's the word on the card for now,' Rigg said.

'See that you don't,' Lehman said to Aria, and headed for the door. Rigg followed him.

'I need a comment on Fernandez,' Rigg said.

'I'll ask my people,' Lehman said, starting down the stairs.

'He's lying,' Rigg said, returning to Aria's doorway.

'If Fernandez had been unproductive, he'd have been released and Lehman would have said that,' she said. 'If Fernandez had been viable, he'd have been announced.'

'Luckily, McGarry is a part of it,' Rigg said.

'He's not strong like Lehman,' she said.

'He can crumble. The question is how to squeeze him,' Rigg

said. 'But first, let's see what the mysteriously reclusive Deputy Glet has to say about all this.'

'All what?' she asked.

'Everything he's keeping secret.' He went to his desk and called Glet. Again, the deputy answered right away. He was no longer dodging Rigg's calls.

Rigg told him about the yellow index card he'd just given Lehman. 'Four distinguishing features, two relating to the girls that have been found, a third matches Anthony Henderson. It's the same kind of index card the Day family received with a ransom request. Same killer, then and now.'

Glet said nothing.

'Why so silent, Jerome?' Rigg asked.

'You're wrong.'

'Things you learned at ATF?'

'Later,' the deputy said, and clicked him away.

A hand touched the back of his shoulder. 'How about dinner and then a look at your file boxes?' Aria asked.

'I've got plans,' he said. He had no plans. He hadn't had plans since Judith was killed. But a plan to have plans with the gorgeous Aria Gamble seemed a most dishonorable thing to do.

He grabbed his laptop and hurried out the door.

He drove west in the dwindling dusk, passing out of the suburbs and into the farmland, as much away from Aria Gamble as toward hope of discovering something new. Three pickups and two cars were parked at the bar at the barren intersection, their owners inside, braced for another evening's merriment of beer, grilled cheese and decorated deer heads. He drove on, trying to focus on what he might have set loose by taunting Lehman about Richie Fernandez, and not imagine anything about Aria Gamble at all.

He cut his headlamps at the last turn and shut off his engine along the side road that bordered McGarry's estate.

The mansion was dim. Only a few low-wattage lights were on. Like when he'd come with Aria, all of the outbuildings were dark.

Five minutes later, headlamps sped through the intersection behind him and slowed to turn on to the drive leading up to the house. Rigg powered down his side window.

The electronic gate opened, the headlights shot up the drive and the car slammed to a stop next to the house. The headlamps switched off. The car's interior light came on as the driver's door was opened.

No new lights came on inside the mansion. Rigg stuck his head out his side window, straining to hear. Footsteps crunched on the snow, growing louder. The driver was crossing the ground at the back of the mansion.

A gentle sound of something being pulled softly across the snow came then. Rigg squinted across the great expanse of the rear grounds but could see nothing. He looked back at the mansion. The interior of the car remained lit. The driver had been in too much of a hurry to close the car door.

The gentle pulling sound continued for another few minutes and then it stopped. Again, footsteps crunched the snow, only this time they grew fainter. The driver was going back toward the driveway.

The car door slammed; the car's interior light went off. A moment later, a new light was switched on inside the mansion.

Rigg started his car, turned it around and drove back to the intersection.

He'd taunted Lehman, and he'd taunted well.

'What are you up to, Charles McGarry?' he asked the night.

EIGHTEEN

Aria Gamble stood grinning by the front desk when Rigg walked into the Pink the next morning. 'I do so love risky behavior.'

Eleanor handed him the small sheaf of pink message slips. 'Deputy Glet has been the most persistent. He said your phone is switched off.'

'Ah, yes, my phone,' Rigg said, fanning through the slips. He'd turned it off at six fifteen, when it rang and he'd recognized Greg Theodore's number on the display. He wasn't surprised; the *Trib*'s media man was just the first of many who were likely to ask if he'd gone nuts by accusing Lehman and McGarry of making an illegal arrest.

The sheaf of slips in his hand proved him right. Besides the half-dozen from Glet and one from Corky Feldott, the dozen other messages were from reporters.

'So, there's a ruckus?' Rigg asked the two women, feigning confusion.

'Luther Donovan called me first thing this morning,' Aria said, still smiling. 'I said that, since the Bastion is so short-staffed, you were able to slip the piece on to our site without my knowledge.'

'The hell you did,' Rigg said.

'Actually, I told Donovan that your reporting will get him readers, and readers will get him advertisers. Greed always shuts him up.'

'Good, because I was going to tell Theodore that my witnesses were society friends of yours, living at the Kellington Arms,' Rigg said.

She laughed. 'We're on the same page, then,' she said, heading for her office.

Eleanor watched her go, then turned back to Rigg, clearly puzzled by the strangely easy banter she'd just witnessed. He wondered briefly if he should wonder about it, too, but pushed the thought out of his mind and went to his desk to call Glet.

'I talked to Lehman,' Glet said. 'I told him I heard about a match between the card the Day family received and the one you gave him listing body marks. He listened, said nothing. I told him you'd been pestering me about some guy named Fernandez. He said you'd been bugging him, too, but he doesn't know what the hell you're talking about. You best be careful around him, Milo. Your Fernandez story crumbles if he wasn't with the Graves girls.'

'It doesn't matter who Fernandez was with. The Fernandez story is about Lehman snatching a supposed witness and making him disappear.'

'Unless he released him right away, like I've been saying,' Glet said.

'Then why doesn't Lehman say that?'

'You're thinking Lehman needs a patsy, someone to soften up, to blame.'

'Or something went real wrong during the interrogation,' Rigg said.

'Or both,' Glet said. 'Damn it.'

'You need to work this Fernandez angle, Jerome.'

'Not now,' Glet said.

'How about that little yellow card I gave Lehman?' Rigg said. 'It links the boys to the girls.'

'That's too fragile,' Glet said.

'What the hell does that mean?' Rigg asked, but Glet had already hung up.

'Greg Theodore,' Eleanor called out behind him.

Rigg pressed the flashing button. 'Hello, Greg.'

'I gotta double-check, Milo: your two witnesses are residents of the flophouse where Fernandez was living?'

'They were clear-eyed.'

'At the time of the bust, or when you spoke to them?' Theodore was smart. He knew memories could be pliable when tempted by a ten-dollar bill, especially when pickled by alcohol.

'Clear-eyed,' Rigg repeated.

'I'm going to be dredging background. What's past is past, except when it isn't.'

'My ejection from the Bastion?' Rigg asked, knowing better.

'Carlotta Henderson and the photos.'

'Lehman made that bust, Greg. I'm sure of it.'

'Then God help us all,' Theodore said, and clicked off.

Rigg called the Dead House and asked for Feldott.

'Are you crazy?' the young man asked in a voice higher than normal. 'You really think my boss and Sheriff Lehman stashed this Fernandez guy? Fernandez must have simply left town.'

'Why is nobody saying that?'

'We're all saying it, Mr Rigg. All except you. Mr McGarry called us into his office. He assured us this Fernandez business is your invention, that, if the guy was arrested, it was by others.'

'What was his demeanor?'

'Sweaty, but can you blame him? Stemec Henderson was a nightmare for him. Now, there's a new nightmare: dead girls. Only, this time, you're also accusing him of a crime, this Richie Fernandez thing, with no proof.'

'Not a crime, not yet. Just a mysterious arrest, seen by two witnesses.'

Rigg looked through Aria's glass wall. She was on the phone, vehemently gesturing with her right hand. Likely the call was about him.

'Two winos? You're killing our credibility . . . Ah, heck,' Feldott said, and clicked off.

Aria, too, had hung up and, for a moment, just stared at her phone. Then she looked out, saw Rigg looking at her and motioned for him to come in. 'That was Donovan,' she said. 'He got a call from someone at the *Sun-Times*. One of their reporters went to the flop.'

'And couldn't find either of my witnesses?'

'You need to be right about Richie Fernandez,' she said.

The guy at the front desk was different, but there'd been different guys at the counter each time he'd come.

'Wally upstairs?' Rigg asked.

'You got a badge?'

'Reporter.'

'Somebody beat you here.'

'I know: *Sun-Times*,' Rigg said. 'Is Wally upstairs?'

'Gone.'

'Gone where?'

'Not my business to ask, not his business to tell,' the clerk said.

'He got to take his stuff?' Rigg said, asking really if Wally had been grabbed.

'Sure,' the desk man said.

'How about visitors? Did anyone come to see him, right before he moved?'

The clerk turned his back to Rigg and pretended to busy himself with the slotted mailbox on the wall. The slots were empty. Residents of the Kell didn't get mail.

'Like a cop?' Rigg asked.

The desk clerk made no move to turn around.

'Mind if I go upstairs?' Rigg said.

'Residents only,' the clerk said to the slotted box.

Rigg headed for the stairs.

Just Wally's room was clean. Nothing was in it except a stripped mattress and a chest of drawers with all of the drawers pulled partially out and empty. Wally had fared better than Fernandez. He'd had the opportunity to take his stuff.

Rigg went back down to the counter. 'Last time I was here, I was talking to the night guy, can't remember his name.'

'Night guys change.'

'Like day guys?'

He shrugged. 'We take turns. Free room for a day.'

Rigg drove to the diner. Lucille was visible inside. Likely Gus was behind the grill window. And neither of them mattered. They'd tipped the sheriff's office about purportedly seeing Richie Fernandez with the two girls, nothing more. And Lehman and McGarry had dutifully come around to the diner, but as far as Lucille and Gus could testify, nothing more. They'd not witnessed Lehman and McGarry combing nearby flops, nor had they seen the bust.

The piece he'd just posted to the *Examiner* was trashed. The witnesses at the Kell to Lehman's and McGarry's bust of Fernandez were both gone.

He called Glet's cell phone when he got out to the sidewalk.

'We just talked, an hour ago,' Glet said.

'We need to talk some more, face-to-face.'

'About what?'

'About Fernandez; about witnesses; about McGarry the keeper, whatever you meant by that.'

'I'm at ATF.'

'I'm fifteen minutes away.'

'I'll be out for a smoke. I'll give you ten puffs.'

Glet was already fouling the air with a fresh cigar when Rigg walked up. The deputy was sweating like always, despite the cold, but there was a slight smile playing on his lips.

'Would Lehman push witnesses out of town?' Rigg asked.

Glet's smile disappeared.

'My two witnesses at the flop that saw Lehman bust Fernandez have disappeared,' Rigg went on.

'Two winos?' Glet blew a smoke ring up into the air. 'Rumor is,' he said, watching it, 'Lehman's got a million in drug money that never made it into the evidence locker.' He smiled a little, meaning it was no rumor. 'He could have paid them, or just threatened them to leave. Look, Milo, I don't know if you shot too fast, accusing Lehman and McGarry of stashing that Fernandez. I sure don't like the implications of it, if it's true. But stick around. There's going to be big news breaking at a press conference right here this afternoon. You've been invited, along with everybody else.' Glet pulled back his coat sleeve to check his watch. 'Any second now.'

'About what you've been up to?' Rigg asked.

Rigg's phone chimed. Glet grinned, pointed to Rigg's jacket pocket. 'Go ahead.'

Rigg took out his phone, saw a text from Eleanor at the Pink: 'Presser at ATF at two this afternoon. Gun distribution case.'

'You got just enough time for a nice cup of coffee and some deep breaths,' Glet said.

'That gun bust you said might link to Stemec Henderson?' Rigg asked.

Glet threw his cigar against the side of the building. 'Lehman might have really done it this time,' he said, and went inside.

Rigg stared at the door for a moment, wondering what Glet had meant, and then went off to find coffee to kill time.

NINETEEN

'Thank you all for coming,' the short man in the brown suit said. 'I'm Special Agent Till for the ATF.'

By 'all', Till meant the seven newspeople gathered in the employee lunchroom. Four were men, three were women. All but Rigg and one other were third-stringers. All had pens or pencils poised above slender wirebound notebooks, and all balanced small digital recorders to catch what they forgot to write. None had video cameras. An ATF presser about gun distribution did not draw television.

The other veteran, besides Rigg, was Greg Theodore of the *Tribune*. He sat at the front table. Rigg guessed that the *Trib*'s media man was there because he'd figured Rigg would show up because of the ninth person in the room. Deputy Jerome Glet leaned his bulk against one of the vending machines for coffee, soda and petrified snacks that lined one wall.

'What we do does not normally elicit much interest from the press,' Till went on, with an acknowledging faint sweep of his hand, 'but it was suggested we reach out to you, and others who apparently could not attend on such short notice, because of an unusual turn one of our cases took a few days ago.'

He paused to look at Glet, who nodded for him to continue.

'One of our illegal firearms distribution investigations reached a satisfactory milestone a week ago, with the arrest of Kevin Wilcox. Ours is part of a multi-state, multi-task force investigation into illegal distributions of firearms throughout the Midwest. That's ordinary stuff for us, here at ATF, but our interrogation of Mr Wilcox took an unanticipated turn when we reached out to the Cook County sheriff's department – as much as a courtesy as anything else, because Mr Wilcox's activities took place in unincorporated Cook County, their jurisdiction. Deputy Jerome Glet began working with us. In the interest of full transparency, he thought it best that we hold this press briefing so he could personally brief you on his part in our investigation.'

Glet introduced himself. 'I was brought into the Wilcox investigation at the request of Agent Till, here, because of jurisdiction, nothing more. And, for some days, that's all it was. I was simply kept apprised of their gun distribution case and allowed to sit in on their interviews. But, because we never give up on a mature murder case and we never quit investigating new cases as well' – he paused to look directly at Rigg, long enough to cause everyone else to turn to look at him, too – 'I began to wonder if there might be something to the close proximity between where Bobby Stemec and the Henderson brothers were found murdered and the Happy Times Stables, north and west of the city of Chicago, where Kevin Wilcox carried out his gun distribution scheme—'

'*Alleged* gun distribution scheme,' Till interrupted.

The third-string eyes turned back to Glet, but not Greg Theodore's. His eyes stayed on Rigg a moment longer. Rigg could only shrug and smile back.

'Alleged scheme,' Glet corrected. 'In the course of Special Agent Till's investigation, I became aware of a number of points of potential contact with my ceaseless investigation' – again he looked at Rigg, to underscore the point – 'into the murders of Bobby Stemec, Johnny Henderson and Anthony Henderson, the October before last.'

By now, all the reporters were writing furiously. This was no ordinary ATF presser about a gun bust. A big break in an old case was being presented.

'It is premature to go into detail,' Glet continued, 'but we expec to request that Sheriff Lehman charge Wilcox with the Stemec Henderson murders.'

Theodore shot up his hand. 'What evidence have you got, and is Wilcox suspected of other murders?'

Instead of answering, Glet looked at Rigg, taunting, almost begging him to follow up on the same question.

Rigg bit. 'The Graves girls? Is Wilcox a viable suspect in the murders of the Graves girls and Jennifer Ann Day?'

'I am investigating other matters. Thank you all for coming,' Glet said, without any mention of why Kevin Wilcox was suspected of the Stemec Henderson murders or any other crimes. He and Till left the room through a side door.

'What ties Wilcox to anything?' Theodore shouted after them.

'Has he confessed?' someone else yelled.

Rigg called out nothing. It would have done no good. Glet's moment was to tantalize, to draw attention to himself and hope to keep it there.

There was a rush to leave the room. No longer did print deadlines dominate. Now all news was hot, aimed for the Internet as short and as fast as it could be typed, from cars or sidewalks or wherever.

Not so with Rigg. He was in no hurry. All he wanted was quiet, a place to think.

'You just got bumped as my next lead,' Theodore said, sidling up. 'I was going to write about your resurrection, flashing your rusted sword of righteousness in the name of Richie Fernandez and his potential involvement in the Graves and Day cases.'

'Nothing else?'

'And your non-existent witnesses,' Theodore said, watching his eyes.

Rigg shrugged and Theodore hurried away.

Heading toward the parking garage, Rigg tried to puzzle Glet's cryptic performance. The deputy came across as positive that Wilcox had killed the boys, but then had suggested he was working an angle to something else, an angle that didn't necessarily point to the murdered girls.

Too many oranges were up in the air, and the juggler was still quite blind.

He wrote the bit from a Starbucks before his coffee had a chance to cool.

STEMEC HENDERSON BOMBSHELL AT THE ATF
Milo Rigg, *Chicago Examiner*

In a confusing performance at an ATF gun case press conference, Cook County Sheriff's Deputy Jerome Glet announced
this afternoon that Kevin Wilcox, currently being held by the
ATF on charges of illegal weapons distribution, was likely to
be charged in the long-unsolved murders of Bobby Stemec
and Johnny and Anthony Henderson. Glet declined to offer
specifics, other than to imply he was investigating other matters
that might, or might not, stem from the arrest of Wilcox.
Efforts to reach Deputy Glet and Sheriff Joseph Lehman for
clarification have been unsuccessful.

He called Aria after sending it to the Pink.

'How the hell can he do that?' she said. 'Toss out a grenade and
then leave the briefing?'

'Maybe to blindside Lehman and pre-empt him from running
with that yellow body-marks card we gave him. And to make sure
all eyes stay focused on him. Glet wants redemption.'

'He's gone rogue to get it?'

'He wants Lehman's job,' Rigg said, 'and that starts with stepping out from behind Lehman. Glet's now the man who's about to
solve Stemec Henderson. But, as he again implied today, he's also
chasing something bigger.'

'Does this affect your story about Richie Fernandez?'

'I'm not sure. He seems interested. He's not outright dismissive,
he's not insisting it's only a catch-and-release.'

'You've got to find this other thing he's chasing.'

'I've got a more immediate problem. My witnesses to the
Fernandez bust have disappeared. Just Wally and the desk clerk
are gone. Lehman could have threatened them or paid them to leave.
I've got to find Fernandez.'

'Best you first find out that big thing Glet's chasing.' She clicked
him away.

His coffee had cooled. He sipped at it, looking out the window
at the sun setting behind the glass towers of Chicago's Loop. An
hour passed, maybe more. And then his cell phone chimed with a
new text message.

How about a drink? it read.

TWENTY

They sat in big overstuffed chairs with warm tumblers of Scotch, served neat. The drapes were pulled and Harold Benten's darkened living room smelled of the books on the two walls of shelves and of cigarette smoke, though there was no ashtray on the table between them, beneath the only lamp lit in the room.

'I called, right after you departed the Pink,' Rigg said.

'My wife said.'

'She was evasive.'

'We're adjusting.'

'You did request time off, right?'

'I'm not sure.'

'What does that mean?' Rigg asked.

'I put in for a week off, for the doctors to run tests. Donovan must have taken that opportunity to ask himself why he's paying me, a wrinkled gent past retirement age. He told me to take a few weeks, but I got the feeling the chute was already primed for the young Miss Gamble.'

'She says her emphasis is on advertising revenue, not editorial.'

'And has she been soliciting new revenues?'

Rigg thought for a moment. 'I can't answer that. I'm not at the Pink much.'

'She's well acquainted with Donovan, I hear,' Benten said.

'North Shore, the two of them,' Rigg said. 'Any test results yet?'

'Prostate, slow growing,' Benten said. 'Chemo and radiation.'

'It's going well?'

'I've just begun.'

There was no cigarette package in Benten's shirt pocket. 'You quit smoking?' Rigg asked.

Benten nodded. They'd been talking more than prostate, just without words.

'So, you saw my afternoon post,' Rigg said.

'Glet said a lot, and not a damned thing.' Benten's right hand started toward the used-to-be pack of cigarettes in his shirt pocket, but there was only habit there now, and he dropped his hand to his lap.

'It's Stemec Henderson, but maybe fourfold,' Rigg said.

'Fourfold? I see only three cases. Stemec Henderson is the first, but Glet's only naming Wilcox, providing no details.'

'I presume he has evidence, otherwise he wouldn't have gone out on that limb.' Rigg told him about the index card listing body marks on Anthony Henderson and the Graves and Day girls.

'Sweet Jesus O'Keefe,' Benten said. 'That seems to link the two cases, the boys and the girls. You really think it's this Kevin Wilcox who's done them all?'

'I would, except Glet doesn't seem to think so. He's only talking Wilcox for the boys.'

'The third case is that Richie Fernandez you say Lehman and McGarry busted,' Benten said.

'Busted, but never booked. He's disappeared, like the two witnesses at Fernandez's flop who saw the arrest.'

'Why make them disappear?'

'Fernandez went awry.'

'He got damaged during the initial interrogation?'

'Lehman's been accused of beating witnesses before. Maybe this time he went too far.'

Benten winced, and asked, 'What's the fourth case?'

'Glet's been hinting he's got something bigger than the boys, the girls and Fernandez. That means there's another case entirely.'

'Then that's what you should be chasing.'

'You sound like Aria.'

'Except she looks better than I do.'

'She wears pearls. Ad revenues are going to rise when she goes out with our advertising peddler.'

Rigg got up and they walked to the door.

'Be careful, Milo,' Benten said.

'Of what?' Rigg asked.

'Of Donovan and maybe Aria. Everyone's expecting the *Examiner* to founder on to the bankruptcy rocks, and they'll throw you overboard if it will save a nickel. Be careful of Lehman, McGarry and Glet, too. They're probably headed for different – and, for you, more dangerous – rocks. Unsolved killings, hidden suspects, disappearing witnesses – those threaten to bring them down.' Benten held open the door. 'And who's threatening them hardest?'

Rigg wanted to crack wise to ease the fear that was in the old man's voice. But he couldn't summon the words, and so he just thanked him for the Scotch.

The memory of the strange, soft swooshing sound he'd heard at McGarry's estate the previous night still nagged, and nothing waited back at the apartment except more futile combing through his files, so he drove west again. Again, he cut the lights before pulling off the side road running alongside the McGarry estate. And, again, he looked out through the darkness at the dimly lit mansion and the almost invisible outbuildings clustered at the back. McGarry's white Escalade was parked on the driveway, up by the mansion's side door.

He powered down his window halfway and then, in a moment, he fell into sleep. Not gently and not into a light doze, but deeper, into a hard sleep borne of too much fatigue from too many nights of being tormented by the black cage; too many too-early phone calls from Carlotta Henderson; the looming shame of the Richie Fernandez story, about to be rendered unproven by the disappearances of his witnesses; and now the warmth of Harold Benten's tumbler of undiluted warm Scotch.

The cold woke him an hour later, confused, struggling at first to understand why he was sitting up. Only slowly did he realize that he was not at his apartment, on his mattress on the floor, but in his car.

He looked out his side window. No new lights had come on in the mansion, and the outbuildings remained dark. McGarry's white Escalade remained parked on the driveway.

A glint came through the pines, from far behind the house, and glinted again. He pressed against the half-opened window, straining to listen. And, like the night before, he heard the soft whoosh, only now he could identify it. It was the sound of snow being moved. Someone was shoveling behind the mansion, using an aluminum shovel that caught the glint of the moon. It made no sense. There were only grounds back there, lawns and gardens and such, but no pavement to clear.

He realized, too, as he should have the night before, that such an opulent estate would have an extensive security system. Motion-sensor lights, cameras, maybe even sirens should have been set off by any movement behind the mansion. But the soft shoveling had triggered nothing. Someone had turned off the system, someone who was now out shoveling in the snow, on the lawn, in the dark. Someone who did not want to attract attention.

Someone who was very likely Charles McGarry.

The shoveling continued for another minute and then it stopped. Rigg strained to hear a house door open, like he had the previous night, but no sound came back from the darkness. He squinted toward the driveway, but it was too dark there to see if someone was moving toward the Escalade.

He waited another moment and then slowly opened his door. The Taurus's dome light had long ago burned out, the result of too many nights of working inside the car. That night, it was a blessing.

He eased out, leaving the car door ajar behind him, and crossed the narrow side road. He paused at the edge of the fence. Nothing glinted. Nothing sounded.

The chain-link fence was only six feet – high enough to keep out animals, but not, he told himself, an intrepid reporter hell-bent on chasing a story that was likely only to trash what little was left of his reputation. As if to underscore the point, the fence tore his pants as he dropped to the ground on the other side.

He stopped to listen. Still, only silence came back.

There was barely enough moonlight to navigate, but enough crusted snow to crunch. He moved carefully, one slow, quiet step at a time, in the direction of where he'd heard the shoveling. It took five minutes to find the mound. Footfalls had beaten down the snow around it.

From what he could see, such a mound in the middle of the back grounds made no sense.

From what he could imagine, it made all the sense in the world.

Big bulbs on high perimeter poles flashed on, flooding the whole property with blinding white light. He ran, casting a long shadow, toward the fence. He jumped up to pull himself over, digging the tips of his shoes hard into the metal mesh, and toppled over to the other side. Scrambling up, he fell, twisting his ankle.

He half-hobbled, half-hopped to the safety of the car parked in the darkness on the other side of the road. He jumped in, swung it around and sped back to the intersection, not switching on his headlamps until he'd gone a hundred yards down the highway.

He'd been seen.

But, more importantly, he'd seen.

TWENTY-ONE

D espite the snow that began falling at dawn, the tiled lobby of the red-brick, white-columned Cook County sheriff's suburban headquarters was mobbed by news creatures at eight o'clock the next morning, as Glet surely expected. And there wasn't a thing Joe Lehman could do about it, also as Glet must have known. Glet was the man of the hour, the holder of the thunder, the cop who was closing in on the killer of the Stemec Henderson boys, and maybe much, much more.

The desk officer yelled at the crowd of newsies that they were wasting their time, that there was no presser scheduled. Announcements would be forthcoming to elaborate on Glet's tease only when more facts were ascertained, he said.

But it was snowing heavily outside and there was no place else for the reporters to go, at least until the snow let up. The reporters, like Rigg, could wait inside, where it was warm, until Glet came in.

They didn't have to wait long. Jerome Glet, dressed for the press in a shiny black suit devoid of the soup spots and cigar ash that adorned his other suits – and brand new, judging by the thin manufacturer's tag he'd forgotten to remove from the left sleeve – pushed his way through the throng at eight-forty and went up the stairs to stand on the landing. He took a moment to drape the equally new-looking tan trench he was carrying on the railing, as if it were a king's robe, and waved his hands for quiet.

'I've got time for your questions, boys and girls, so wait your turn and I promise to call on each of you.'

And so he did, until almost noon.

STEMEC HENDERSON MURDERS SOLVED?

Milo Rigg, *Chicago Examiner*

Cook County Sheriff's Deputy Jerome Glet held an impromptu, far-reaching briefing at the sheriff's headquarters today to follow up on his surprise announcement yesterday that the alleged killer of Bobby Stemec and the Henderson brothers, the October before last, was arrested by the Federal Bureau of Alcohol, Tobacco, Firearms and Explosives on an unrelated weapons distribution charge. Kevin Wilcox, a worker at the Happy Times Stables in northwest Chicago, was arrested there by the ATF ten days ago for the unlawful distribution of firearms. Deputy Glet was called in simply as a courtesy but soon began to suspect that Wilcox might have been involved in the murders of Stemec, 14, Johnny Henderson, 13, and his brother Anthony, 12. Wilcox has denied any involvement in the three murders that galvanized all of Chicagoland, but Glet announced that his investigation, which he termed 'tireless and never-ending', has turned up evidence, still unspecified, that at least one of the three boys came in contact with Wilcox sometime immediately prior to being murdered.

Glet was pressed for comparisons to the murders of the Graves sisters and Jennifer Ann Day. 'I admit there are compelling similarities to the murders of the Stemec Henderson boys,' he said. 'The three girls were found naked, similarly close to roads and bodies of water, and all were young, aged twelve or in their early teens. Also, all three girls had gone missing well before Wilcox was arrested by the ATF.' But Glet stressed that any efforts to link Wilcox to the girls' slayings was premature, and reiterated what he'd said at his ATF press conference, that his focus for the present was on investigating the murders of the boys, and, he said, on other, perhaps related, matters that had come to his attention. Pressed as to what those were, Glet said only that his responsibilities as the sheriff's most senior deputy required him to be alert to all crimes of consequence in Cook County. Neither Cook County Sheriff Joseph Lehman nor Cook County Medical Examiner Charles McGarry was at Deputy Glet's briefing, and both were unavailable afterward to comment for this story.

'Sounds like Glet's saying DNA links Wilcox to the boys,' Aria said.

'Interesting that there's been no official word from the M.E.'s office, but McGarry must have gotten a swab from Wilcox and tipped Glet that it matched the unidentified DNA that was found on one of the boys. It's also interesting that Glet said at least one of the boys had come into contact with Wilcox, when foreign DNA was found on two of the boys: Bobby Stemec and Johnny Henderson. Glet wouldn't elaborate, and McGarry hasn't returned my calls.'

'Work Feldott. He's normally available, isn't he?'

'He is, and he's straight up, doing a credible job. You like him, too.'

'What does that mean?'

'You wrote a couple of admiring profiles of him for the *Examiner*. You implied he's the hope of Cook County.'

'He's young, fresh and dedicated.' She shrugged. 'Any progress on this other business Glet is being so coy about?'

'None, other than he keeps hinting that it's big.'

'Not Fernandez,' she said.

'He's not disinterested, but he's chasing something else.'

'Not the girls,' she said.

'He doesn't talk about them much.'

'Despite the card listing the body marks on both the boys and the girls,' she said.

'Despite that.'

'So, this other thing, not even the faintest idea what it might be?' she asked.

'No,' Rigg said.

'Maybe he's just showboating. There are politics raging here.'

'No kidding,' he said. 'New trench coat, shiny new suit.'

'I don't like Glet.'

He laughed. 'Nobody likes Glet, but they'll love him if he solves Stemec Henderson.'

'Something about the guy . . .'

'He plays angles, cuts corners?' Rigg said.

The hint of a smile worked around her lips. 'Like others?'

He told her about last night's drive out to McGarry's estate, the glint of a snow shovel, and climbing over the fence to find the mound of snow behind the mansion.

'Richie Fernandez?' she asked.

'Whoever I saw wasn't burying anything, not with a wide-blade aluminum snow shovel. But he could have been scooping snow on top of something that was already buried, to help the dirt settle when the ground thaws.'

'Lehman, always suspected of beating suspects, went too far this time, as you've been wondering? And McGarry helped him bury the body on his estate? Isn't that too risky?'

'It's perfect. The estate is secluded, fenced and protected by a security system. No one can stumble across the dig.'

'You did.'

'I didn't stumble,' Rigg said.

Aria pursed her lips, thinking. 'If you're right about Fernandez, change could come to Cook County. Glet could replace Lehman. So why isn't Glet more interested?'

'As I said, he thinks he's got something even bigger.'

'And, at the M.E.'s, Feldott could replace McGarry,' she said. 'What an odd couple they'd be: Glet and Feldott. Still, Glet's like that new suit – too shiny.'

'Feldott's got the backing of the heavies at the Citizens' Investigation Bureau, which means they already have him tapped for bigger things than the M.E.'s office. Maybe that means they're eying him for sheriff.'

She nodded slowly. 'We could help that along. A positive paragraph or two.'

'We should help things along with more paragraphs about Richie Fernandez.'

'You've got nothing on that, Milo. No witnesses.'

'Corky hasn't risen to anything yet, other than being affable,' Rigg said. 'He's hiding stuff.'

'Like what?'

'Beatrice might have been penetrated.'

She caught her breath and leaned back in her chair. And for a moment she appeared to be looking past him, unfocused. And then she said, 'That can't be.'

'Glet told me the same night he tipped me to the cabbie.'

'He got it from where?'

Rigg shrugged. 'Somebody at the M.E.'s, or maybe Lehman. He wouldn't say.'

'But not Feldott?' she asked.

'Don't know.'

'Nobody's said anything about a sex crime,' she said.

'Nobody wants the sex crimes unit involved in this,' he said, 'but, if they found penetration, maybe they found semen.'

'And that's why Glet is shying away from linking Wilcox to the girls? The semen doesn't match Wilcox's DNA?'

'If there's semen at all,' Rigg said.

TWENTY-TWO

'GoPro,' Pancho Rozakis said. Pancho, whose real first name was Juan, was half-Mexican, half-Greek, and all clever. He had been the *Examiner*'s chief photographer before he got laid off, six months earlier. Since then, he'd been scrounging freelance work for the *Examiner* and Chicago's dozens of local neighborhood rags.

'Those little cameras?' Rigg asked.

'Everybody's using them. Realtors, surveyors, men living next door to ladies sunning topless.'

'You've got one?'

'Several, and two drones.'

'Legal?'

'Sure, but since when did you care about that?'

'I don't want you to get arrested.'

Rozakis laughed. 'So long as you're not around, I'm safe,' he said, and clicked off.

Rigg called Glet's cell phone again, but the cell phone only wanted to take a message. He called the sheriff's department and asked for the man of the hour. The operator didn't hesitate before saying Glet was not in. Glet had been unavailable ever since his star appearance on the stairs of the sheriff's headquarters.

He didn't bother asking for McGarry when he called the Dead House, because McGarry was likely to remain a shadow until things settled down, much as he hoped the mound would settle down in his backyard. By now, Rigg was sure there was nothing else that would explain why McGarry had twice gone behind his mansion to move snow.

Rigg asked for Corky because, as he and Aria had agreed, Corky was almost always available.

'At the beginning of the Stemec Henderson investigation,' Rigg began, 'McGarry said there was unidentified DNA on two of the boys. I assume you swabbed Kevin Wilcox.'

'Mr McGarry won't allow the release of information without his approval,' Feldott said.

'Since McGarry's never available, you'd rather I speculate about why Glet is so positive Wilcox killed the boys?'

'I can tell you off the record that we took a DNA sample from Mr Wilcox, but it's out for analysis.'

'It's being compared to the foreign DNA found on both Bobby Stemec and Johnny Henderson?'

'Mr McGarry—'

Rigg cut him off. 'Someone from your office must have encouraged Glet, for him to sound so positive about Wilcox.'

'The DNA is out for analysis, Mr Rigg. There's been no encouragement that Wilcox's DNA was found on Johnny Henderson.'

'Or Bobby Stemec?' Rigg asked.

'The DNA is out for analysis.'

Rigg gave it up. 'Glet's not sounding like he's seeing any link between Wilcox and the girls.'

'As you know, nothing was recovered from the Graves sisters.'

The pup was fencing. 'Not even from penetration?'

'There's been no mention of penetration.'

'You're sure? No signs of forced sexual activity?'

'Darn it, Mr Rigg, you're just throwing out wild questions.'

'Jennifer Ann Day,' Rigg said. 'She was too long in the water to give you anything?'

'Mr McGarry is rigid in instructing us to—'

'When will McGarry be available?' Rigg interrupted.

'Off the record, he hasn't been here in days,' Feldott said. 'He's probably at Sheriff Lehman's office.'

'Helping to ready Lehman's own warrant to arrest Wilcox, like Glet inferred?'

'I don't know.'

'You don't know where McGarry is, do you?'

'I can't comment, Mr Rigg.'

'I'll take that as a no, meaning McGarry's gone underground. Which leaves us with Richie Fernandez,' Rigg said, mostly because he'd run out of other things to ask.

'I can't comment—'

'McGarry accompanied Lehman to bust Fernandez.'

'So you say, Mr Rigg. So nobody else corroborates.'

Rigg thanked him for nothing and hung up.

*   *   *

Pancho's email came at five fifteen. He'd taken two dozen aerial pictures of McGarry's estate. Seventeen of them showed the ground behind the last of the estate's outbuildings. Despite the falling snow, the high mound far behind the house was easily visible.

Rigg's cell phone rang a moment later. 'See the pictures?' Pancho asked.

'They're swell. No signs of life out there?'

'It was snowing. Nobody was outside and, as you can see, no car was in the driveway.'

The evening, though young, was dark. Rigg made one more call.

'I'm going to write that you're blowing smoke,' he said to the voicemail.

Glet eased on to the passenger seat of Rigg's Taurus an hour later. Again, the deputy had parked elsewhere in the Robinson Woods.

'You're offering no proof. I'm thinking you got the wrong guy, Jerome,' Rigg said.

Glet laughed. 'Don't bet against me on this one. Otherwise, you'll be writing for that suburban stuffer for the rest of your life.'

'What's making you positive?'

'About Wilcox doing the boys? How about proximity?'

'Proximity of the stables to Robinson Woods isn't enough,' Rigg said. 'How about DNA?'

'I was straight up with all of you reporters,' Glet said, evading.

'You weren't straight up at all. You're teasing, offering nothing concrete. You know you need more than proximity to charge Wilcox for the boys. You're acting like you got a heads-up on a DNA match.'

'I got plenty working for the boys.'

'And for the girls?' Rigg asked. 'The fact that the yellow index card links the boys' killer to the girls?'

Glet shifted his bulk on the seat. 'More than that.'

'What could be more than that, especially if the Feds already have in custody the person you're convinced killed the boys? A little more work and you've got the guy who killed the girls.'

'I'm looking into things.'

'You're holding back, or you're bluffing.'

'Wilcox was selling handguns out of a stable less than a mile from here.'

'Proximity is nothing. All you've got is a suspicion that the boys were at the Happy Times Stables that day and saw something they shouldn't have. DNA is more.'

Glet turned to face Rigg squarely. 'I'm being very careful. You of all people should appreciate that. No mistakes this time, Milo.'

'Feldott's being cagey on the DNA. He's saying it's still out for analysis, that you've not been tipped to any match.'

Glet laughed. 'Like I keep saying, Milo, I'm being careful. One step at a time.'

'Richie Fernandez,' Rigg said. 'Lehman's afraid of Richie Fernandez. And so is McGarry. He's disappeared from the Dead House.'

'I don't know about McGarry.'

'You need to chase Richie Fernandez.'

Glet pushed his way out of the car and turned to lean back in. 'I ain't saying Fernandez ain't important, Milo.'

'I need you to make a phone call,' Rigg said.

He pulled into a drive-thru. It could have been a McDonald's or a Burger King or something else. It didn't matter, so long as they had cheeseburgers. He ordered two and a Coke. The Coke was good. The first burger was easy to eat as he drove, because it was thin and he was famished. But he had no appetite for the second. When he passed two raccoons ambling alongside a wood, he unwrapped the second burger and threw it at them. Likely enough, they'd be surer of their next steps than he was.

In his apartment, he sat for some minutes, staring at his wall of file boxes. And then he called Carlotta. She'd still be up. She was like him. She was always up.

'Come over,' she said.

'Did your boys ever go to stables?'

'Come over now,' she said.

'Did your boys go to stables?'

'Those stables where that Wilcox man worked? I suppose. My boys went all over, bowling, swimming in the summer, Cubs games when they could sneak in.' She started crying. 'I don't know about horses.'

He said he'd call soon, and, despicably, he hung up.

He made a weak Scotch and sat some more, staring at the files. He'd conned himself, thinking they held answers. There was nothing in them about any stables.

TWENTY-THREE

McGARRY ILL, STEPS BACK
Milo Rigg, *Chicago Examiner*

Cornelius Feldott, assistant Cook County medical examiner, announced this morning that he has assumed management of the department following the sudden illness of Medical Examiner Charles McGarry. Details of McGarry's illness will not be made public, Feldott said, in respect for McGarry's privacy, but he said that the illness is not life-threatening and that McGarry is expected to return to head the medical examiner's office within the next month. 'Our hopes and wishes are for his complete and speedy recovery,' Feldott said.

McGarry's illness comes at a difficult time, as his office is in the midst of assisting the Cook County sheriff's department in investigating the murders of the Graves sisters and Jennifer Ann Day, and in the re-examination of the killings of Bobby Stemec and Johnny and Anthony Henderson, as announced two days ago by Sheriff's Deputy Jerome Glet. The status of Richie Fernandez, who, according to witnesses, was arrested as a person of interest in the Graves case by Cook County Sheriff Joseph Lehman in the company of Charles McGarry, remains unknown.

'Again, Richie Fernandez!' Aria said, throwing her arms up in mock exasperation.

'For now, and maybe for quite a while,' Rigg said.

'Feldott caught you by surprise with his announcement?' Aria asked.

'He gave no hint of taking over when we talked, even going so far as to pretend confusion about where McGarry might be.'

'And about Beatrice Graves being penetrated?'

'He didn't flinch at that, either.'

'How do we find out if the Day girl was sexually assaulted?' she asked.

'She was in the water for a long time. Even if evidence survived, I bet he'd quash it. He wouldn't want Sex Crimes anywhere around.'

She turned to her keyboard, tapped keys and sent Rigg's piece off. 'You can't say that last business about Richie Fernandez. You have no witnesses now.'

'Fernandez is a story.'

'A story that has no corroborating witnesses. You said Greg Theodore is watching you. He'll sniff out the weakness and crucify you for sloppy reporting.'

'McGarry is complicit in Fernandez's disappearance. His hinges are coming loose. That's why he's pretending to be sick.'

Her desk phone rang. She picked it up. It was a short conversation, consisting twice of, 'I'll tell him.' She hung up.

'The Bastion beckons,' she said.

He hadn't been back to the *Examiner*'s headquarters since Donovan exiled him under the shadow of Carlotta Henderson, early the year before. Never as foreboding as the *Chicago Tribune*'s Gothic tower, as detailed as the Art Deco magnificence of the old *Daily News* headquarters or as boxily efficient as the former *Sun-Times* building, the majesty of the six-story, fortress-style brick Bastion always held, for Rigg, the scrappy resoluteness of the city's third-largest newspaper.

'Milo!' Edna, the woman behind the reception desk in the Bastion's grand marble lobby, smiled. She loved all the *Examiner*'s reporters.

'I'm back!' he said.

'To stay?'

'Probably just for minutes. I'm here to see Donovan.'

Her smile disappeared. Things had got steadily worse for print reporters since Rigg's first day at the paper. Fresh-faced out of Chicago's Columbia College, the school for scrappy but broke aspiring journalists, he'd realized only when he came through the doors that first day that he'd never thought to ask what his salary was going to be. It had been of no matter; he was going to be a reporter at Chicago's third-largest paper and that was all that counted. Not that many years had passed since then, but they'd been years of brutal transformation, and, by now, Edna must have been seeing reporters leaving in greater numbers than ever before.

He got out of the elevator at the newsroom, three floors shy of his destination. At eleven fifteen, the floor should have resonated with keyboard clacking, shouted snippets of conversations and muttered profanity. Maybe long gone were the days of 'Hat and coat!' – meaning, *Get your ass out on the street* – or 'Get me rewrite!' but there should have been more modern incantations of a live, bustling newsroom crackling across the low-walled cubicles. But the third floor, the reporters' floor, was now a ghost town. Half the cubicles were empty and the other half was occupied by bent-over people speaking in whispers, as if to avoid notice that they were speaking at all. There was no mystery to their futures. More lay-offs were coming – there at the *Examiner*, but also at the *Trib* and the *Sun-Times*. People no longer read the ink of the news; more and more, they wanted less and less of it, and they wanted that in tiny bits on screens that they could delete in an instant if it was too upsetting or demanded too much concentration, bits like Rigg himself had been reduced to writing.

He walked through the newsroom, stopping at almost every occupied cubicle with a smile. He knew them all and they knew him. He'd never ruled this room, but he'd been a force at one time, before Carlotta.

Several people stood in front of a giant electronic screen that showed the day's online stories and the number of hits each had received. It was the new age of readership accounting, assessing which stories drew attention – and, as Rigg and everyone else on that floor knew, which reporters didn't draw much attention and were likeliest to be axed in the next round of lay-offs.

He paused in front of his old cubicle in the corner. It was still empty, never filled.

A rumpled, gray-haired fellow in corduroy pants and a plaid shirt walked up. He was the *Examiner*'s City Hall reporter, and was, he often proclaimed, too old to fire. 'What the hell have you done now?' he asked with a smile.

'Meeting with Donovan on the sixth floor,' Rigg said.

Those that had turned at the sound of their voices frowned. No one went up to Donovan's floor simply to chat.

The rumpled fellow stuck out his hand, no doubt in farewell. 'Ah, hell, Milo.'

Rigg took the stairs up one floor and poked his head in at the advertising and sales department. No matter how good any news-paper was editorially, it was nothing without the money to pay for its people, ink, paper and Internet sites. The *Examiner*'s fourth floor had always been filled with hotshots, snappy dressers talking fast on the phone to potential advertisers. Now, the fourth floor was even more deserted than the newsroom. The battle had been lost; the advertisers had gone away. A woman he didn't recognize sat in a cubicle halfway across the floor. She didn't look up.

He climbed the last two flights. There were no cubicles on the top floor, just polished old oak secretarial desks and private offices behind polished old oak doors. Most of the doors were closed on empty offices. Donovan's cost-cutting had decimated his own executive floor as well.

The publisher's office was in the corner. Donovan was lanky, narrow-faced and had the small eyes of a ferret. Anecdotes abounded about the driven bastard who'd made great wealth in commercial real estate. He was an everyday tennis player with his own key to a downtown club so he could practice his serves at six in the morning. He drove hyper-expensive Porsches that his secretary traded in for new ones every six months and, when she wasn't doing that, she took frequent cab rides to the bank, because Luther Donovan wouldn't touch paper money unless it had never been touched before.

But, nowadays, word was that Luther Donovan was scrambling for any kind of money. The sense of invincibility that had taken him past real-estate development into newspaper publishing, thinking his roughshod managerial style and relentless cost-cutting would turn the teetering *Chicago Examiner* into a profitable business, like every financial endeavor he'd approached before, had gotten him into deep trouble. He and his minority investors were getting creamed by the *Examiner*'s falling circulation and rising printing costs.

Donovan's door was open. His secretary, who'd been with the paper through three publishers, two of whom had cared not one whit for tennis, Porsches and pristine paper money, managed to force a smile and waved for him to go right in.

Unlike the venerable old oak paneling and furniture that was everywhere else on that historic sixth floor, Donovan's inlaid walls had been painted over in flat white enamel and a desk had been brought in consisting of two bright chrome pillars supporting a smoked glass top. The computer screen on the adjacent, matching glass and chrome table was blank.

'Milo,' Donovan said without inflection, not glancing up from the sheet he was reading. Donovan's rudeness was a tactic, a delay meant to be unnerving and give the publisher an advantage. No doubt it had worked with contractors, listing agents and the other denizens of his real-estate world, but Rigg didn't see much point in allowing it to work on him. His career had already plummeted to the Pink.

'Luther,' he said, sitting down and crossing his legs with what he hoped was the nonchalance of a man about to doze.

Donovan finally looked up. 'Back in the game?' The publisher was a man of millions of dollars, but only a few words.

'The usual at the Pink.'

'More than that.'

Rigg shrugged. 'Car wash openings and murders. Such is the news.'

'Your treatment of them is off-putting.'

'Which? The car washes or the murders?' Rigg said.

The great man did not frown at the sarcasm. 'This, in particular,' he said. He turned to his computer, tapped a key to bring the screen to life and began to read aloud. '"The status of Richie Fernandez, who, according to witnesses, was arrested as a person of interest in the Graves case by Cook County Sheriff Joseph Lehman in the company of McGarry, remains unknown."'

It was a surprise and a delight. He'd thought Aria had deleted the offending last sentence.

'Part of the big story,' Rigg said. 'Lehman and McGarry busted Fernandez, but never booked him. That's important.'

'They deny it and, according to your boss, Mrs Gamble, you have no corroborating witnesses to the supposed Fernandez arrest.'

'Lehman made them disappear.'

'You know this?'

'I conclude this.'

'I say again: you have no witnesses.'

'To which I say again: Lehman made them disappear. He's dirty on this. So is McGarry, which is why he's pretending to be sick. He needs to be squeezed.' Rigg paused, knowing he was about to do wrong, and then went ahead anyway. 'I don't know the man, Luther, but I hear you do.'

It was a feint and it worked. Donovan's face flushed red. 'Only from business dealings. Real-estate partnerships, trade associations and the like.'

The desk phone buzzed, no doubt a prearranged signal from Donovan's secretary that the time allotted for an annoying pebble like Rigg was up. 'McGarry is to be removed from your reporting, do you understand?' Donovan said.

'You're the publisher.'

'We don't want a flare-up,' Donovan said.

'There are no Carlotta Hendersons here, Luther. There was no Carlotta Henderson the last time, either.'

'And there is no McGarry now, because there are no witnesses to Fernandez.'

Donovan's phone buzzed again, insistent. Rigg got up.

'Be wise, Milo,' Donovan said, without bothering with the pretense of picking up his phone to a dead line. He'd turned back to the sheet he'd been studying when Rigg came in. The sheet was filled with numbers. Likely, they were bad numbers.

'Wisdom – of course,' Rigg said, and stepped out, but it was way too late for that.

TWENTY-FOUR

Aria called just as he got to the *Examiner*'s rear parking lot, a prime piece of downtown real estate with a huge *For Sale* sign in one corner.

'Perfect,' Rigg said, before she could speak.

'What?' she asked.

'Your timing,' he said. 'I just finished with Donovan.'

'How's that perfect?'

'I assume you, too, just finished with Donovan.'

'As a matter of fact, he just called me,' she said.

'You left in my last sentence about Richie Fernandez.'

'Futile. Donovan deleted it,' she said.

'As you were sure he would.'

'I'm in your corner, Milo, even when it's futile. You're coming in?'

'I need to clear my head,' he said.

'You're thinking another drive will help?' She was smart, damned smart.

'Glet's managing Stemec Henderson. Lehman doesn't appear to be managing anything.'

'Leaving McGarry managing to be sick in his city house?'

'And leave Richie Fernandez unattended? I hope not,' he said. She hung up, laughing.

He called Pancho Rozakis before starting his car. 'Are you free right now?'

'I'm free almost always.'

Rigg told him what he wanted. 'Probably nobody's home and nothing will happen,' he added.

'Whatever,' Rozakis said.

The long driveway up through McGarry's estate was thick with six inches of the new snow. The Escalade was still parked at the end of the drive and was also thick with snow. It hadn't been moved since he was last there. Rigg hoped that meant McGarry was remaining vigilant.

He left his car at the side of the highway, climbed over the gate and high-stepped in street shoes up to the long porch, stomping the snow from his feet loud enough to be heard. He rang the front doorbell. When there was no answer, he beat on the door with his fist. Still no answer.

He walked around past the Escalade and knocked on the side door. When no one answered, he began to wonder if McGarry really was ill and had been taken to a hospital. If so, Rigg was wasting his time. But he reminded himself that he was already scraping by on part-time wages and frugal withdrawals from Judith's small life insurance. And his shoes were already soaked. He had little left to waste.

The sky was clear, and that was good. He resisted the urge to look up as he crossed the snow in back to the mound.

As he'd seen in Pancho Rozakis' drone photos, the fresh snowfall had obliterated any footsteps and sweep marks, but not the rise of the mound itself. It rose up a good eighteen inches above the ground, several inches higher than when Rigg had snuck on to the estate.

Footsteps crunched on the snow, back by the house.

'Mr McGarry,' Rigg called out, 'you look splendid.'

'I'm ill.' McGarry cradled a shotgun in the crook of his right arm, pointed down. He wore high boots, a long black coat and, incongruously for a man who worked in a morgue, a red knit hat with a purple pom-pom on top.

'I knocked on all the doors I could get to.'

'I gave the staff the day off,' McGarry said, trudging closer.

'And the days before, judging by all the unshoveled snow.'

'Didn't you see the *No Trespassing* sign by the road?' McGarry got to within ten feet and stopped.

'Ah, but we're associates, you and I. Fellow seekers of the truth. Friends even, I like to think. I'm concerned about your sudden illness.'

'And when there was no answer at the door, you thought to come all the way out here to see if I was playing in the snow?' The shotgun wavered in his arm, but did not rise.

'You have lovely grounds. Surely you don't maintain them all by yourself?'

'Why are you here, Rigg?'

'As I said, I was concerned about your sudden illness.' He reached into his coat pocket and brought out the can he'd bought on the drive out. 'Chicken noodle soup, generic, the cheapest I could find.' He held out the can. 'Plus, Glet's been talking to us in the press. I want your comment. Do you think ATF has bagged the boys' killer?'

'I hope so.'

'How is your analysis of Wilcox's DNA progressing?'

McGarry stared at him, but said nothing.

'What about the boys?' Rigg prompted.

'What about them?'

Rigg gestured down at the mound. 'Or was Richie Fernandez able to tell you anything about the girls?'

McGarry tilted the shotgun up just an inch or two, but it was enough.

'Interview's over?' Rigg said.

The shotgun rose another inch.

Rigg risked another gesture at the mound. 'A toboggan hill, or something more?'

McGarry didn't answer. He just met Rigg's eyes, but that was fine. Rigg put the soup can back in his pocket and high-stepped around the man, through the snow, back to the house and down to the highway. He didn't look back, but he didn't need to. He could feel McGarry's eyes and both barrels of the man's shotgun hot on the back of his neck all the way to his car.

And that was fine, too.

HEALTHY ENOUGH?
Milo Rigg, *Chicago Examiner*

Cook County Medical Examiner Charles McGarry appeared in the snow outside his far west suburban mansion to express hope that Cook County Sheriff's Deputy Jerome Glet's claim that Kevin Wilcox, being held in custody by the Chicago office of ATF on charges of illegal gun distribution, is also the prime suspect in the murders of Bobby Stemec, Johnny Henderson and Anthony Henderson a year ago last October. But he refused to confirm that Wilcox's DNA has been submitted for comparison to evidence found on their bodies. The interview was cut short without McGarry commenting on whether Wilcox is suspected of being involved in the murders of the Graves sisters and Jennifer Ann Day, or whether that investigation led to the arrest of Richie Fernandez by Lehman, accompanied by McGarry.

'You're not yet forty, Milo,' Aria said. 'You're sure you can afford to retire at such an early age?'

'I'm already semi-retired.'

'You're back in full swing.'

'At half-wages,' Rigg said.

'Which delights Donovan, and, these days, is better than no wages at all.'

'What publisher warns a reporter off a key angle to the biggest story in the Midwest?' Rigg asked. 'He's protecting McGarry.'

'It's the way of the world,' she said.

'Or is it just the way of the North Shore?' he said. 'Your turf, Aria.'

She fingered her pearls. 'My family isn't like Donovan and McGarry. Steel companies and an oil refinery were very lucrative for my grandfather, but my father made bad investments.' Then, 'Why doesn't McGarry want to talk about comparing Wilcox's DNA to the Stemec Henderson samples?'

'I wanted to think it was because he was in a hurry to get me off his property, but nobody wants to talk about matching Wilcox's DNA to the boys. Glet avoids talking about it and Feldott's evasive about it, too, though he did say that only one foreign DNA sample was being compared to Wilcox's. Two foreign DNA samples were recovered, one from Bobby Stemec and another from Johnny Henderson. Running both foreign DNA samples against Wilcox would be standard procedure, but, for some reason, only one is being analyzed.'

'There's problems with the Stemec Henderson DNA?' she said.

'Of course.'

His cell phone rang. He glanced at the number, stood up and stepped out of Aria's office.

'It's been four hours,' Rigg said. 'Why so long to send me pictures?'

'Plenty happened after I got pictures of McGarry greeting you with a shotgun,' Pancho Rozakis said. 'He took a cab to O'Hare Airport right after you left. I followed him. Luckily, it must have taken him some time to decide on a destination. I was able to park and catch up to him inside. He finally bought a one-way to Paris. I couldn't go past security, so I've been watching the board. His plane just took off.'

'Pictures of him at O'Hare, too?'

'Plenty. Check your phone.'

He brought up the photos as he walked back to Aria's doorway.

'Breaking news?' she asked.

He selected one of the pictures and handed her the phone. 'Charles McGarry at O'Hare a couple of hours ago, buying a one-way ticket to Paris.'

She studied the photo. 'This could have been taken anytime.'

'Dial back a few photos until you get to him with a gun, ten feet from me.'

She clicked back, nodded and asked, 'This could have been taken anytime, too.'

'Pancho Rozakis. It was his drone. He'll corroborate.'

'Still not enough.'

'Probably, but notice the mound.'

'What about it?'

'I set McGarry to running by suggesting I knew what was beneath it.'

'Richie Fernandez,' she said.

'Forever on my mind.'

'What are you doing tonight?'

'I haven't decided,' he said.

'Like hell,' she said. 'You'll be looking through your famous wall of boxes for mention of Happy Times Stables.'

'I don't think it's in there.'

His shoes squeaked as he shifted on his feet. She leaned forward so she could see them. They were still wet and the leather had bubbled. 'Aren't your feet cold?'

'I'm going to the shoe store down the block.'

'Dinner afterward sounds fine,' she said.

TWENTY-FIVE

He awoke confused by the sunlight. He never woke to sunlight, not in his apartment, not since the cage began coming. But there'd been no cage this past night.

He felt the floor for his phone. It was 8:15.

She shifted beside him.

Startled, he rolled over, thinking he was dreaming, hoping that the grandmother of all nightmares was over. Praying that Judith was there.

Aria's eyes were wide open, fully awake.

He felt shame. 'How the hell did we get here?' he said.

A slow smile formed on her lips. 'I'm not memorable?'

'It's not that, it's . . .' He stopped. Her face was simply and totally beautiful.

She smiled widely then, or, rather, she leered. 'The living-room floor was too littered.'

'What?'

'You asked how we got here.' She rolled on to the floor and stood up, magnificent now in only pearls. He remembered exactly how they'd gotten there.

She walked to his closet slowly, perhaps to not agitate the pearls, more likely to agitate his memory. 'Why do you have nothing but white shirts?'

'I got rid of most of my stuff.'

'Everything even remotely festive?'

'I was thinking of moving full-time to the dunes.'

'And moving away from Chicago memories, I suspect,' she said. She pulled a white shirt from a hanger. 'Coffee?' she asked, slipping it on with no haste at all.

'In the cabinet above the stove.'

A moment later, she called from the kitchen. 'It's instant.'

'The kettle is on the stove.' He got up and slipped on trousers and yesterday's shirt, wishing for the first time since Judith died that he had a blue shirt, or red, or one of any other color except white.

'Yuck to instant.' She came back into the bedroom, picked up her clothes and walked into the bathroom. 'Real coffee is essential,' she called through the door.

And so, now, would be searing regret, but he didn't call that back to her.

She emerged, dressed, a moment later. They left the bedroom and began stepping across the files they'd scattered on the living-room floor.

He remembered then.

'Peter Tanson,' he said.

She looked at him, startled to realize he'd just now remembered. 'Of course, Peter Tanson,' she said. 'Peter Tanson, thanks to me.' She went out the door without a kiss or another word.

Peter Tanson. Horses, the Happy Times Stables, the vaguest note in one of his files. Peter Tanson.

He knelt to cram all the files into the boxes, in a hurry to stuff them away as worthless. All except one, but even that one was unnecessary to leave out. He'd never again forget the name.

Peter Tanson.

He sat on the love seat to rethink the evening. Not what came with Aria afterward, borne of an odd conflict of elation and desperation, a mix that kept them up so late that the cage hadn't the time to come – but before.

He'd bought black Oxfords and a pair of socks at the shoe store down the block from the Pink, and then headed to meet her for dinner, as agreed, at a Chinese restaurant out by the highway. But, when he arrived, she was standing inside the door, holding a paper bag. General Tsao chicken, and pot stickers, fried rice and lemon chicken – takeout, she said, so she could see his wall of files. They got to his apartment at six thirty.

'Minimalist,' she'd said, stepping inside.

'It used to have furniture,' he said, of the living room.

'Now it has only the love seat . . .'

'Yes.'

'And that tall wall of file boxes with a small television balanced on top.' She went over to the boxes and began reading their labels. '"Discovery",' she began, and then, '"Autopsy" . . . "John Henderson, Senior: life and associates" . . .?' She turned. '"Life and associates"?'

'The father was in the building trades, a contractor. Not particularly wealthy, but successful enough, perhaps, to have angered someone along the way. It was a theory that went nowhere.'

'Thorough you,' she said. 'What do you do with all these, exactly?'

'Look for something I missed.'

'Incessantly?'

'I suppose.'

'And now stables and Kevin Wilcox?'

'I'm sure there's no mention of them in any of the files.'

She pointed to the only item hung on the walls – the framed front page of the last edition of the *Chicago Daily News*, its headline bold: *SO LONG, CHICAGO*.

'March 4, 1978. Neither of us was born yet.' She turned to him. 'This resonates with you?'

'A eulogy, almost an elegy, written by the great Mike Royko.'

'We read it in college,' she said. 'Do you ever wonder if one will be written for the *Examiner*?'

'I fear we'll just slip away unnoticed.'

They took down boxes and sat on the floor, resting their backs against the seat cushions of the love seat, and passed the four containers of Chinese food back and forth – she'd spurned his offer of paper plates and plastic forks, his only dinnerware – eating with chopsticks and looking through the files he'd looked through so many times before.

She found it at ten o'clock, faint and easily missed. 'What about this kid, Peter Tanson?'

He didn't remember the name.

'On a list of Bobby Stemec's classmates,' she said, holding out a sheet. 'You wrote *horse rides* next to his name.'

He looked at the list. 'It was just a note, something I probably got from someone else. I didn't make any connection.'

'Nor should you have. Nobody had interest in horses or stables at that time.'

Something oily worked up his throat. 'Anything in there about

'I suppose it could be, though women serial killers are extremely rare.'

'We're more cautious,' she said, fingering her pearls, 'so that probably means it's a man. A woman would have been more worried about being spotted and wouldn't have dumped the boys and the girls so close to a road.'

'Now who's speculating? You're linking the boys to the girls.'

'Glet seems to be speculating, too,' she said.

'About more than the boys and the girls, apparently.'

'You've got no progress on that?'

He shook his head and stood up, anxious to leave her office before anything could be said about the night before.

'Milo?' she said.

He stopped and turned back around.

'You're not overstepping, are you? Spooking McGarry enough to flee? Newsman becoming newsmaker?'

There was nothing he wanted to say to that. The question no longer mattered to him.

Glet hadn't been at the discovery site that morning, and he wasn't answering his cell phone. Corky Feldott was in his office, ever accessible, and said Rigg could come in for a chat. He got to the Dead House thirty minutes later.

'You're sure: three freckles, tightly clustered?' Rigg asked.

Feldott was nervous, close to being distraught. 'Just as you expected, apparently. They look like one bigger freckle, behind her knee.'

'Just like the yellow card said.'

'Not for publication, Mr Rigg. Sheriff Lehman was firm about me insisting on that.'

'Understood.'

'This is a damned bad time for Mr McGarry to be off sick,' Feldott said.

Rigg brought out his phone to show Feldott some of Rozakis' drone pictures. 'I went out to his estate, brought him soup. He came out into the snow, spry as a chicken and, as you see, carrying a shotgun. After I left, he cabbed to O'Hare.'

Feldott's face froze. 'None of this is on the *Examiner*'s website.'

Rigg had checked the website before walking into the Dead House. As expected, Donovan had clipped the mention about

which stables . . . which stables . . .?' He didn't want to finish the thought, frightened at what he might have missed.

She fanned some papers, shook her head. 'No. Just that one *horse rides* reference on a list of classmates.' She smiled. 'Do you have anything to drink?'

He got up and walked – horrified or ecstatic, he didn't know – to the kitchen. A kid, one he'd never bothered to chase down, might have been linked to the Happy Times Stables; a kid who might have known something about Kevin Wilcox. A link – maybe *the* link – had been there, in the damned boxes, all the time, waiting for him to see it, to interview the kid, Peter Tanson, to learn maybe that Bobby and John and Anthony had gone riding at the Happy Times Stables the last damned day of their lives.

His hand shook as he took the Scotch from the cabinet. If he'd seen, maybe more kids – girls, this time – would be alive.

He poured two small Scotches and brought them back to the living-room floor. 'Why is my gut sure Peter Tanson knew the boys went to Wilcox's stables?' he said, slumping down against the cushions.

'Because you want it to be so, for closure, and because the Happy Times Stables is so close to Robinson Woods, and because Glet is so sure Wilcox links to the boys.' She took one of the glasses. 'How long do you expect to live like this?' she asked, motioning with her free hand at the barren living room, littered now with folders strewn on the floor.

He looked around, trying to see it fresh with her eyes. 'I haven't wondered about that.'

'You ought to store these boxes where it won't be so easy to access them.'

'If I had, you wouldn't have come up with the name of a potential witness linking Wilcox to the boys, someone I should have found months ago.'

He wasn't sure what happened next, whether she shifted, or he did, but their shoulders had touched. And, after a time, she touched his hand and they got up off the floor. It was to be a night of frightening new discoveries all around. Good or bad, he could not tell.

'This way?' she asked.

He nodded. They walked into the bedroom.

She laughed. 'Don't you have a bed?'

He tried to pretend confusion. 'It's that rectangle,' he joked.

'A mattress on the floor, no matter how neatly made up with a bedspread, does not make a proper bed.' She turned to him, her face serious. 'You're still married, aren't you?'

'Very much.'

'Oooh, risky,' she said. 'I'm here with a married man.'

Neither of them said anything more. The time for that, for him, had just passed.

Now, in the morning, she called three minutes after she left the apartment. 'Turn on your television! Route 83, just south of Plainfield Road!'

'What's—?'

'Maybe three clustered freckles,' she screamed.

TWENTY-SIX

GIRL FOUND SLAIN
Milo Rigg, *Chicago Examiner*

The naked body of a girl found early this morning by a couple hiking along a creek in the woods beside Route 83 has been tentatively identified as Tana Damm, 15, of Villa Park. She was reported missing six days ago by her grandfather, Jeffrey Damm, with whom she lived. Miss Damm was a freshman at York High School and was last seen alive by a classmate last December 29 or 30, leaving a McDonald's restaurant on Route 83, 500 yards south of where she was found.

According to an aunt, who also lives at the Villa Park home, Miss Damm had a history of running away. Authorities at York High School repeatedly inquired about her frequent absences, she said. Miss Damm last attended classes in early December.

The victim had been decapitated. Acting Cook County Medical Examiner Cornelius Feldott supervised a brief, preliminary autopsy this morning. It failed to determine a cause of death, or whether the girl was alive at the time her head was removed, though Feldott said it's almost certain she'd been

dead for some time. A more thorough examination is scheduled for later today, to be conducted by the same forensics experts that were brought in for the autopsies of the Graves and Day girls. Miss Damm was found less than two miles from where the Graves girls were discovered.

In a related matter, Cook County Medical Examiner Charles McGarry – rumored to have become ill following the disappearance of Richie Fernandez, a suspect in the cases of a string of recently murdered girls – was spotted at O'Hare International Airport yesterday, purchasing a ticket for a flight bound for Paris, France. It has not been determined whether his departure was planned.

Rigg watched Aria through the glass as she read what he'd forwarded to her. She looked calm enough and waved for him to come in.

'Oh, what the hell are you doing, Milo?'

'Reporting all the news that's fit to print,' he said, quoting some ancient newspaper's motto.

'You don't know that McGarry was actually fleeing.'

'I showed you the pictures Rozakis took at O'Hare.'

She shook her head. 'He bought a ticket for Paris. He could be on vacation. And, in case you've forgotten, Donovan told you to lay off McGarry. He'll cut the McGarry part. Ah, hell,' she said, tapping a key to send the entire piece downtown.

In a perverse way, he was faintly relieved for the distraction of the latest discovery. Aria had gone home to change before coming in, and he'd left his apartment to race directly to the discovery site. Now, at the Pink, the bad breaking news swept away any opportunities for awkwardness about the previous night.

'At least you were somewhat circumspect, only hinting at a connection to the other girls' murders,' she went on.

'Another girl who disappeared at the end of December, foun nude, decapitated like the last one, beside a shallow creek along well-travelled road like the first two? When we learn Tana Dam has a tiny cluster of three freckles, the last unassigned physical m on the yellow card, we'll know it's our man.'

'Or woman,' she said.

'A woman?' he asked, surprised.

'Women kill, Milo. Surely you've considered our killer cou a woman?'

McGarry fleeing, as well as one of the photos of McGarry at
O'Hare.

Rigg showed him more of the photos on his phone. 'McGarry
has friends at the Bastion,' Rigg said.

'Has Mr McGarry gone nuts?' Feldott asked.

'Hard to tell. He didn't take the soup, but he didn't shoot me,
either.'

'What does all this mean?'

'Nothing I'm able to report, apparently.'

'Stop with the mysteriousness.' Tiny beads of sweat had broken
out on Feldott's unlined brow.

'McGarry blew town for Paris and, from there, who knows? I
think you're going to be medical examiner for a long time.'

'Nobody signs up for this kind of grief,' Feldott said.

'This is exactly the kind of grief you sign up for.'

'Not *headless*, for God's sake. Not butchery, not young girls.'

'I don't suppose Northwestern prepares you for that sort of thing,'
Rigg said, glancing at the drawing of the campus on the back wall.

Feldott fingered the day's sleek, narrow tie, a yellowish thing
with blue dots that hung a little too loose around his neck. The
gesture reminded Rigg of the way Aria sometimes fingered her
pearls.

'Why wasn't Deputy Glet there for the Damm girl this morning?'
Feldott asked. 'Too busy at ATF?'

'Don't you talk to Lehman?'

'I don't think he knows what Deputy Glet's up to. He always
changes the subject.'

'Speaking of changing subjects, what's the status of comparing
Wilcox's DNA to the foreign DNA you got from Bobby Stemec
and Johnny Henderson?'

'The analysis is incomplete.'

'How incomplete?'

'Mr McGarry says no information is to be released—'

Rigg held up a hand. 'McGarry's in Paris, damn it.'

'He's still in charge, even if nominally, Mr Rigg.'

'Glet's talking like he's solid on Wilcox killing the boys.'

'Not because of DNA results,' Feldott said. 'I told you: they're
incomplete.'

'Any hope of recovering foreign DNA from Tana Damm?'

'We haven't autopsied her yet. I can tell you that, based on when her family says she disappeared, I assume she was killed the same time as the others.'

'One fast, murderous spurt?'

'And well before your Richie Fernandez was supposedly picked up, so he could be the killer.' He managed a small laugh, but it was nervous. 'Have you noticed that everyone in this case seems to be betting on a different horse? Deputy Glet has Kevin Wilcox, at least for the boys. Sheriff Lehman has, or had, Klaus Lanz. You've got Richie Fernandez.'

'No. Lehman and McGarry have, or had, Fernandez. I just want to know what they did with him.'

'Beyond probably just questioning him and letting him go?' He shook his head before Rigg could protest. 'Actually, I believe you're right to investigate his disappearance.'

'I think he was questioned too aggressively.'

'Sheriff Lehman and Mr McGarry? What are you thinking they did?'

Buried him on McGarry's estate, beneath a mound of dirt and snow, Rigg wanted to say. It was the only scenario that explained why McGarry would play sick to stay home. He needed to guard the mound with a shotgun, to keep scooping snow on it to settle the dirt until spring brought grass to cover up the wounded earth. It must have seemed like a wise strategy, until Rigg showed up with soup.

'I'm not sure yet,' Rigg said, evading.

'Whatever you're thinking, it can't be made public yet,' Feldott said. 'It will destroy our credibility.'

'When are you going to tell me about the DNA?' Rigg said.

'Let's see what Tana Damm tells us,' Feldott said.

TWENTY-SEVEN

Rigg turned at the peeling, painted sign that showed a grinning horse and an even happier horseman, and drove up the rutted gravel alley behind the Walgreen's drug store. The Happy Times Stables had once occupied all the land at the intersection just north of the Kennedy Expressway and east of the Des Plaines River, but real-estate values gone exponential had prompted the sale of the choicest part at the corner. Now, the stables were invisible from the road. He pulled into the clay parking lot and parked next to the only other vehicle there – a dusty green Ford 150 pickup truck.

The wide, central door was closed against the cold. Nobody was riding that day. But the side door was unlocked. Rigg went in and stopped. And, for an instant, he could not breathe.

A framed, full color newspaper page hung on the rough-planking wall inside. He knew the picture. He'd seen it a long time ago. And he'd seen a part of it for hundreds of horrible nights since . . . well, he didn't know when it started, but it must have been at least a year.

It was a page from an old issue of the *Examiner Sunday Magazine*, run when the paper still had a Sunday magazine. It showed a teenaged girl, in full horse-riding regalia, holding a silver trophy. But it wasn't the girl or the trophy that stopped him now. It was the wrought iron door in the background. He was looking into a nightmare. His nightmare.

The bars on the door were the bars of the black cage.

He clenched his fists to keep his hands from shaking. He leaned closer. The photo had been published six months after Rigg joined the *Examiner*. He read everything in every issue of the paper in those rookie days. He'd read the article about the young equestrienne. He'd seen the picture.

And, years later, those iron bars in that picture had emerged from his subconscious, to try to nudge him to a name in a file he'd once thought to write down, but never to think of again. A name only Aria could find. It hadn't been Judith's arms beckoning from beyond those iron bars. They'd been the arms of one of the murdered boys, begging him to see the wrought-iron door, begging him to see the Happy Times Stables. Begging him, perhaps, to see Peter Tanson, a kid, Rigg once noted, who knew something about horse rides.

'Son of a bitch,' Rigg said, and then he laughed at the relief of it.

'What the hell?' a man's voice said. Rigg spun around. A man had come up to stand ten feet away.

He was wearing worn Levis, a fleece-lined, dirty suede jacket and a black cowboy hat. He could have been the buckaroo pictured in the sign out front, except nothing about him looked happy.

'I was just enjoying your article,' Rigg said. He supposed he very much would, from that instant on.

'What do you want?' the unhappy cowboy asked.

'I was hoping to see Peter Tanson about horse rides,' Rigg said. The cowboy offered up only confusion.

'A kid who comes here?' Rigg said, because he didn't know anything about Tanson.

'Don't know the name, mister. I'm just watching the place, temporary. Best you beat it.'

Wilcox's notoriety would have shut the place down, at least for a time. Rigg took the man's advice and beat it back to his car, but he whistled the short two miles to the home address he'd gotten from the Internet for a Peter Tanson, Senior.

A woman in her mid-forties answered the door. 'I know who you are,' she said, after he introduced himself. 'I thought you got fired.'

'Then you can see how deeply I'm still committed to finding the killers of Peter, Junior's classmates.'

'I remember how disgusting your behavior was, taking liberties with the bereaved,' she said.

'You can't always trust what you read in the papers,' he said.

Her face cracked with a frown. 'Besides, only one was a class-mate, and they weren't really friends.'

'I'd like to talk to your son about that,' he said. 'In your presence, of course.'

'My son's not home from school yet, and my husband is not home from work. You can come back at six tonight, for ten minutes and ten minutes only, Mr Rigg.'

He thanked her and left.

He found a Walmart, bought a multiple-meat sandwich that looked to have been made recently, and killed an hour eating it at one of the small scratched tables in the five-booth dining section. He got back to the Tanson place at six sharp.

They sat in the living room. The kid's father was a big fellow, six foot and at least 250 pounds, who leaned forward on his chair as if ready to pounce if Rigg stepped out of line. The boy looked to be sixteen, and was almost as big as his father. Mrs Tanson sat farthest away. 'Ten minutes,' she said.

'Football?' Rigg asked the kid.

The kid nodded. 'Right guard.'

'I'm one of the reporters that has been following the investigation of your friends' killings for the past fifteen months.'

'I didn't know the other two boys,' Peter said. 'Just Bobby. We were in the same homeroom.'

'Do you know if Bobby ever went to the Happy Times Stables?'

'I don't work there anymore.'

'You worked there?' Rigg cursed the sloppy note he'd made about the boy, months earlier. The kid could have been questioned thoroughly then, for sure.

The boy looked at his father. The father nodded.

'Bobby would come around to the stables, sometimes by himself, sometimes with other kids. I was allowed to let kids work for an hour of riding.'

'By Kevin Wilcox?'

'He was the boss.'

'He was always around?'

'I hardly ever saw him. He stayed up in the office.'

'Were the boys there the weekend they went missing?'

The father moved closer to the edge of his chair. 'Peter was sick that weekend.'

'We made him quit right after, because it was so near where the boys were found,' Mrs Tanson said.

'Did Bobby Stemec ever bring the Henderson kids around to work for free rides?' Rigg asked Peter.

'Bobby brought kids around, but I didn't pay attention to them so long as they did the work. I didn't recognize the Hendersons from their pictures in the paper.'

'It's been ten minutes,' the father said, standing up. 'You will not give out our names.'

'Under no circumstances. One last thing,' Rigg said, still sitting, because it was the most important thing. 'Has anyone from law enforcement ever come around to question you?'

'Never,' the father said.

'What about your friends, anyone at school?'

'Not for over a year,' the boy said.

'Time's up,' the boy's father said.

Rigg called Glet from the car. He didn't answer, so Rigg talked to his voicemail. 'I know something you'll want to trade for.'

Glet called back in a minute. 'What?'

'Wilcox confess yet?'

'Soon, real soon.'

'And his DNA matching to Bobby Stemec and Johnny Henderson?'

'What do you want, Rigg?'

'I don't think you're solid on Wilcox, Jerome. You don't have his DNA on the boys.'

'Horse shit.'

'Quite apropos,' Rigg said. 'But I think you're having a problem proving he did the boys.'

'Don't you worry about the DNA.'

'You overlooked something last time, big time,' Rigg said, 'but you'll have to trade for it.'

'Trade what?'

'Trade for that phone call I asked you to make.'

Glet sighed. 'Whatcha got?'

'Happy Times Stables,' Rigg said.

'The former employer of our murder suspect and gun peddler. I'm ahead of you on that one, pal.'

'Do you have witnesses who'll testify that kids, including Bobby Stemec, worked there for free rides? I just talked to one who said Bobby brought other kids around.'

'What's this kid's name?'

'I promised I wouldn't say, but you can find him and probably others by interviewing Bobby's homeroom classmates. How the hell did you miss this last time?'

'I didn't know we had. Lehman coordinated all that. I was responsible for sightings. But I'll make sure your classmates angle gets chased.'

'Do it yourself.'

'I got other things working at this minute.'

'What's so big you couldn't show up at the Tana Damm discovery site?'

Glet dodged. 'Your witness puts boys inside the stable with Wilcox?'

'No. He just puts Bobby inside. But there's no doubt Wilcox was there. He ran the stables. Interview the classmates, Jerome.'

'Lehman was a damned fool. You won't put this in the paper yet?'

'Only if you do me that favor I already asked you for,' Rigg said. 'What do you think about McGarry taking off?'

'Taking a vacation from the heat, or maybe not. Him and Lehman, they're both crooked.'

'Did he tell you there were problems with the DNA recovered from the boys, or was it Feldott?' It was a shot in the dark.

Glet laughed, loud.

It wasn't the response Rigg expected. 'You're not worried?' he asked.

'Here's what you need to know for now: McGarry's a moron.'

'He's not that something you're chasing that's more important than the boys and the girls?'

'Off the record on this for now, Milo?'

'Of course,' Rigg said.

'I'm chasing enough fireworks to set the whole county ablaze.'

'We have a deal, Jerome. My tip about Bobby's classmates in return for that phone call I've been asking you to make.'

'Get your pencil sharp, Milo; hell's going to pay,' Glet said. 'But I'll make your call.'

TWENTY-EIGHT

'**M**ilo?'

He held the cell phone up to see the time. It was five-fifteen, before dawn, a usual time for Carlotta to call. But he'd been sound asleep, and his first thought was relief. There'd been no cage. He knew about the bars now, and the arms behind them – arms that had never been Judith's.

'What is it, Carlotta?'

'I got another yellow card. In a blank envelope, no postage, like the last one. But, Milo?'

'Yes?'

'This one is different. And I think there's someone down by the cross street, watching the house.'

'Right now?' He rolled on to his knees and stood up.

'I think so, yes. I heard the mail slot, found the envelope. I looked outside, saw somebody walking away fast.'

'Where is he now?'

'I think at the corner. The darkest corner, opposite the street lamp and in the shadows of the big bushes. I lost sight of him there. He's small.'

'Someone out walking a dog?' he said.

'There was no dog.'

He said he'd be there in thirty minutes.

It was still dark by the time Milo got to Carlotta's neighborhood. He parked two blocks away and came up the sidewalk, watching the houses on both sides of the street. No one lurked behind any bushes. It was cold, barely twenty degrees. It was not a time for anyone to linger.

He crossed into Carlotta's cul-de-sac. There were a dozen cars and three panel vans parked along the street. Someone could have been hiding inside any one of them, slouched low. He was sure that was what had happened the last time, when the pictures of him leaving Carlotta's were taken.

He saw no one.

Like always, she opened the door before he got to the house. Like always, he stepped into suffocating heat. Like always, she was dressed in thick fleece pants and at least two sweatshirts to ward off a chill that would never go away. And, like always, her face was drawn tight by the grief that had hollowed out her life. They had that in common, that hollowing. He supposed it was why he always came when she called.

They sat next to each other at the dining-room table and he put on fresh latex gloves. She handed him a Ziploc bag.

'It's blank, of course,' he said, of the yellow card inside.

'I don't understand,' she said.

'Someone used you to get me here, and hung around to make sure I came.'

'To take pictures?'

'Most likely,' he said.

'They did their damage last time. What's left to lose?'

'Credibility, in case I discover something.' He reached for the Ziploc bag that held the blank envelope.

She put her hand on his wrist. 'Tell me what's going on.'

'They might be getting closer to solving the case,' he said, but that wasn't the whole of it.

'That Deputy Glet?' She pressed down harder on his wrist. 'I've seen him on TV, but all he says is that Wilcox will be arrested for the murders.'

He pulled his hand away. 'He's got new leads, Carlotta.'

'On the boys?' she said.

'Of course, for the boys,' he said, trying to not snap at the woman. He was in a hurry, now; he wanted no more talk. He wanted to get outside, out from the stifling heat of her house, away from the heat of her desperation. But, mostly, he wanted to get outside for another look to see if someone might be waiting.

'That deputy keeps saying he's investigating other things. But those things might distract.'

He stood up. 'The cops should have interviewed every damned one of the boys' classmates. Your boys went horseback riding, I think. The cops should have discovered that. They should have learned about Wilcox.' Sweat from the heat was dripping into his eyes. He wiped it away. 'I should have learned it, too.'

She followed him to the door.

'We must be careful, Carlotta,' he said.

'Careful?'

'Careful that we don't become a distraction again. Careful they don't focus on us.' He stepped out into the cold and pulled the door closed behind him.

Outside, in the growing light of the dawn, he saw no one lurking. But, as he headed down the sidewalk, the devil took his hand. He stopped, raised his middle finger, and took a slow turn in all four directions before continuing on to his car.

He went back to his apartment for a shower and coffee. On his way to the Pink, he called Glet's cell phone to remind him of the phone call the deputy had promised to make. But he got Glet's voicemail, so he reminded that instead.

He called the Dead House for an update on Tana Damm.

'My God, her neck's a mess, hacked,' Corky Feldott said. 'The bastard was no surgeon. Chunks of flesh are missing.'

Rigg thought again of Aria's musing that the killer might be a woman, and Carlotta's description of the person watching her house being of slight build. 'How much strength was needed to cut her head off?'

'Not that much, if the killer was patient. We're pretty sure it was a saw, but dull.'

'Could a woman have done it?'

'Mr Rigg, you're not suggesting a woman . . .?' He let the question dangle.

'I'm trying to keep an open mind. Any hope for recovering foreign DNA?'

'The body was so frozen . . .'

'You're sure about the freckles?'

'A tiny cluster behind the knee, as I told you before,' Feldott said.

'That's the last of the body marks listed on the yellow card. Let's hope that means Tana Damm is the last of our victims.'

'Let's hope,' Feldott said.

'And killed within the same brief time as the others?'

'So I presume.'

'Why stop at four girls?' Rigg asked. 'Why kill in a short spurt and then quit? Why write down body marks, as if on a shopping list? And why include Anthony Henderson's birthmark on that list? To tip us that it's the same killer?'

'I can't fathom this,' Feldott said, clicking Rigg away.

Rigg held up the Ziploc bag for Aria to see through her glass wall. She was on the phone, but gestured for him to come into her office.

'Of course, Luther,' she was saying. 'Of course.' She hung up.

'Luther loves me?'

'He wants to make sure you lay off McGarry.'

'McGarry's potentially a big story if he links to Lehman and Richie Fernandez. That can draw readers.'

'He's got a big balloon payment coming due.' She arched her eyebrows almost comically, nudging.

A thought began to grow in his mind. 'We've talked about Donovan having other investors . . .' he said slowly.

'Donovan formed a limited partnership to buy the paper. The identities of the other investors are shielded,' she said, but her eyebrows remained high. She knew something she wasn't saying.

'If Charles McGarry is among them, it would explain a lot,' he said. 'He needs McGarry's cash, and I chased the man right out of the country . . .'

'As I said, the identities of the other investors are shielded. But they do know each other very well, Milo.'

'Donovan killing my Fernandez reporting to protect an investor would trash our credibility.'

'It might not matter if he can't meet his balloon payment,' she said. 'What's in your new bag?'

He set the Ziploc on her desk. 'Carlotta got another card.'

'Blank on both sides,' she said, picking it up. 'Why?'

'To get me to go to her house in the wee hours.'

She groaned. 'For pictures?'

'Even worse, I paused outside to raise a finger.'

She laughed hard enough to open a drawer for a tissue. 'I'm sorry, none of this is funny,' she said, dabbing her eyes. 'So, was it the killer again who dropped off the card, or some hound who got tipped about the yellow cards and saw a way to snap a picture to sell to the *Curious Chicagoan?*'

'The lid's on the yellow cards; there's been no mention. I think it had to be the killer, like the first time, but now he'll submit pictures anonymously to ruin my credibility.'

'Maybe Donovan will frame one of you and your upraised finger to remind him why he should never have bought the *Examiner*. And you can hang one in your caboose, which is where you'll be exiled for forever, to remind you of the journalist you'll never be again.' She leaned forward across her desk. 'You need a huge story. You need to learn what Glet's chasing. No idea what's bigger than the boys and the girls?'

'He won't say.'

'But he's still acting solid on linking Wilcox to the boys, right?'

'For reasons I don't understand. He says the proximity between the stables and the forest preserve matters, but, according to Feldott, he doesn't have DNA. I just tipped Glet to have Bobby Stemec's classmates interviewed to see who worked for rides at the stables. He'll come across Peter Tanson.'

'He won't do it himself?'

'Too busy with that mysterious bigger stuff.'

She said nothing, and Rigg got the feeling that she was looking right through him, as if she couldn't see him.

'Aria?'

She shook her head. 'Sorry. I'm worried that Glet and his hack boss, Lehman, will drop the ball on the girls like they did on the boys.'

'I'm hounding Glet to make a call. I need some digging.'

'Oh, no,' she said, but she said it without surprise. She'd expected it.

'You said you like risk, Aria.'

She stared straight back, forming a slight smile. 'Wouldn't that be . . . crossing a line?'

'Risks often are.'

'Poor Donovan,' she said. 'Call Lehman to come get the latest card before you break out your shovel. And see if you can make some progress on those other stories I'm expecting.'

He left her office, but he looked back through the clean glass and saw that she'd turned to look at Benten's woods poster, and she was smiling full out now.

He called Lehman. He was put right through. 'I got another yellow card. It's blank on both sides.'

'Those cards, they're being left for you how, again?'

'My car.'

'Bullshit. You're at the Pink?'

'Yes.'

'I'll send somebody by.'

'Have you talked to McGarry lately?'

Lehman hung up.

Rigg called Glet's cell phone and this time got through. 'You're moving on my tip about the classmates?'

'I got men on it.'

'I got another yellow card. Lehman is sending someone to pick it up.'

'What's this one say?'

'Nothing. Blank, front and back. Stick your nose in it, Jerome. See if Lehman gets fingerprints.'

'Why send a blank card?'

'To take pictures of me picking it up. How are you doing on my phone call?'

'I'm on it,' Glet said.

Rigg picked at the stack of stories he'd been dodging and was on the phone, interviewing the owners of a new carwash, when two of Lehman's deputies came to pick up the envelope and the card. After that, he was to call a school district superintendent about the need for a new swimming pool in a high school, and then he supposed he ought to write something about a miserable stretch of road that contained a miserable number of new potholes. The afternoon ahead looked like what his career had become – a miserable road of potholes.

It was too much. Without a glance through Aria's glass wall, he left. He drove into the city, found a cabbie who took ten dollars to call his dispatcher. Rocco Enrice was still on vacation or off sick or something.

There was yet another new desk man at the Kellington Arms who didn't know a damned thing about any damned thing.

Potholes, every one of them, deep enough to stall a story.

He drove home. After climbing the exposed central stairs, he had the thought to go to the balcony rail and look out over the street.

Someone was there, in a black hoodie and a long black coat, beside a tree. A man or a woman, he couldn't tell.

He stood still in the cold night air, knowing he was backlit by the new lightbulbs and totally exposed. The person across the street could have been out for a walk, or waiting for a ride, or doing any of a number of different, innocent things. Not all the people out in the night were evil.

He was tired. It was late. He went to his door and his Scotch.

TWENTY-NINE

The sun was out when he woke up. No cage, not anymore. Cops were interviewing kids, forging links to Kevin Wilcox. The arms that had beckoned in his subconscious had been satisfied.

Digging for Richie Fernandez, though, still beckoned.

Glet's cell phone sent him to voicemail. He left his name and number and called the sheriff's department. 'Deputy Glet's not in,' the operator said, adding, 'It's Saturday.'

Saturday. Another Saturday. The second since the Graves girls were found.

'Sheriff Lehman, then,' Rigg said.

He was put right through, because Lehman couldn't afford to be known for taking a Saturday off, not with the murders of four girls remaining unsolved, and because Lehman needed something from Rigg about the latest yellow card.

'It would help if you were precise about how you got the card,' Lehman said.

'I leave my car open.'

'You lie.'

'Did you get anything off the card?'

'Nothing; no prints. Nothing off the Ziplocs either; thought they must be your bags.'

Like last time, he'd switched Carlotta's for new ones. 'They are. I used gloves.'

Lehman clicked off.

Rigg called ATF and was told Deputy Glet was unavailable. He asked if that meant Glet was in. He was told it simply meant Glet was unavailable. He took that to mean that Glet was there. He drove downtown.

'Jerome Glet?' Rigg asked at the desk.

The guard checked his sheet. 'Unavailable.'

'Does that mean he's here?'

'That means he's unavailable.'

'Is Agent Till unavailable, too?'

'Name?'

'Milo Rigg.'

The guard shrugged, made a call. Rigg expected the dust – it was Saturday, as had been pointed out to him several times already – but the desk man surprised him. 'Agent Till will be down in a minute.'

He wasn't. Agent Till took a full half-hour to come down in the elevator. He hadn't used the thirty-minute delay to spruce up. Even though it was a Saturday, he was wearing a brown suit and brown tie – perhaps the same suit and tie that he'd worn to the presser a few days earlier. His white shirt looked to have been changed, though today's seemed to be more yellowed than the one he'd sported the last time.

'The infamous Milo Rigg,' Till said, not bothering to extend his hand. He motioned to a cement bench against a blank cement wall. 'What brings you here on a weekend?'

'Jerome Glet's investigation.' He wanted no such thing. He'd come to breathe on Glet to make sure he made the call he'd asked him to make.

'Here's the update: we are progressing.'

'On your gun case?'

'That's the only case that officially interests the ATF.'

'You didn't come down from your office just to tell me that.'

'How can I locate Glet?' Till asked.

'He's not here?'

Till shook his head.

'Glet can be elusive,' Rigg said. 'I had to resort to coming down here in hopes of finding him.'

'We scheduled an important status meeting on Wilcox for this morning, one that Glet would be sure to attend. He did not show up. I assumed illness, and had our secretary call his office and his cell phone. No answer, either one. When I was told you were here, looking for him, I tried his cell phone and his office again. Still no luck. Glet's not one to skip a status meeting on his own prime suspect, even on a weekend.'

'He's working other cases, he's fond of saying,' Rigg said.

'He could still answer his cell phone.'

'Glet say anything about those other cases he's working?'

'You'd have to ask him about that.' Till stood up. 'Let me know when you find him.'

'Best you phone before you knock,' the ever-vigilant old crone next door said. Despite the cold, she'd stepped out from behind her weathered wood door.

Rigg stopped at the base of Glet's front steps. 'Why?'

'Remember the last time you were here, you asked if Jerome had a sweetie?'

'Yes.'

'Remember I laughed?'

'Yes.'

'Well, he might have got someone,' she said.

'You know this?'

'Someone came around last night. Jerome, he don't get visitors on account of his personality. Except last night. Someone came at nine o'clock, right up his steps to ring the bell.'

'Man or woman?'

'Couldn't tell. Long coat, hood or big collar or something. Could have been a man, could have been a woman. An escort whore, maybe. Even that slob must have needs.'

'You just told me to call him first. You're telling me the visitor is still in there?'

'I didn't see anybody leave.'

'When did you go to bed?'

'Maybe later than them,' she cackled.

Rigg climbed the steps, rang the bell, and braced himself for the horror of Glet with a cigar, in a robe, perhaps with lipstick smeared on his cheeks and bite marks on the folds of his neck.

There was no answer.

He rang again. Still no answer.

He went through the gangway between the two bungalows, to the garage at the alley. He wiped the filthy window clean enough to see Glet's black county car parked inside.

The door to the enclosed wood rear porch was unlocked. He went up the steps, went in and crossed to knock on the kitchen door. Hearing nothing, he tried the knob. It turned easily. He stepped inside.

'Jerome?' he called out. 'It's me, Rigg.'

The kitchen was a mess. Dirty dishes were stacked in the sink, a box of bran flakes sat on a porcelain-topped table next to a bowl of dried spaghetti.

'Jerome, damn it – it's me, Milo Rigg,' he yelled.

The house gave up no response.

A back bedroom opened off the kitchen. It was furnished as an office with a yellow metal desk topped with plastic fake woodgrain, a black four-drawer file cabinet and a brown fabric desk chair that leaned forty-five degrees to the right.

Rigg stepped back into the kitchen. 'Glet!' he shouted, but, again, there was no response.

The dining room was empty – no table, no chairs, no chest for good dishes. Another bedroom opened off it. It held an old dresser and a scratched nightstand. A three-year-old calendar from a bank was tacked to the wall. There was no bed. Probably Glet had gotten what furniture was in there for free.

Rigg walked into the front parlor.

And found Jerome Glet.

THIRTY

Two Chicago cops in a blue-and-white SUV raced up first, followed five minutes later by Lehman, two of his deputies and two of Feldott's forensics people. Corky came last, alone, white-faced, small and frail, looking like he was going to throw up.

He wore no stylish, slender necktie that Saturday, but his shirt was a deep burgundy, the color of long-dried blood, as if he'd known the day was going to be bad.

Lehman must have been quick about claiming jurisdiction, because the Chicago cops left within minutes. Corky Feldott went in, but was out in a couple of minutes.

'I'm no forensics man,' he told Rigg. For a man running a morgue, it might have seemed a strange thing to say, but it was honest. He was the CIB's kid, destined for bigger things.

'Besides,' Feldott went on, 'what's to see besides he blew half his head off?'

Rigg nodded. An instant's look had been plenty before he bolted back through the house and out the kitchen door to call the cops. 'But you'll autopsy, right?'

'Suicides don't need much of an autopsy, but I won't be in the room then, either.'

'You better get used to this stuff. If McGarry never comes back, you'll be in charge for a good long while.'

'I can't reach Mr McGarry,' Feldott said.

'Richie Fernandez,' Rigg said. 'You saw the pictures. Him with the shotgun, then at O'Hare, just an hour or so later.'

'I still can't believe that.'

'When's the last time you talked to Glet?'

'Late yesterday,' Feldott said. 'I was upset.'

'About what?'

Feldott turned to face Rigg. His eyes were glassy. 'About nothing I can share right now.'

'DNA?'

'I can't—'

'Come on, Cornelius. The man's dead. Off the record, if you like.'

'It's all so disappointing.'

'Disappointing?' It was an odd choice of words for a man just discovered dead. 'Glet?'

'Some time ago, one of our technicians confronted him where he shouldn't have been. Down in the basement, outside the lab where we store the DNA samples. I called him to demand an explanation. Again.'

'To demand to know what he was doing down there?'

'He hung up on me.'

'Are the samples OK?'

'Johnny Henderson's was missing.'

'That's the problem you haven't wanted to explain?' Rigg said. 'Glet took it?'

'I believe so, yes.'

'You were able to have the foreign DNA taken from Bobby Stemec analyzed?'

'It didn't match to Kevin Wilcox,' Feldott said. 'We don't know whose it is, so Deputy Glet's taking a key sample was inexcusable, because now that sample is particularly vital. But yesterday, like previously, he lied, denying he took Johnny Henderson's sample.'

'And of course there are no samples from the Graves girls and Jennifer Ann Day,' Rigg said.

'We got nothing from Tana Damm either, so there are none from any of the girls. The Graves girls were scrubbed with bleach, and Jennifer Ann Day was too long contaminated by the oil residue that was in her barrels, so there's nothing from any of the girls.'

'Cautious, knowledgeable killer.'

'You bet.'

'Why would Glet take the Johnny Henderson sample? What would he do with it?'

'I don't know, but obviously he was upset when I accused him of taking it.'

'Are you seeing that as reason for killing himself?' Rigg asked.

Lehman stepped out from the front door. 'Your people are done in here, Cornelius,' he said.

Feldott blanched even whiter as Lehman came down the stairs to join them.

Rigg looked down at the cement urns, domed white from the most recent snow. One recently snuffed cigar, standing particularly straight up from the crusted snow, reminded Rigg of the childish way he'd raised his middle finger the last time he left Carlotta Henderson's house.

Nothing felt childish now. Despite what Rigg had seen inside the bungalow – Glet's arm dangling above a revolver fallen to the floor – and despite Corky's far-fetched suggestion that Glet had panicked at being accused of pinching DNA evidence, suicide was a non-starter. Glet wouldn't have let a pup like Feldott intimidate him, let alone sour him into suicide. Glet was on the road to his own redemption, cocksure he was about to prove Wilcox was the doer in the boys' murders. And, trumping it all, Glet was hell-bent on setting off fireworks on an even bigger case. A man aiming that high didn't aim for his own head. His suicide had been staged.

Feldott walked quickly to his car. Lehman stayed at the base of the front stairs, next to Rigg.

With almost anyone else, Rigg wouldn't have noticed. But Feldott was a lithe, streamlined young man. His clothes fit like they were custom-made. But, that morning, he had a bulge. He'd jammed something partway into his left coat pocket. It was one of the county's distinctive orange and tan paper evidence bags.

Lehman didn't seem to have noticed. 'He's just a damned kid,' he said as they watched Feldott drive away. 'Exactly how much did you see inside?'

'I'm not good with shattered heads. I saw, I went out the back, I called the cops.'

'You saw the gun?'

'On the floor, and his right hand hanging down above it.'

'I can't stop you from reporting this, Rigg. All I ask is that you not sensationalize.'

'Like Fernandez, you mean?'

'This isn't one of your fancies, Rigg, nor is it murder. Glet shot himself.'

'Glet was on a roll, excited about chasing new leads.'

'What do you know about those new leads?'

It was no surprise Lehman was fishing. Glet despised the sheriff and had kept him as far away as he could from what he was chasing.

'He told me only that he was chasing fireworks.'

'What does that mean?'

'It means something more than Kevin Wilcox, Bobby Stemec, the Henderson brothers and the girls. He said he was chasing something that would upend Cook County, something that would set the whole county ablaze.'

'Don't speculate in your paper,' Lehman said.

'You'll want to talk to the neighbor,' Rigg said, nodding at the lace curtain fluttering next door. 'She saw somebody, dressed in a long coat and maybe a hoodie, knock on Glet's door last night, about nine o'clock.'

'Man or woman?'

'She wants to imagine it was a rented woman. Carlotta Henderson saw a figure that might fit the same description watching her house the night she received that last yellow card.'

'That's where you've been getting them? Carlotta Henderson?'

Rigg nodded. 'He's using her to get to me.'

'What is it: a him or a her? You just implied it could have been a woman that visited Glet and the Henderson woman.'

'You should call Carlotta, get it straight from her.'

'You should have called me when she received the first card. She cost you everything last time.'

'I'm expecting new pictures, maybe taken by the killer.'

'We're not the enemy, Rigg.'

'You'll have Carlotta Henderson's house watched?'

'I'll have a word with her locals.'

'And McGarry?'

'What about McGarry?'

'Richie Fernandez.'

Lehman scowled and went up the steps to go back in the bungalow.

Rigg went out to his car and called Till.

SHERIFF'S DEPUTY FOUND DEAD

Milo Rigg, *Chicago Examiner*

Cook County Sheriff's Deputy Jerome Glet was found dead this morning in his home on Chicago's northwest side. Cause of death is presumed to be gunshot, but the official finding is pending the results of an autopsy scheduled to be conducted later today. Sheriff Joseph Lehman issued a statement saying, 'Jerome Glet served our department with honor and professionalism for twenty-eight years. Words can't describe our sense of loss, and we will investigate his untimely death with all of our resources.'

Glet drew attention most recently in his re-examination of the Stemec Henderson murders that occurred fifteen months ago. On two separate occasions, he announced that he was close to bringing that investigation to a conclusion following the arrest of Kevin Wilcox by the Federal Bureau of Alcohol, Tobacco, Firearms and Explosives on charges of gun trafficking. Though circumspect, Glet also implied he was making excellent progress on other things that, he said, 'would set the county ablaze.'

'This last sentence reads like a scandal sheet,' Aria said. 'You have no proof that he was closing in on anything substantive at all. Feldott told you there was no match between Wilcox and Bobby Stemec's foreign DNA, and you have no clue about that bigger thing he was working.'

'I can't see Glet killing himself.'

'His mysterious visitor killed him?'

'We got lucky with the neighbor seeing someone. Lehman wants that withheld until he can check that out.'

'We're running out of time, Milo.'

'Now that I've sent McGarry off to points yonder, none of Donovan's other investors are lining up to cover the slack?'

'You'd best remember we don't know if McGarry had money in the *Examiner*.'

'We can guess accurately by Donovan's behavior.'

'Do not breathe a word about any of that,' she said.

'Greg Theodore at the *Trib* is about to, or at least some of it. He called, left a message that he's doing a piece about our imminent demise.'

'How can we find out what Glet was working on?' she asked.

'As you just said, there might not be time,' he said.

THIRTY-ONE

Peter Tanson's mother opened the door only a crack.

'Did anybody come by?' Rigg asked.

'On TV, they said that dead deputy was the one working on the boys' murders.'

'He was in charge, but his people never came by?'

'You said you'd keep us out of it.'

'I need to know if sheriff's deputies are questioning Peter's classmates.' Rigg doubted it, like he doubted Glet had made the phone call he'd requested. Glet acted too cocksure he already had Wilcox in the bag for the boys' murders, and was too hell-bent on chasing his mysterious fireworks to bother with Rigg's request.

Mrs Tanson turned to yell out her son's name and then closed the door. A moment later, the kid opened the door wide.

'Ma said you want to know if cops have been asking about Happy Times.' He shook his head. 'Not that I heard.'

'I won't mention your name, but tell me who else knew that Bobby traded work to ride there?'

The kid gave him three names and approximate addresses.

The first kid, a boy of about seventeen, an age Bobby Stemec never got to be, was in the driveway alongside his house, filling the rear tire of a rusted minivan with a small electric compressor.

'Sure, Peter got us rides sometimes,' the kid said. 'If we worked a couple of hours, we got thirty minutes on a horse. I went with Bobby twice.'

'How about the Henderson boys?'

'Those other dead kids? I just knew Bobby.'

'You knew Kevin Wilcox?'

'The guy in the news for selling guns and maybe killing Bobby and the others? Maybe he was in the office. I don't remember him.'

'But you're positive Bobby Stemec went riding there sometimes?'

'Like I said, I went with him twice.'

'Any cops ever ask you about that?'

'Nope.'

The second boy on Tanson's list was just pulling into his driveway when Rigg arrived. He got out of his car dressed in sweats and carrying a basketball. Like the first kid, he'd gone riding with Bobby Stemec in exchange for work, didn't know either of the Hendersons and didn't remember Kevin Wilcox. And, no, no cops had come around asking about any of that.

Nobody was home at the third kid's place. It was no matter. Rigg had enough. He called Lehman before starting his car.

'I got nothing to tell you about Glet,' the sheriff said.

'I got something to tell you, Sheriff. I tipped him that Bobby Stemec and some of his friends traded work for rides at Wilcox's stable.'

'You gave this to Glet?'

'Yes, and I asked him why he never bothered to talk to classmates the first time around. He said you dropped the ball on that.'

'That son of a bitch.'

'He never mentioned my tip?'

'Not a word.'

'I don't think he ever followed up on Richie Fernandez either,' Rigg said.

Lehman didn't bite. 'I'll see about those kids,' he said, and hung up.

Rigg called Till for the second time that day.

'Thanks again for calling me about Glet,' the ATF man said. 'He was coarse and stunk of cigars, but there was no mistaking his dedication. I called Lehman to get his take.'

'And?'

'He said it was suicide.'

'Do you believe Glet could do himself?'

'I told Lehman Glet had no potential for suicide.'

'Glet ever say anything about DNA?'

'Glet could bluster, but he hammered Wilcox with that DNA, time and again. He seemed real strong on the link.'

'That's troublesome. Feldott says one of the two samples is missing, and the other came back negative to Wilcox.'

'Glet acted otherwise around here, like the match was solid.'

'What about the girls?'

'He tried coming at Wilcox with DNA about them, too. Told him preliminary DNA was good there as well. Wilcox laughed like he didn't laugh about the boys. He knew Glet was bluffing about the girls.' Till paused, then asked, 'What haven't you said?'

'That sample that's missing? Glet was spotted too near the M.E.'s storage lab.'

'It . . . might make sense,' Till said slowly.

'What do you mean?'

'Nothing I want to share yet.'

'Glet kept saying he was on to something bigger than the boys and the girls. Did he ever mention what that was?'

'No, but I got the feeling Glet was using us as a dodge. He wasn't here much, just enough to convince that hack Lehman that he was working alongside us every minute. He wasn't. He was gone from here most of the time.'

'Where?'

'I don't know. We work our side of the street, he worked his.'

'Except you know something you're not saying about DNA,' Rigg said.

'I need to check it out. If it's worthwhile, I'll get back to you.'

'I tipped Glet about a link between Bobby Stemec's classmates and the Happy Times Stables. Glet didn't work it and Lehman says he knows nothing about it. If my tip doesn't get worked, without DNA the whole boys' case against Wilcox might go back in the dumper.'

'Not my jurisdiction.'

'Glet had a visitor last night,' Rigg said. 'He didn't have friends, I don't think, and I doubt he entertained women.'

'Glet's death is not an ATF matter either.'

'It's Lehman's, and that's troubling.'

'You're thinking someone from county did him?'

'I think someone was worried Glet was getting too close to those fireworks he was so secretive about.'

'I keep telling you: these aren't ATF matters,' Till said, but there was a new hesitation in his voice. He knew where Rigg was headed.

'You can't investigate the murder of someone working on a federal task force involving the illicit sale of guns?' Rigg asked.

'He was ancillary, sitting in on our interrogations of Wilcox, not relevant to our . . .' The phone went silent for a beat, and then Till said, 'What do you want, exactly?'

Rigg told him.

'Don't post anything to your site until tomorrow,' Till said after a moment. 'It'll be Sunday and I won't be in the office.'

ATF TO INVESTIGATE DEPUTY'S DEATH
Milo Rigg, *Chicago Examiner*

Special Agent Till of the Chicago branch of the Federal Bureau of Alcohol, Tobacco, Firearms and Explosives announced today that his office will conduct an investigation into the death of Cook County Sheriff's Deputy Jerome Glet. Glet was found dead of a gunshot wound yesterday at his Chicago home.

'While Jerome was most actively involved in the investigation of the murders of Bobby Stemec and John and Anthony Henderson that occurred over a year ago, he was providing valuable counsel to our own investigation into the illicit sale of guns in the Chicago area,' Till said. 'We need to rule out any potential that his death might be related to our investigation.'

It has been rumored that Glet's investigation into the Stemec Henderson murders produced links to other crimes that were, in Deputy Glet's words, 'explosive'. Till promised a wide-ranging investigation into any and all matters that Glet may have been working on as part of his service with ATF, to include interviews with those of Bobby Stemec's classmates who might have gone horseback riding at the stables managed by Kevin Wilcox, currently in ATF's custody on gun trafficking charges.

Cook County Sheriff Joseph Lehman was unavailable for comment, but Acting Cook County Medical Examiner Cornelius Feldott released a statement thanking ATF for their 'willingness to get involved in examining the troubling life and death of their and our cherished colleague, Jerome Glet.'

Meanwhile, Medical Examiner Charles McGarry remains on leave due to an unspecified medical condition, and was unavailable for comment about Glet's death, as well as the disappearance of Richie Fernandez, a purported suspect in the Graves case.

It was 8:30, Saturday night. Aria had waited in her office for his copy.

'Lots to love here, Milo,' she said, with almost a straight face. 'Especially your insistence on bringing up McGarry and Richie Fernandez in everything you write. Feldott's buying into a "troubled life"?'

'He's seeing what's too obvious: suicide.'

'And you're seeing murder?'

'Glet was chasing fireworks. I think he got too close.'

'That man who came to Glet's house?'

'Or woman, as you suggested,' he said. 'His visitor could have been the same person who dropped off the two cards at Carlotta Henderson's home, and another one for the purported ransom request to the Day family.'

'Someone who knows too much about body marks on both Anthony Henderson and the girls?' she said.

'Whoever it is, it wasn't Kevin Wilcox. He was in ATF custody when the cards were delivered to Carlotta.'

'But not to the Day family. Their card came right after the daughter disappeared. So . . .' she went on slowly, 'Wilcox had an accomplice?'

'I'm guessing Wilcox is good for the boys, but not the girls,' Rigg said.

'So, a different killer for the girls?' she said. 'And it's that person who killed Glet?'

'That's where I'm stopped. What's the motive? Glet showed no real interest in the girls. He was closing in on his fireworks.'

'So, it couldn't have been the boys' killer who killed Glet, and it wasn't the girls' killer. It was whomever Glet was closing in on for his fireworks – fireworks which we know nothing about?'

'And don't forget—'

She groaned. 'Don't say digging. Don't say Richie Fernandez.'

'Fernandez was not explosive to Glet, either. He was interested, but not enough. He was chasing something else.'

'But yet . . . Tell me, Milo: did you make Fernandez interesting to Till?'

Rigg smiled.

She smiled. And then she sent Rigg's piece to the Bastion.

THIRTY-TWO

H e called Corky first thing, when he got to the Pink, Monday morning. 'Have you examined Glet?'

'Soon.'

'I thought you'd be in a rush,' Rigg said.

'We're being careful. And I'm in no hurry to release results that characterize Deputy Glet as unstable.'

'I already reported your belief that he was troubled, even if I disagree.'

'So I saw, yesterday,' Feldott said. 'This is off the record?'

'Isn't most everything, these days?'

'I can't understand why he stole Johnny Henderson's foreign DNA.'

'It makes no sense,' Rigg said. 'Like suicide makes no sense.'

'He got very upset when I called to confront—'

Rigg cut him off. 'You said he hung up on you, I know. Forget the mystery of why he took Johnny Henderson's foreign DNA, for now. Forget that Bobby Stemec's foreign DNA doesn't match to Wilcox. Glet was working other angles to Wilcox, witnesses that could place the boys in the stables. And don't ignore the grand prize – those fireworks Glet was so secretive about.'

'What the hell are those fireworks?'

It was the first time Rigg had heard Corky Feldott swear.

'I'll find them,' Rigg said, like he believed he could.

He killed the rest of the morning and half the afternoon working the fillers that he'd owed Aria for days. He wrote up the telephone interview he'd conducted about a new car wash, the repair of the long-leaking swimming pool, and the pothole repair program.

He was about to call the organizer of a Fourth of July pet parade when, most mercifully, Till called. 'Sheriff Lehman phoned me this morning about your piece yesterday.'

'Enraged that I reported you're doing what he should have done fifteen months ago?'

'No,' Till said. 'He was very controlled, very polite, almost timid about us looking to find kids that could place Kevin Wilcox close to those boys.'

'And you are?'

'And we did, at least to Stemec, from the three kids you told us about. And, as you damned well know, one actually worked at the stables. His mother was furious. All three kids were very respectful, and very certain. The one who worked there said Bobby Stemec occasionally showed up with other kids to work in return for free horseback rides. The other two kids said they each worked at Happy Times Stables twice for free rides. I just messengered the sworn statements to Lehman.'

'I'm amazed he wasn't furious.'

'Maybe he doesn't want to get called out for screwing up, this time around,' Till said.

'Or he doesn't want to invite attention that might lead to other scrutiny.'

'Richie Fernandez?' Till said. 'I haven't forgotten.'

WITNESSES TIE ATF GUN SUSPECT TO STEMEC HENDERSON

Milo Rigg, *Chicago Examiner*

Investigators for the Federal Bureau of Alcohol, Tobacco, Firearms and Explosives announced today that they have secured eyewitness testimony tying slain Bobby Stemec, 14, to the Happy Times Stables, where Kevin Wilcox was manager.

One witness stated that Bobby Stemec and his friends occasionally worked at the stables in exchange for riding horses.
Wilcox is now in federal custody, charged with illegally selling
hundreds of firearms. Stemec and two other boys were found
murdered less than two miles from the stables. The case
remains unsolved.

'No Fernandez? No McGarry?' Aria said. 'Well, this won't excite
Donovan. He's convinced your mentions of McGarry show you
want to keep thumbing your nose at him.'

'What did you tell him?'

'That I'd quit if he reined you in, and that would be a shame
because I just booked advertising for a local supermarket and a used
car lot, demonstrating my potential to rescue the *Examiner* from its
financial woes all by myself.'

He looked at her, surprised.

She laughed. 'No chance,' she said, fingering her pearls. 'Our ad
revenue barely covers our rent here.'

'Did you mention we suspect Donovan is tied to McGarry
financially?'

'I reminded him that Stemec Henderson and the girls' cases are
heaters, and that your nose is good and Richie Fernandez fits in
somewhere. And maybe, I said, so does McGarry, and we need to
stay on top of it all.'

'If the paper doesn't go down next week,' Rigg said.

'I told him the *Trib* and the *Sun-Times* would soon sniff out the
fact that McGarry left the country.'

'He was concerned?'

'Not at all,' she said. 'The man has no taste for news.'

'You seem unconcerned,' he said.

'About my job?' She sighed. 'There is that, yes.'

'My goodness, the phantom returns!' Blanchie said, bringing water
to his booth. Things at the diner had improved, hubbub-wise. Three
other booths and four of the tables were occupied.

'Busy times,' he said.

'I've been reading your posts,' she said, pointing to the laptop
he'd set on the table. 'Are they going to get him?'

'Wilcox, for Stemec Henderson?' He nodded.

'And that missing Fernandez, for the girls?'

'I wish I knew,' he said, instead of saying Fernandez was likely a dead patsy, like Glet.

She left and he opened his laptop to puzzle again over the piece posted that evening on the *Examiner*'s website.

CORNELIUS FELDOTT, QUIET MASTER?
Aria Gamble, *Chicago Examiner*

As the Cook County sheriff's investigation into the deaths of Beatrice and Priscilla Graves, Jennifer Ann Day and Tana Damm drags on with no discernible results, hopes are turning to Cornelius Feldott, Cook County's acting medical examiner. Sources say he has begun carefully examining all the previous evidence collected in the Stemec Henderson murders of a year ago, the more recent killings of the girls, and the untimely death of Cook County Deputy Sheriff Jerome Glet. He's released no new findings but his methodical assembling of previously verified facts offers the best hope that all of these cases will be brought to successful conclusions.

It might have been the damndest piece of worshipful essaying he'd ever read in the *Examiner*, but Aria was cunning. She was nudging the Citizens' Investigation Bureau, the heavies who'd installed Feldott at the M.E.'s office, to get cracking at the sheriff's department as well, to push Lehman out of the way and put someone else in charge, even a pup like Feldott, to direct a full team of aggressive, intelligent investigators in all three cases.

He looked through the large front window, out at the parked cars and the railroad station beyond. A slim figure stood across the street and seemed to be looking in, straight at him.

He got up quickly and hurried to the door, but, when he got outside, the figure was gone.

'You all right, Milo?' Blanchie asked, clearly alarmed, when he came back in.

'Just peachy,' he said, of his frayed nerves.

But, of course, his nerves weren't peachy at all.

THIRTY-THREE

R igg climbed the front steps to Glet's neighbor's brown brick bungalow the next morning and knocked on the door.

Two bolts slid back in the next instant. Ever vigilant, she must have spotted him getting out of his car.

'I was the one who found him,' he said. With her antennae, he figured she already knew that – and that he was a reporter.

'You snuck in the back way,' she said, 'other side of the porch, where I can't see.'

'The front door was locked, but the back door was open.'

'Dead of gunshot, according to the newspaper and TV,' she said. 'There's no yellow police tape, and no cops have been back to investigate.'

'They don't see a crime.'

'Suicide? They're damn fools.'

'You told them about the visitor?'

'Sheriff himself came over to talk to me.'

'What did you see, exactly?'

'Jerome wasn't much for electric bills. Night-times, the only light was from his TV, so it was hard to see in. Like I told you last time, whoever came to see him was just a shadow from the street light at the corner, done up in a long coat, high collar, a hood pulled down the sides of the face. Could have been the Grim Reaper himself, come to fetch Glet's soul, except I didn't see a scythe and I don't think Jerome had a soul. One thing's for sure: the cheapskate didn't switch on any more lights when the guest went in.'

'Glet let the visitor in right away?'

'He or she was expected,' the woman said.

'You heard nothing unusual . . .?'

'Gunshot?' She shook her head.

'And you never saw the visitor leave?'

'The TV went dark, so there was nothing to see in his front room. I figured they were off to do the hooty-tooty in one of the bedrooms on the far side, where I can't see. One thing's for sure: nobody went out the front; the street light would have told me that. And Jerome's back porch door is on that same far side, as you damned well know from sneaking in. I was thinking his visitor must have left that way, out to the alley, meaning she was a hooker and took off on account of him having some peculiar requirements and lacking even the most basic of masculine charms. Of course, now I'm thinking he was murdered, and I don't know what to imagine.'

'I'm going to look around inside.'

Comprehension tightened the wrinkles around her eyes. 'You don't want me to call the cops that you're snooping.'

'As you said, there's no yellow cop tape. Case is closed for them.'

'But not for you?'

'I want to know about that visitor.'

'Jerome would kill others before he'd kill himself,' she said, and closed her door.

Lehman's deputies had locked the doors, but they'd not checked the windows. The lowest one in the gangway between the two houses was unlatched. He raised the sash and crawled into the dining room, the empty room he remembered from the morning he'd discovered Glet. He took a breath and went to the front of the house.

The living room had two chairs. One, upholstered green in a nubby fabric and greasy at the arms, was splattered dark with dried blood at the top and side. It was where Rigg had found Glet slumped back against the cushion with his right arm dangling over the armrest, above the revolver on the floor.

The other chair was smaller and had been orange before it faded into a dirty beige. Too narrow for Glet's bulk, it held a stack of newspapers two feet high. On top was the first section of an *Examiner*. Once again, Rigg was startled by his paper's thinness and narrowness. Long gone for all the queens was the broadsheet thick with national coverage, in-depth local reporting and investigative reports. But, even before the hatchet-wielding Donovan had taken over, the *Examiner* had been shrunk more than its remaining competitors. Donovan had reduced it even more, into a ribbon of blurbs and fast paragraphs.

One of Rigg's short pieces was on the front page, right below the fold. It typified the paper's new age. It wasn't solid reporting so much as a news blip written for restricted attention spans.

A scratched pine table was between the two chairs. It held a green ashtray the size of an automobile hubcap, filled with a half-dozen foul-smelling stubs of Glet's cigars. One stub looked to still be damp. Glet's last rope, Rigg supposed.

A can of Miller Lite was next to the ashtray. Rigg pinched its top with his thumb and forefinger and raised it. It was almost full. Rigg doubted the crime-scene team wondered about that in their rush to conclude they were seeing a suicide.

Across the small room, a big-screen television was aimed at the greasy green chair. A small artificial Christmas tree rested on the floor next to it, either a month late to be taken down, or – more likely, given the indifference of the slob that was Glet – it was a year-round accoutrement of the bungalow's front room.

Rigg looked again at the newspapers piled on the orange chair. Glet hadn't cleared them away to offer his visitor a place to sit down. That, and the fact that the neighbor saw the living room darken immediately when the TV was switched off, could have supported her theory that Glet, a bachelor, had welcomed a visitor whose expertise was not best conducted sitting down.

Or Glet had been ordered to sit back down by a visitor who'd come with a gun.

The front bedroom opened off the living room. Rigg hadn't looked in it, the morning he'd found Glet; he'd seen only the body slumped in the chair before he ran out the back. The double bed was made, sort of, its peach-colored coverlet pulled carelessly over the pillows and sheets.

There could have been activity there, if Glet had been the type to welcome a working girl, but it didn't seem logical that he would have made the bed afterward and then gone to sit in the living room and kill himself.

The dresser and nightstand looked to have been found in the same alley as the junk furniture in the middle bedroom. Rigg looked through the drawers and saw two frayed sweaters, huge underwear, and socks. A Hawaiian shirt festooned with tropical birds and flowers was balled up on the shelf in the closet. Below it hung several garishly bright blue, green and yellow shirts, and three dark suits.

He fingered the newest of them, the shiny black suit with the manufacturer's sleeve tag still attached that Glet had worn to his impromptu press conference on the stairs of the sheriff's headquarters. Frugality like Glet's was reflexive, deeply ingrained. He would have spent money on a new suit only if he thought he was about to draw substantial press attention from breaking something big.

Rigg walked back through the barren dining room and cluttered kitchen to the rear bedroom Glet used as an office. The rubber wastebasket was empty. Giveaway advertising pens, paper clips and small scratch pads were jumbled in the desk's center drawer. Paid utility and property tax bills, income tax returns and other financial documents filled the two drawers on the right side.

The two drawers on the left side of the desk were as empty as the wastebasket. Jammed-full desk drawers on one side and empties on the other meant things like Glet's checkbook, cancelled checks and bank statements had been removed by Lehman's deputies. And maybe Feldott. He remembered the bulge in Feldott's left coat pocket the day Rigg had discovered the body. The acting chief medical examiner had taken something, too, in an evidence bag.

The basement was empty, the place of a man with no hobbies. It held only a rusting washing machine, a dryer and a tiny metal workbench with a cluster of cheap hand tools lying in its center.

He went back upstairs and outside, locking the kitchen door behind him, and crossed the small lawn to the peeling white clapboard garage. The side door was unlocked.

Glet's black county car was still inside. Rigg reached in to open the glovebox. It was empty. No papers or pockets were jammed under the seats. That Glet had an immaculate automobile was inconceivable. Lehman's people had searched the car and scooped up everything to take it away.

A push-type reel lawnmower, good enough for the tiny lawn, was leaned in the corner next to a cracked red plastic snow shovel. Glet, forever penurious, had bought none of the things – garden tools, fertilizer, salt for winter sidewalks – that typically cluttered suburban residential garages.

Rigg left the garage. As he went up in the narrow gangway between the brick sides of the two bungalows, he fought the urge to wave at the lace next door. He understood lace curtains. They were thick enough to conceal interested eyes, yet thin enough to see a visitor who should have left by the front door.

He got in his car. He'd seen nothing and maybe a lot in an almost-full can of Miller Lite. He doubted anyone about to kill himself would open a beer and take only a tiny sip before pulling the trigger.

What he did not doubt was Glet's nose. A feral hunter, Glet

had smelled something major, something that would give him
redemption and praise enough to perhaps become the next sheriff.
He'd said several times that he was on the trail of explosive, career-
rocketing things. Such a man would not have offed himself, certainly
not in fear of a pup like Feldott threatening to accuse him of pinching
DNA.

But it was the visitor that trumped everything. The visitor left
by the back door. Front-door arrivals didn't leave by back doors.

He called Feldott from his car. 'Got a verdict?'

'I pronounce the *Examiner* delightful. Thank you.'

'Check the byline. Aria Gamble wrote it.'

'I thank everyone at the *Examiner*,' Feldott said.

'She wrote that you're becoming the go-to guy in the
investigations.'

'For the record, I merely want to support Sheriff Lehman. I want
to help in offering the citizens of Cook County absolute assurance
that all these matters are being investigated fully.'

It was a nascent politician's speech, a chick emerging from the
egg.

'So, a verdict?'

'Not for publication.'

'Agreed.'

'I was there when the doctor tested the swab. GSR was on Deputy
Glet's right hand.'

'Officially, it will go down as him firing into his own temple?'

'I'm not going to put out a release, Mr Rigg. Deputy Glet was
a good man, an honorable man. Let this fade away.'

'You tipped Lehman?' Rigg said.

'Of course. The sheriff is heading that investigation as well, and
Deputy Glet was his most senior deputy. But Sheriff Lehman is no
more anxious than I am to stir up anything embarrassing.'

'Glet's house reeks with evidence that contradicts suicide.
Lehman – and you, if you're serious about a thorough investigation
– must comb it for evidence. And the neighbor's got to be questioned
exhaustively about the visitor she saw.'

'You went back?'

'The neighbor says Glet's visitor came in the front and went
out the back. What innocent person does that?'

'A hooker.'

'A hooker would arrive at the front and leave by the front, or arrive at the back and leave by the back. Focus on what Glet was chasing. He was on to things that were explosive.'

'He stole Johnny Henderson's foreign DNA like he was trying to ruin the case. When news of that got out, it would probably have forced his resignation and maybe resulted in his prosecution.'

'I'd just tipped him that witnesses could put Bobby Stemec and other boys at the stables, and that meant right to Wilcox. Yet he was excited about bigger things than that. He didn't kill himself.'

'Maybe the fireworks didn't pan out,' Feldott said.

Rigg took a breath. It was time. 'I'm assuming Lehman's team was in charge of removing evidence from Glet's house?'

'Standard procedure.'

'I'm correct about that, right? Only Lehman's team would have removed evidence?'

Feldott paused for only a second, but it was long enough. He'd sensed what Rigg had not said, that Rigg had seen Feldott leaving Glet's bungalow with an evidence bag jammed in his coat pocket.

'Please, Mr Rigg, mum's the word on the gunshot residue,' Feldott said, and hung up.

The acting M.E. had dodged. Whatever he'd taken was important enough to still keep hidden.

Milo sat in Aria's office twenty minutes later. 'So that's it,' he said, after briefing her. 'Feldott's not going to release an official finding, but he's ruled Glet a suicide.'

'Which you doubt because of a full can of beer?'

'And the fireworks he was chasing, and the fact that his visitor left by the back door.'

'And the uncleared chair?' she asked.

'Who invites a visitor into his house, doesn't clear off a place to sit?'

'Someone who takes a woman directly to bed, as the neighbor suggested?' she said.

'Who doesn't rumple the bed?'

'So, he's a neatnik, or—'

'Glet?' he interrupted. No one had ever thought of Glet as being neat.

'Or,' she said, a faintly suggestive smile forming on her face, 'maybe he likes the floor.'

He fought the urge to say that his was a mattress, not just a floor, but said instead, 'Feldott left Glet's bungalow with a small evidence bag stuffed in his pocket.'

She opened her mouth to say something, but her desk phone rang. She picked it up, still looking at Rigg.

'Of course, he's right here.' She handed the handset over to Rigg.

'You got your call, Rigg,' Agent Till said.

THIRTY-FOUR

Yellow police tape was strung across the gate to McGarry's estate. Beyond it, three blue-and-white Winthrop County sheriff's patrol cars, a black Chevrolet Suburban, a white crime-scene investigator's van and a red ambulance were lined up along the snow-packed driveway behind McGarry's Escalade. Uniformed officers and crime-scene investigators were bringing tarps and shovels to the van and the cars, getting ready to leave. The ruckus, if there'd been one at all, was over. Rigg parked on the road and walked up.

A sheriff's deputy saw him and came down to the gate. 'You can't be here, sir.'

Rigg showed his press ID.

'Your credentials don't matter,' the officer said. 'This is private property. You can't be here.'

The sheriff must have spotted Rigg, because he came walking down the drive. The Winthrop County sheriff was a tall man, blond, with a ruddy complexion. His name was Olsen. Rigg had interviewed him once, several years earlier, about a missing persons investigation. 'The famous Milo Rigg?'

'How are you, Sheriff?'

The sheriff told the deputy he could leave and said to Rigg, 'Not at all delighted to see you, Rigg. You trashed us, some months back.'

'Only those who weren't helping in Stemec Henderson, and that wasn't you. That case was off your turf.'

'Trash one, trash all, and now you've come to do him?' Olsen said, jerking a thumb toward McGarry's mansion.

'He must be livid, you guys showing up,' Rigg said, for the show of it. McGarry was in Paris, or at points far from it, but that had not been published, thanks to Donovan.

'He's unavailable.'

'Care to give me a statement?' Rigg asked, pointing to two deputies carrying shovels back to their cars.

'How did you find out about this?'

'A tip,' Rigg said, because Till hadn't ratted him out.

'Your tipster wasted your time.'

'About Richie Fernandez?'

'You can write that we arrived here this morning with a duly executed warrant authorizing us to search these grounds, based upon credible information that a person might be buried on this property. We knocked, but received no answer. We tried calling Mr McGarry's various homes and his office, but could not locate him. In accordance with our authorization, we proceeded to conduct our search of his grounds. We have concluded our search. We are leaving, and so are you.'

'You found nothing?'

'Oh, we found something, Rigg, and now we've found you, right here where you don't belong.'

'What did you find?'

Olsen gave him only a smile, and turned and walked back up the driveway. Vehicle doors began slamming shut. An officer came down, removed the yellow tape and opened the gate.

Rigg waited in his car as the van, the ambulance and the cops backed down the driveway and drove away. The last squad car backed down, but stopped outside the gate. An officer got out. He was different than the first officer Rigg had talked to – younger, maybe twenty-five, which was right for a rural sheriff's department.

Rigg got out of his car and approached the gate. 'How do you guys manage to open locked gates?' he asked in what he hoped was a conversational voice.

The officer smiled. 'We always request security codes to keep on file. This owner complied.'

'What was all the activity up there?'

'Sheriff got a credible call that there was a body buried in a shallow grave. But it was just a dog.'

'A dog?'

'Sheriff was furious.' He pointed to the keypad on the wood post. 'You'll have to leave, sir,' he said. 'I've got to reset the code.'

Rigg got in his car and drove away, but only to the next side road. When the young officer's car disappeared down the highway, he parked, put on the running shoes he'd thought to leave in the car, and walked back to the gate. The gate was made of tubular metal, set low, meant only to stop a car. He climbed over, walked up the driveway and on to the vast back grounds.

Their search area had not been widespread. Hundreds of footprints circled only the mound where McGarry had swept up snow. That mound was a tiny mudhill now, from being excavated and refilled.

The garage was the closest of the outbuildings. The side door was unlocked. Several red-tipped prong holders were screwed into a two-by-four along the wall. One held a pointed shovel. He brought it to the mound and began digging.

The dirt, already loosened by the sheriff's team, was now muck, the heavy sludge of wet cement. Still, it took him only a couple of minutes to hit bone and just another to lift away enough to reveal a leg. It was about two feet long, and covered with fur. A dog, like the deputy had said.

He leaned on the shovel, staring down. No matter how beloved that pet might have been, its grave did not warrant McGarry coming out on two successive nights to sweep snow on to that dirt, nor to come out cradling a shotgun when Rigg approached the mound in daylight.

He dug around the entire animal. It was a collie. He shoveled around it until he was able to lever the stiff corpse up and on to the side of the shallow grave.

The dirt beneath the dog's grave was harder, but didn't seem as solidly frozen as it should have been that many weeks into winter. He poked at it carefully, digging up fist-sized chunks of dirt, bit by bit. He began sweating, despite the cold, but he kept shoveling, one small, careful bladeful at a time. And then an ear appeared and a patch of matted hair above it.

He shoveled back just enough dirt to cover it, dropped the shovel and went down to his car. He was trembling, whether from sweat or from fury, he did not know. He started the car, turned the heater on full blast and drove to the bar at the intersection down the highway.

He needed a drink, but he needed Pancho Rozakis more. He called him from the car. 'Meet me at the bar down the road from McGarry's estate. Bring every camera and drone you've got.'

He went inside. Only two people were at the bar – the dark-bearded bartender and a white-bearded fellow wearing denim overalls and a yellow-and-green DeKalb Corn cap. Rigg ordered a Scotch and took it to the farthest table, the same table where he'd sat with Aria.

Pancho Rozakis stepped in forty-two minutes later. He had a scruffy, untrimmed beard, like the denizens on either side of the bar, but there the similarities ended. Instead of thick denim and flannel to ward off the cold, Pancho wore his usual outfit of cargo shorts bulging with small gear, a tufted orange down jacket and a bright red Nebraska Cornhuskers ball cap.

'Greetings and salutations, stalwarts,' he said to the bartender and the customer, grinning as he headed to Rigg's table. 'Tell me again,' he said as he sat down.

Rigg told him what he'd told him from his car.

'Zowie,' the photographer said.

Rigg phoned the Winthrop County sheriff's department tip line and told the personable voice that answered that her sheriff hadn't dug deep enough at McGarry's estate and ought to get back there before the very human corpse the sheriff had missed got up and left. He clicked off and smiled at Pancho.

'I haven't had lunch,' the photographer said.

'My treat,' Rigg said. He got up, went to the bar, ordered the house specialty and, in less time than bagged food should need to become bacteria-free, he brought the puffed cellophane back to the table. He dropped it on the laminate like something snagged from a polluted river.

Pancho, who was known to eat anything, looked at the bag bloated with steam with alarm. 'What's inside?'

'It's been nuked and will squirm no longer.'

'Zowie,' Pancho said.

THIRTY-FIVE

Yellow cop tape was again strung across the gateposts and the driveway up to the house was again lined with official vehicles. But, this time, no cops were returning digging implements to their cars. And no one was guarding the gate. Rigg and Rozakis walked up the driveway.

Sheriff Olsen spotted them when they got up to McGarry's
Escalade. He charged across the broad back lawn, red faced. 'I could
arrest you for tampering with our crime scene,' he said to Rigg.

'That crime scene I discovered because you couldn't?'

The sheriff glared at Pancho, who'd begun snapping pictures of
him.

Rigg gestured toward the house. 'Have you begun to wonder why
nobody's around?'

'They're out,' the sheriff said.

'Tell yourself that this evening, or tomorrow, or the next day,
when no one has called to complain about you digging up the yard.'

'I told you: I called McGarry's office, talked to some assistant,
left a message that we have a warrant. They say they don't know
where he is.'

Pancho started to walk past the drive, toward the cluster of men
in back.

'Hold it!' Olsen yelled at him. 'No pictures.'

'He's got drones,' Rigg said. 'He can get what we need from up
above.'

'Ah, hell.' Olsen motioned for them to walk with him toward
the mound, but stopped a dozen yards short of the dig. 'Wait here,'
he said.

Several people surrounded the site. Two of them, crime-scene
technicians, were kneeling in the hole, hammering gently with
wide chisels and then using hand trowels to clear away the dirt
surrounding the body. Four sheriff's deputies stood watching,
farther back.

'What should we do with the dog, sir?' one of the deputies called
out.

'Put it in Rigg's car,' the sheriff said. 'Front seat, where it will
thaw when he turns on his heater.'

'Huh?' the deputy managed, clearly startled.

'Just put the damned thing aside!' the sheriff yelled.

The sky had darkened and a light snow began to fall. 'You said
you don't know this guy we're digging for?' Olsen asked.

'I won't be able to identify him,' Rigg said.

'Who will, then?'

'A husband and wife that own a diner on Chicago's old Skid
Row, and a cabbie.'

'They witnessed the bust?'

'No. Only two residents at a flop a few blocks away did, but they're on vacation.'

'What's that mean?'

'It's Cook County. Those two have disappeared.'

'Besides Lehman, who I expect to be uncooperative, McGarry should also be able to identify him,' Olsen said, looking straight at Rigg. 'This is his property, after all.'

Pancho Rozakis shook his head. 'Paris, France,' he said.

Olsen looked at the photographer, who was standing serene in cargo shorts, without a trace of the shivers. 'What?'

'Paris, France,' Pancho said. 'I followed him from here to O'Hare, slipped up behind him at the counter when he bought a ticket for that night's flight. I didn't buy a ticket for myself because Rigg here was too cheap to pay for international surveillance and, besides, I didn't pack a beret.' Pancho pulled his phone out of one of the many pockets in his shorts, brought up the picture of McGarry at the ticket counter and held it up for Olsen to see.

The sheriff turned to Rigg. 'What set McGarry running?'

'Me. I'd come here to show interest in his mound. He showed interest in me by waving a shotgun.'

Pancho held out a cell-phone photo of McGarry with the shotgun.

Olsen turned to look at the men circling the dig. 'He'd figured what's in the hole could stay hidden for all time, even if someone came digging.'

'Because they'd stop at the dog, like you did,' Rigg said.

'We're ready, Sheriff,' one of the forensics men called out, straightening up from the hole.

'Stay here,' Olsen said, and walked to the hole. He stared into it for a long minute and then turned around and waved for Rigg to come up. Even from a dozen yards away, Rigg could see the shock on the sheriff's face.

Pancho came too. 'No damn pictures,' Olsen said to him.

Pancho nodded and took another one, of Olsen looking at Rigg now with a slightly bemused expression.

Rigg looked down at the frozen face, contorted in fear, speckling fast with flakes of falling snow. He didn't know Richie Fernandez.

But this face he knew.

He stared at it, trying to understand how he could have gotten so much so wrong.

The sheriff took Rigg's elbow and guided him away so the body could be removed. 'Who's been fooled now, Rigg?'

Rigg turned to the closest forensics man. 'Cause of death of the dog?'

'Gunshot to the head.'

'How long do you think the dog's been dead?'

'Long enough to freeze solid.'

'Much longer than the man?'

'The man's more recent.'

'Cause of death gunshot, too?'

The forensics man shook his head. 'Blunt force trauma to the head.'

'Like from the blade of a shovel?' Rigg asked.

'Sure, but we need to examine to be certain.'

'Talk to me, Rigg,' Sheriff Olsen said.

It seemed so horribly clear. 'The first or second night I came out, McGarry must have spotted me watching him scooping snow on to this mound. He called Lehman to say I'd come snooping. They'd buried Fernandez deep, covered him with dirt and topped him with the dog to explain the grave if someone got too nosy. But their precautions didn't calm McGarry, roosting nervous out here by himself. He kept watch. And, when I came back during daylight, he waved his shotgun, but he knew that wouldn't be enough to keep people away. He panicked. When I left, he did, too. He took off for O'Hare. He must have called Lehman from there to tell him he was fleeing. Lehman couldn't let him go off wandering, even overseas. McGarry knew too much. So Lehman must have promised him he'd take care of everything, and picked him up at O'Hare.'

'Telling him they'd simply move Fernandez, replant the dog in the same place, and all would be well?' Olsen asked.

'Sure,' Rigg said, 'except, after they dug Fernandez up, Lehman whacked McGarry and put him in Fernandez's former place, under the dog.'

'No sense wasting a good hole,' Rozakis said.

Olsen shook his head. 'You know, when I first got tipped that the Fernandez fellow might be buried out here, I re-read your old posts in the *Examiner*, trying to figure how you could think McGarry would get involved with Lehman in the bust in the first place.'

'McGarry must have had dreams of a greater political future, and Lehman must have played on that.' Rigg waved his arm toward the vast expanse of the estate. 'What better place to soften up a suspect without the bother of booking him right away? No lawyers, no neighbors, nobody to interfere.'

'Lehman would have had to book him eventually,' Olsen said.

'He must have beat on him too much.' Rigg paused, remembering what Feldott had told him. 'Or maybe that was Lehman's plan all along. To kill Fernandez for his DNA.'

'You're not making sense,' Olsen said, but then his radio crackled. He listened and said, 'Let him through.' Turning to Rigg, he said, 'Can you sit on this until noon tomorrow? I'll hold a press conference then, but I'd like to search for Fernandez as much as I can before then.'

'You think you'll find him here, Sheriff?' Rigg asked.

Olsen looked startled. 'Why not?'

Rigg gave a shrug. McGarry's little mound had just taught him how wrong he could be. 'I get notified before other press if you find anything else here?'

'Fair enough.'

Corky Feldott hurried up to them. His grim smile disappeared when he looked down into the hole. When he looked up, he was wild-eyed.

Sheriff Olsen nodded down at the corpse. 'Stupid bastard,' he said.

THIRTY-SIX

He woke in the dark because, like so many nights, a hand beckoned. But it was not like the cage. This time, there was only one hand. And it was real.

'Sleeping on the floor excites my thinking,' she murmured.

'We're not on the floor. There's a mattress. It's a proper bed.'

'It's been a most improper bed for us.' She laughed low.

'You can't sleep?'

'I keep wondering what Glet knew,' she said.

'Something big, he called it,' Rigg said.

She snuggled closer. 'You really have no idea?'

'Not yet,' he said.

'But you know who might know?'

He lifted up on one elbow. 'Someone who was willing to interview Bobby Stemec's classmates. Someone who was willing to call Sheriff Olsen to request a dig.'

'Till.'

'He was amenable. He'd made an odd comment when I said that Glet might have taken Johnny Henderson's foreign DNA samples, and that Bobby Stemec's came back negative to Wilcox.'

'What?'

'He said that might make sense. He wouldn't elaborate.'

She snuggled closer, found his knee with a hand. 'Let's stop thinking.'

'I'm fully awake.'

She moved her hand beneath the covers. 'I'm like Glet,' she said.

'How?'

'I'm working something bigger, too.'

He went to her office doorway as soon as she got in. 'I meet with Feldott in an hour,' he said.

She'd gone home to change into gray tweed, and he had the thought that there was no color, no texture in which she looked anything less than stunning. The ever-present pearls helped, too. If ever there was a woman whose beauty and erect, confident bearing justified pearls, it was Aria Gamble.

She set down her purse and a tall Starbucks coffee. 'What's shakin'?'

'I called him first thing, asking for his take on what he saw at McGarry's estate yesterday.'

'Surely not first thing?' she said, lowering her voice. 'I know what you were doing first thing.'

He supposed he might have blushed. 'OK – second thing. I called second thing, after the first thing.'

She sat down, smiling, wicked and victorious.

'He's holding a news conference at four this afternoon, but he agreed to tip me beforehand. He's formally launching his own investigation into the murders of the Stemec Henderson boys, the Graves girls, Jennifer Ann Day and Tana Damm. And he's going to pursue the disappearance of a potentially key witness.'

'That's—'

'That's exactly what you were trying to goad him into with your piece in the paper,' he said. 'Congratulations are in order.'

She took a sip of the Starbucks. 'You're saying the lowly editor of the lowly supplement of the third-largest paper in Chicago has the muscle to move the CIB?'

'Maybe it's the pearls,' he said.

'It's the obvious, as you well know,' she said. 'The CIB dropped Feldott into the M.E.'s office for seasoning. With Lehman's future cloudy, his most senior deputy and McGarry both dead, it's time to move Cornelius into the limelight. The question is, when will people start thinking Lehman killed McGarry?' she asked.

'And Fernandez, of course?' he said.

She bowed her head in acquiescence. 'And Fernandez, of course, but Sheriff Olsen has to find him first.'

'He's going to have trouble,' Rigg said.

'Why? All he needs is recently broken ground.'

'It's just a hunch. Olsen's press conference is at noon. He'll announce McGarry's death, but won't say a word about Fernandez.'

'All he needs is recently broken ground,' she said again, 'and perhaps Cornelius. He'll push things into a higher gear.'

'The sky might be the limit if Feldott pulls all the killings together,' he said. 'Sheriff, then governor, then senator, maybe.'

'We'll support him,' she said.

'If we're around,' he said. 'How's Donovan's balloon?'

'Still set to pop if he doesn't get new money,' she said. 'Work Till, see if you can find out what Glet was up to.'

The Dead House was dead. No press was bustling about.

Feldott welcomed him right in. 'The Winthrop County medical examiner determined Mr McGarry died of blunt force trauma to the head.'

'So they said at the site,' Rigg said. 'Olsen called me as I was driving here. He's going to announce it straight: death by shovel blade.'

'The sheriff gave me the scenario you outlined about what could have triggered Sheriff Lehman to kill Mr McGarry. Will there ever be proof, even when Sheriff Olsen finds your Richie Fernandez?'

'Even *if* Olsen finds Fernandez,' Rigg said.

'What do you mean?'

'Risky, for Lehman to leave Fernandez on McGarry's estate.'

'My God, you think he took him?'

'Time, and a thaw, will tell,' Rigg said.

'What else do you know, Mr Rigg?'

'Glet was no suicide. His bungalow needs to be thoroughly examined.'

'You keep saying that.'

'That scene seems so staged, for one thing.'

'What else?' Feldott asked.

'Maybe the evidence that left there in your pocket.'

'How do—?'

'I saw a small evidence bag jammed in your coat.'

Feldott's face reddened. 'I didn't want it to get lost,' he said, but his lower lip was trembling. He was lying.

'Why would Lehman's people lose it?'

'Not now, Mr Rigg.'

'What was it?'

Feldott stood up. 'Cut me some slack, Mr Rigg. I'll tell you when I'm ready.'

'Ready about what?'

'I'll see you at four o'clock,' Feldott said.

Rigg called the sheriff's office before starting the car, doubting that Lehman would talk to him.

He doubted right. Lehman's secretary, a woman he'd pestered mercilessly during the shamble of the Stemec Henderson investigation, said that the sheriff was in meetings.

'Don't you want to know if I'd like to leave a message?' Rigg asked.

'Would you like to leave a message?' the secretary asked, with the warmth of granite.

'Just a request for comment on a rumor going around, really,' he said. 'If you could write it down exactly?'

'Just go ahead.'

'Ask Sheriff Lehman when he's going to confess to killing Charles McGarry and Richie Fernandez.'

THIRTY-SEVEN

MEDICAL EXAMINER McGARRY DEAD.
NINE OR TEN DEATHS RELATED?
Milo Rigg, *Chicago Examiner*

Cook County Medical Examiner Charles McGarry was found dead yesterday, buried on the grounds of his country estate, according to Winthrop County Sheriff James Olsen. The county's medical examiner is conducting an autopsy and is expected to release his complete findings in the next several days, but all signs point to death by blunt force trauma to the head. Investigators from several Cook County agencies are eagerly awaiting Sheriff Olsen's investigation, to see if McGarry's death links to their investigations into other recent killings.

Cook County Sheriff's Deputy Jerome Glet was found dead in his Chicago home three days earlier. At the time of his death, Glet was working closely with the Chicago branch of the Federal Bureau of Alcohol, Tobacco, Firearms and Explosives in its investigation of the activities of Kevin Wilcox, former manager of the Happy Times Stables of northwest Chicago. Wilcox is currently in federal custody, alleged to have been illegally selling firearms out of the stables. But, working on a lead developed by Deputy Glet, ATF personnel have found witnesses who place murdered Bobby Stemec, who was often accompanied by friends, at those same stables at the time Wilcox worked there. The three boys were found dead fifteen months ago, in a field two miles from the stables.

Glet was also believed to be assisting in investigating the recent murders of Beatrice and Priscilla Graves, Jennifer Ann Day and Tana Damm. Leading those investigations has been Cook County Sheriff Joseph Lehman, who, after making an initial arrest of Klaus Lanz in the Graves case, was identified by eyewitnesses as arresting another suspect in the same case, Richie Fernandez, in the company of McGarry. Fernandez was never booked. Both Lehman and McGarry denied arresting Fernandez. Fernandez's whereabouts are not known.

Sheriff Olsen said today that he regards the suburban McGarry estate as an active crime scene and is hopeful of recovering more evidence there in the coming days.

In another related development, it is expected that Acting Cook County Medical Examiner Cornelius Feldott will formally announce later this afternoon that he is launching his own series of investigations into the murders of the Stemec Henderson boys, the more recent killings of the Graves, Day and Damm girls, and perhaps the deaths of Deputy Glet and Medical Examiner McGarry. Feldott is strongly supported by members of the Citizens' Investigation Bureau, an ad hoc group of influential Chicagoans formed to spur progress in investigating the killings of the past fifteen months. Feldott is expected to assemble a small team of independent investigators to assist him in his inquiries.

'Whew!' Aria Gamble said. 'Still, it's more straightforward than your scarlet pieces on Stemec Henderson used to be.'

'I was enraged. I'm more meticulous now, like Feldott.'

'You implied that both the sheriff and the dead medical examiner are crooked. Did you really ask Lehman if he killed McGarry and Fernandez?'

'No. I asked his secretary to ask him that. And, you'll note, that's not in my piece. Sheriff Olsen's got to prove that out in Winthrop County, but, first, he's got to find Fernandez.'

'You keep saying that. Surely Lehman reburied him on the grounds right after he killed McGarry.'

'If it's that simple.'

'Surely you don't think he took him?'

He told her what he'd told Feldott. 'Risky, leaving Fernandez where he was sure to be found if McGarry was discovered.'

For a moment, she said nothing, then, 'Nothing new on Glet's fireworks?'

'Feldott tossed me a tantalizer. He admitted to taking evidence from Glet's bungalow, ostensibly to protect it.'

'Something to do with that shadow of a visitor at Glet's door?'

'He wouldn't say.'

'Do you still think Glet's visitor was the same person that hung around Carlotta's after dropping off the last card?'

'To take my picture? Sure.'

'Think those pictures will ever show up?' she asked.

'They'll show up when he thinks I'm getting too close. But, if Donovan's balloon pops before that, it won't matter.'

'We'll all be out of work,' she said.

Carlotta's place was changed. The snow had been freshly shoveled from her driveway, her car brushed clean and a realtor's *For Sale* sign was stuck in the middle of the front yard.

Carlotta had changed, too. She was outside, bundled up in a black ski jacket, hauling cartons out for garbage pickup. For the first time since her boys were killed, she'd attempted something with her appearance. Her hair was brushed, though lopsided at one side, and her lipstick was smeared at the corners of her mouth, but she was trying to regain control. It was an encouraging start.

'Milo,' she said, as he got out.

'Cleaning house?'

'Getting rid of the past and accepting what little I'll need in the future,' she said.

He nodded. He'd thought that way since Judith was killed.

'I stopped by to see if you've been keeping up with the news,' he said. 'There are new investigations.'

'Good leads?'

'Too soon to tell,' he said.

She smiled too little of a smile and walked into the garage to get more of her past to take to the curb.

He had the thought to call after her, to say getting rid of stuff wouldn't cut any pain, but those sorts of things were only learned in solitude.

A brand-new podium had been placed in the lobby of the Dead House. Corky Feldott strode up to it as confidently as a politician running unopposed for a tenth term.

Greg Theodore of the *Tribune* came up to stand beside Rigg at the back of the room. 'Hail, hail, the gang's all here,' he whispered. And they were. Two dozen reporters, including a full camera crew from WGN, Chicago's premier local station, stood clustered in front of the podium.

'I'll be brief,' Feldott began. 'As Winthrop County Sheriff Olsen reported earlier today, Cook County Medical Examiner Charles McGarry was discovered dead yesterday on his Winthrop County estate. Sheriff Olsen is conducting a thorough examination, but he did announce that Mr McGarry died of blunt force trauma to the head sometime in the last several days and was buried behind his house. A more thorough report will be issued in the next few days. Now,' he said, clearing his throat, 'as to the future of our department here, I have assumed its direct management. I will use all the resources we have at our disposal to initiate comprehensive investigations into the murders of the Stemec Henderson boys, the Graves sisters, Jennifer Ann Day, Tana Damm and, of course, Mr McGarry.'

'What about Glet?' someone shouted from the back of the room. 'Was he murdered, too?'

'That case is also under investigation.'

'Murder is what's being said. Somebody came to Glet's, right before he was killed.'

Feldott shot an angry look at Rigg. Rigg shook his head. He hadn't touted his thinking to anyone except Aria. But Glet's vigilant neighbor would have shared her description of Glet's visitor with any reporter she spotted stopping by.

'We've not substantiated that anyone visited Deputy Glet,' Feldott said.

It was premature. Feldott was publicly giving the visitor theory the dust without checking it out thoroughly – unless whatever Feldott lifted from the bungalow was evidence against it.

Theodore raised his hand. 'Are you looking into the disappearance of the Graves suspect, Richie Fernandez, that Rigg, here, keeps harping about?'

'We're conducting a wide-ranging series of investigations,' Feldott said.

'How does Lehman feel about you going off on your own?' another reporter asked.

'I assume the sheriff is glad to have more eyes on these killings.'

'Exactly how many eyes are you going to add?' Theodore asked. 'Your people are forensic, they evaluate. You have no investigators.'

Feldott gave him a smile, but nothing else. He raised his arm in a half wave and said, 'That's it for now. I'll be holding more brief-ings as new information comes in. Thank you for coming.'

And, with that, the much-in-control acting medical examiner left the reporters to their cameras and notepads.

Theodore turned to Rigg. 'I haven't gotten around to writing about you, Milo,' he said.

'Please tell me why I've been so blessed.'

'For one, I like your hounding. These girl murders have gone cold and, despite what the boy wonder just announced, they seem destined to stay cold. Everybody except you – and perhaps, now, Feldott – seems to have moved on.'

'And?'

'You might not be around long enough to matter. LaSalle Street says Donovan's other investors aren't stepping up to bail him out on his balloon payment. They want bankruptcy and liquidation to recover what they can.' Theodore patted him on the shoulder and walked away.

Rigg went out to his car. He was done for the day and, if Theodore was right, about to be done for longer than that. Yet, driving back to his apartment, he felt oddly at peace. He thought of Corky Feldott, relentlessly ambitious, tilting his lance at Lehman, seizing control of cooling cases, taking over the fight. Maybe Aria was right: maybe the lad would bring real justice to Cook County. And maybe that meant it was time for Rigg to step back and watch things from the sidelines. He thought of grabbing a burger at a fast-food franchise and looking for a comedy on television; he wanted to let his mind blank from thinking about anything at all.

Except that wasn't quite true. He wanted to think of Aria Gamble.

THIRTY-EIGHT

First thing the next morning, Rigg walked.

He walked a full block in each direction from Glet's bungalow, looking for security cameras that might have captured an image of his visitor. He saw none. He wasn't surprised. It wasn't that kind of neighborhood. The neighbors felt safe enough on their blocks or they didn't figure they had anything worth stealing.

He was just a hundred yards from getting back to his car when a dark sedan pulled up alongside him and the driver's window powered down.

'Looking for security cameras?' Corky Feldott asked.

Rigg nodded, stepping into the street.

'I already checked, Mr Rigg. There aren't any. Hop in.'

Rigg went around to the passenger's side. 'So, what are you doing here, Cornelius?'

'Hoping the sight of Glet's house will incite clarity.'

'About what?'

'About everything, about anything. But first, how did I do yesterday afternoon?'

'You projected confidence and control, probably just what the M.E.'s department needs at this moment.' It came out as pabulum, but it was probably true.

'I held back ninety percent of what I know or suspect,' Feldott said. 'I'm becoming a real pol.'

'Have you heard from Lehman?'

'Not a peep.'

'He should be enraged at your encroachment on his turf.'

'Then he should be getting angrier. I've gotten approval to hire two investigators. Regular investigators – former cops.'

'The Citizens' Investigation Bureau is funding?'

'For six months, but that's off the record. On another note, I talked to Sheriff Olsen this morning. Because McGarry's estate is so vast, he's going to wait for the snow to melt before looking for recently disturbed ground.'

'I suppose that's good,' Rigg said.

'Why so unenthusiastic? You still think Sheriff Lehman took Richie Fernandez away?'

'It would be prudent to remove any evidence the corpse might provide,' Rigg said.

'Sheriff Olsen said the best he can do is hourly drive-bys.'

'If I'm wrong, if Lehman reburied Fernandez on the estate, he can find him in the dark. As soon as any sheriff's headlights go away, he can haul him out of there.'

'I already thought of that,' Feldott said. 'The CIB has also approved my request to hire a private security firm. They'll be driving by more frequently.'

'It's wise.'

'I'll tell you what else seems wise. I'm beginning to share your belief that Richie Fernandez is the key to Deputy Glet's fireworks.'

'You want to see if Glet was worried that Fernandez's DNA was substituted for Bobby Stemec's foreign DNA in your freezer.'

'Yes. I think Deputy Glet saw Sheriff Lehman and Mr McGarry building a frame on Richie Fernandez, probably after they accidentally killed him,' Feldott said.

'Perhaps not accidentally,' Rigg said.

Feldott turned on the seat, startled. 'They killed Fernandez on purpose?'

'Lehman had no suspect for the girls and he saw the cases cooling, like Stemec Henderson. He must have been frantic, seeing himself being driven out of office by the likes of the CIB and you, Cornelius. And then he got tipped to Fernandez, living in a flophouse, a guy who was identified as being with the Graves girls by the owners of a diner. He enlisted McGarry to help in the arrest because he wanted to use his estate to sweat Fernandez with no interruptions. He must have realized almost right away Fernandez was no killer. Maybe he didn't mean to kill him, maybe he did, but he saw Fernandez would do just fine as a patsy, especially dead.'

'And, around that time, you reported back to Deputy Glet that Sheriff Lehman and Mr McGarry had arrested, but not booked, Richie Fernandez,' Feldott said. 'It's no wonder Deputy Glet snuck into our lab. He wanted to grab one of the Stemec Henderson samples for safekeeping before Mr McGarry could switch the foreign DNA.'

'Not for safekeeping, because he knew he'd be destroying its chain of custody and therefore its admissibility in court. Glet wanted its reassurance. He wanted to be sure he had the right guy, Kevin Wilcox, under wraps at ATF. It was a desperate move.'

'Sheriff Lehman didn't know about Wilcox at that point?' Feldott asked.

'No, and Glet wasn't yet ready to tell him. He wanted to know for sure that Wilcox did the boys.'

'And, once he began to suspect what Lehman and McGarry were up to – arresting but not booking Fernandez, likely to use his DNA – he saw his fireworks. Pretty amazing.'

'He must have foreseen Lehman saying he was about to book Fernandez when Fernandez escaped. Later, of course, Fernandez would be found long dead, well away from McGarry's estate. But Fernandez's DNA would be run against the Bobby Stemec foreign DNA sample, and there would be a match, thanks to McGarry. And that would tell the tale: the dead Fernandez had killed the boys. By implication, he'd be tagged for the girls as well.'

'I can imagine Sheriff Lehman's and Mr McGarry's shock and fear at Deputy Glet's first ATF presser when he announced he was confident Mr Wilcox killed the boys.'

'Maybe not,' Rigg said. 'Lehman and McGarry still controlled the situation. McGarry had to go through the motions of obtaining a swab from Wilcox and sending it out to be compared with Bobby Stemec's sample. It was no worry, because he knew there would be no match to the doctored Bobby's slide. Lehman and McGarry could still dismiss Wilcox and put the blame solidly on Richie Fernandez for the Stemec Henderson murders. And they could keep implying that he also did the girls.'

'What if the Johnny Henderson sample that Glet took showed up?'

'As I said, Cornelius, when Glet took it, he destroyed its chain of evidence. There could be no telling where the slide had been.'

Feldott stared ahead through the windshield. It was a lot to consider. But then he asked, 'So, who killed the girls, Mr Rigg?'

'I don't know if we'll ever know. The last of the birthmarks on the yellow card has been accounted for. Maybe that means the spree has been over since last December. But, if our killer does start up again, there'll be no way of telling if it's the same perpetrator. As you found, there've been no DNA traces on any of the girls.'

'So, you're pretty sure Sheriff Lehman got wise to what Deputy Glet was learning about their plans for Fernandez?' Feldott said.

'That would explain Lehman, or someone acting on his behalf, murdering Glet. And now, Cornelius, it's time to tell me what you found in Glet's bungalow.'

'Index cards,' Feldott said. 'A packet of one hundred yellow index cards. I counted them, with gloves on, of course, when I got back to the office. Three were missing.'

'Absent the two sent to Carlotta Henderson and one to the Day family? Isn't that too obvious?'

'They were wedged behind his desk. At first, I worried they'd disappear if Sheriff Lehman found them. He wouldn't want that stain on his department. The fingerprints of all sheriff's employees are in our databases. I had one of our technicians run the comparison.'

'They were Glet's prints?'

'Of course, and it seemed so obvious – too obvious. You kept saying the GSR on Deputy Glet was manipulated. So, too, could have been his fingerprints. Someone could have pressed the deputy's fingertips on to the card packet.'

'Any thoughts as to who killed him?' Rigg asked.

'As you suggest, it could have been any of a number of thugs who wanted to curry favor with Sheriff Lehman, someone who the sheriff is hounding for a murder or something. Quid pro quo: kill Deputy Glet, get a free pass to get out of town with no warrant for anything to follow.' Feldott sighed. 'If any of this gets released improperly, it will destroy people's faith in us at Cook County law enforcement.'

'I get what you're doing, Cornelius. You and the CIB are trying to restore the M.E.'s and then the sheriff's department, but you're going to have to go after Lehman to do that.'

'Allow me time to investigate everything, Mr Rigg. Ideally, we'll find leads to the girls' killer.'

'And pursue Wilcox for the boys.'

'I expect my new team to solidify the case against him. Just give me time.'

Till led him to a small conference room. 'What's too urgent to discuss on the phone?' he asked as they sat at the small table.

'I told you Glet took Johnny Henderson's foreign DNA sample from the M.E. lab,' Rigg said. 'You told me that might make sense, that you'd check it out and get back to me. You haven't gotten back to me. And now I've just spoken with Cornelius Feldott.'

'The kid who's taken over the medical examiner's office and soon the world.'

'He's got GSR that purports to show Glet was a suicide, and other evidence that shows Glet might have been involved in the girls' murders.'

'Too convenient?' Till said.

'He agrees everything could have been manipulated. But he and I have got questions about what Glet was doing with the missing DNA. And that, I think, is what you were going to get back to me on.'

'Glet asked if we ever used an independent lab for DNA testing, which we have, on occasion. I told him about Richmond Laboratories.

They mostly do paternity and ancestral stuff, but they're top-notch with everything.'

'He didn't say what he was up to?'

'No. As I've told you, we work our side of the street, he worked his. But he took his own swab from Wilcox, and, after a time, he became more persistent with him. He badgered him relentlessly, saying his DNA was found on the boys, trying to get him to confess.'

'But not the girls?'

'He tried, but as I said, Wilcox laughed; he could see Glet was bluffing. Hell, we could all see Glet was bluffing about the girls. After I told you that Glet's little theft might make sense, I called Richmond. They know me; they were candid. Glet came in twice. First, he brought in two samples to be compared to each other, a swab and a medical examiner's vial, neither labeled. The results matched. He paid five thousand dollars for that and told them to keep both the swab and the vial.' He paused. 'I had to wonder about a cheapskate like Glet shelling out five grand of his own money for that.'

'Lehman and his deputies have access to unlogged evidence money,' Rigg said.

Till smiled faintly. 'Ah, yes. Cook County.'

'That second time?'

'He brought in a soda can and a paper coffee cup.'

'To be compared with each other?' Rigg said.

'No. He wanted them kept safe until he returned with whatever he wanted them compared against, but he said it might be a while. He wanted them kept safe until he could return.'

'What was he waiting for?' Rigg asked.

'A new DNA sample to appear, obviously.'

'From a girl,' Rigg said. 'A girl yet to be discovered, a girl who would point to her killer or killers.'

'Killers whose DNA was on that can and that cup? Most likely we'll never know, Rigg. I don't have the authority to order them tested, and, even if I did, it would prove nothing.'

Outside, Rigg stood in the cold, indulging a thought, a long shot that had begun to form in his mind. And then he called Feldott, because there seemed nothing else to do.

'I have to believe Glet left traces,' Rigg said.

'What traces?'

'Traces – notes, memos, something – of those fireworks,' Rigg said.

THIRTY-NINE

The chirp of his cell phone echoed loudly off the cement walls of the parking garage.

'Mr Donovan will see you downtown,' the publisher's secretary said. 'Can you be here in one hour?'

'I'm already downtown. Shall we lunch in his office?' Rigg asked, but she hung up instead of answering.

Likely it was confirmation of what Aria had said and Greg Theodore had heard from his LaSalle Street contacts. The *Examiner* was turning *Titanic* and Milo Rigg would be one of the first to be slid off the deck. He killed time with a coffee at Starbucks, thinking about soda cans and other paper coffee cups, and got to Donovan's office at 12:45.

Donovan wasted no time. 'Our printing plant also does the *Curious Chicagoan*,' he said.

'And Christian membership directories and two porn magazines,' Rigg said, though the observation didn't appear to lighten the man's mood. His face stayed drawn, his eyes squinty, and Rigg had the insane thought that perhaps the desperate Donovan had been up all night rootling beneath his sofa cushions for lost pocket change.

'One of our more loyal production guys thought to grab this,' Donovan said. 'The *Curious Chicagoan*'s business people think differently than ours, that online will reduce print sales. So they've not posted this to their website yet.' He handed a sheet of copy entitled 'Primer's Take' to Rigg.

The *Curious Chicagoan*'s Primer, the sleaziest of their sleazy reporters, had breaking news:

BACK IN THE SADDLE AGAIN?

Used-to-be respected *Examiner* journalist Moral-Milo Rigg is back doing what got him in trouble following the murders of the Stemec Henderson boys. Remember how Rigg, the oh-so-pure voice of impatient conscience, castigated Cook

County Sheriff Slow-Go-Joe Lehman and Chief Medical Examiner No-Luck-Chuck McGarry for their turtle-like investigation that led to Nowheresville? That Moral-Milo? Loyal Readers of Primer's Take will remember pictures that showed Milo to be a Not-So-Moral Milo, nocturnally visiting Mother Victim Carlotta Henderson, former exotic dancer and belle of New Orleans' rentable ladies, so recently widowed after her husband keeled over on his youngest son's corpse at the county's Dead House. Following our scoop, Not-So-Moral Milo disappeared from view, banned to the hinterlands of the *Examiner's* ever-shrinking empire to write no-byline, less-than-mesmerizing paragraphs of bowling alley openings and Cub Scout parades.

As we've known for a couple of weeks now, Moral-Pretender Milo is back, rightly concerned about the latest horrors in Chicagoland's kill history, the murders of Beatrice and Priscilla Graves, Jennifer Ann Day and Tana Damm. Berating, as in days of old, Slow-Go and No-Luck for their dismal progress, and hinting that they've been perpetrators in nefarious goings-on in our Windy City, including the questioning and disappearance of a mysterious Graves suspect, Richie Fernandez. Now Lehman's deputy, Jerome Glet, has turned up dead of self-inflicted lead poisoning, followed to Croaksville by the aforementioned No-Luck, the late Charles McGarry, whose luck finally ran out in a grave in the back yard of his country estate.

And Not-So-Moral Milo? He's not had much to say about Glet, maybe because he's been too busy midnight-visiting the lovely Carlotta Henderson, as the photos below show. Doubt not, the pics are not oldies from the Stemec Henderson days. Check out the new set of old wheels the Moral Man is driving to those rendezvous. Current state license plate proves this is up-to-date evidence of up-to-date lust.

Damned shame on Milo and Carlotta for dirtying the current investigations!

'Look at that!' Donovan screamed as he pointed to one of the photos. 'The hand in the air?'

'It's more like just one finger.'

'You're ruining me!'

'I've understood,' Rigg said, a little surprised that Aria hadn't tipped Donovan to the pictures they both knew were coming.

His phone buzzed in his pocket. He let it go.

'Understood what, damn it?' Donovan said.

'I understand why Carlotta Henderson was tipped.'

'What the hell are you talking about?'

'I was set up,' Rigg said. 'She got key evidence. I went to her place to retrieve it and ultimately gave it to Lehman.'

'Aria told me about the cards.'

'They were sent to Carlotta Henderson to get me there to be photographed for just such a moment as this.'

His phone buzzed again. Something was urgent.

'Leave!' Donovan screamed. 'Leave here before people know you've been here. Do not go to the Pink. Go to whatever the hell rock you live under and stay there. I will continue to pay you to stay the hell out of sight, to keep your damned mouth shut, to not go to another paper, at least for now. Do not talk to anyone, do not profess your innocence or your beliefs or your stupidity. Get out!'

'You're going to pay me not to jostle any potential investors?' Rigg said, still sitting.

'Out!'

'I got set up to be silenced, Luther. That should concern you. As the publisher of a newspaper, rendering one of your reporters inoperative should concern the hell out of you.'

'Out!'

'It should concern the hell out of everybody,' Rigg said. He stood up and walked out.

His cell phone buzzed again as he passed Donovan's secretary. 'No lunch,' he said.

He took out his phone in the elevator but didn't recognize the number that had buzzed him so insistently, three times in the last ten minutes. Outside, he called the number but got no answer, and the voicemail at the other end had not been activated. It wasn't unusual; he'd often been tipped anonymously by people calling from burner phones.

He'd just pulled on to the expressway when his phone buzzed once more. It was the same number.

The voice was muffled. The caller was talking through Kleenex or thin cloth, just like in old movies. 'McGarry's estate, seven tonight;

wait an hour so I can be sure you're not followed.' The line clicked dead.

He called the Pink. Aria picked up. 'What the hell, Milo?'

'The day has not been without developments,' he said.

'Are you canned or just suspended or what? Donovan was frothing on the phone so much I couldn't understand him, other than to make out "the *Curious Chicagoan*".'

'The photos we've been waiting for are about to be published,' he said. 'I'm suspended for now, but I'll be fired if the *Examiner* somehow survives.'

'The killer is cleaning up,' she said.

'Exactly,' he said. 'The first card sent to Carlotta was meant to show, bona fides, that he was the real deal. The second sent to her was to draw me back for another photo, to show I made routine visits. Clever.'

'And the ransom note sent to the Day family?'

'That was the card sent at the beginning, the most horrible card of all. It was meant to show authenticity, I guess, validating that the two that would then be sent to Carlotta were genuine. I'll bet Jennifer Ann was already dead when her family got the card.'

'What makes you so important to the killers?' she asked.

'Killers, plural? Why do you think there are two?'

'I don't know,' she said. 'I guess I was thinking two were needed to heave each of the Graves girls up and over the guard rail, down into the ravine? This is so unnerving.'

'I'm important to the killers because I stuck with Stemec Henderson longer than anyone else. Silence me, maybe silence or at least slow the girls' investigation, not that anyone's been doing much anyway.'

'Cornelius Feldott won't be silenced.'

'He's hiring two investigators. And at last he's looking at Glet as something other than a suicide.'

'What changed his mind?'

'He found evidence in Glet's bungalow that could have been planted, making him wonder what else was staged.'

'My God.'

'You're the one who wrote Corky is methodical. He's being methodical,' he said.

'Let's have dinner,' she said.

'I have an appointment.' No good would be served if he told her about the phone call he'd just received. She'd want to come along and there was no knowing if an armed crazy had made it.

'I meant we could have dinner and . . .'

'Dinner and . . .?' he asked, but he knew. Absolutely, he knew.

'You seemed to enjoy that "and",' she said, her voice low. 'It could take your mind off things.'

'I do like that "and",' he said.

'So how about it?'

'I need to check something out.'

'I'll come along.'

'Maybe I'll call you later,' he said.

She laughed. 'And maybe I'll be waiting by the phone.'

McGarry's place was in darkness. Servants were no longer around to turn on lights since the master of the house had been found planted beneath the snow.

There were no automobiles on the highway or the side road. That wasn't necessarily a surprise, but Olsen's cops and Feldott's private security were sure to come along. Rigg wondered if his caller would get spooked and run.

He angle-parked on the shoulder of the side road and cut his engine. The moon was almost full, bright enough for him to see across the snow to where Charles McGarry, trucking company inheritor, political aspirant, murder victim and fool, had been shoveled into the ground he'd spent many of his father's millions to acquire. He'd been played for that ground, by a bastard sheriff that needed its quiet seclusion to sweat and perhaps purposefully kill a suspect.

He wondered, too, if he was being played by Lehman or the girls' killer to come out into the night – though, for what, he could not imagine. It was too much of a muddle. He'd wait the hour the caller requested and then leave.

He leaned back, let his mind drift on to the half-formed idea he'd blurted out at Feldott. Traces, he'd called them – traces of what Glet ought to have left behind, somewhere.

He ran the notion through his mind, again and again. It was all he had, all he could think to do.

He looked at his watch. Forty minutes had passed. No cars had passed by – no cops, no private security. It was enough. He'd been played again, to come, to sit in his car, to wait. But maybe not for nothing.

He smelled the Chinese food before he got up to his apartment.

She'd heard his footsteps and come to the top of the staircase. 'Dinner and "and"?' she asked.

'You must be cold. How long have you been waiting out here?'

She laughed. 'I just got here. I took a chance you'd be home.'

'I'm very hungry,' he said, pushing away the plan he'd begun imagining back at McGarry's estate.

She smiled.

Afterward, they ate as they'd eaten before, on the floor, leaned up against the seat cushions of the tiny love seat, and he told her about his afternoon and evening.

'I could try to change Donovan's mind . . .' she said, but she sounded doubtful.

'So I can go back to what I did with Benten? I write, you take the byline? No. I'm done at the *Examiner*.'

'It might not matter, if Donovan doesn't get his money. You're sure you have no ideas about your mysterious caller?'

'I can only think he got spooked. I sat in the car, I thought, and, forty minutes later, I drove away.'

'What did you think about?'

'What Glet left behind.'

She reached to squeeze his wrist. 'You found something at last?'

'I don't know,' he said. She couldn't be a part of a plan he didn't yet understand. She had a career to lose. A career with another paper, no doubt, but still a career. And there could be danger.

Her grip tightened on his wrist. 'What did you find?'

He put his hand over hers. 'Only musings of traces.'

'I don't understand.'

'Me, neither,' he said.

He looked at his wall of file boxes, the rows of files that had done him no good. And then he looked at her.

'You've done me good,' he said.

'Then let me do it again,' she said.

FORTY

They came for him before dawn, beating on his door, yelling for him to open up.

He found his pants on the floor, his shirt in the living room. He opened the door barefoot.

Four uniforms stood outside. Two Cook County sheriff's deputies, one Winthrop County deputy and Winthrop County Sheriff Olsen.

'Milo Rigg,' Olsen said.

'What the hell?'

'I'd like you to accompany us.'

Rigg rubbed his eyes, unsure if he was dreaming.

'Milo?' Aria appeared ten feet behind him, wearing one of his shirts and, most obviously, nothing else. Except her pearls. Always her pearls.

She was no dream. He turned back to Olsen. 'What the hell is going on?'

'With or without handcuffs?' Olsen said.

Aria walked up to stand next to Rigg. 'What's the damned charge?'

Olsen met her stare. 'You are?'

'An editor of the *Chicago Examiner*, in charge of making sure travesties get posted online immediately. What's the damned charge?'

'No formal charges yet,' Olsen said to Rigg, 'but, if we do file, it will be for arson, obstruction of justice, and destruction of evidence – and those are just for openers.'

'Whose fire?' Rigg asked, but it was for show. Now he understood the previous night's call.

'Cuffs, or no cuffs?' Olsen said.

'I need clothes,' Rigg said.

Aria, challenging, taunting, confronting, tousled and so obviously naked beneath Rigg's shirt, didn't step back from the cops when Rigg turned to go into the bedroom. The two Cook County deputies and Olsen stayed put – the deputies grinning, Olsen remaining taciturn. Only the Winthrop County deputy frowned, when he was directed to leave the view to follow Rigg.

Rigg found socks, shoes, a clean shirt and the small digital recorder he carried everywhere, and came back to the living room in two minutes.

There were two police cars parked down in the parking lot, neither with bubble lights flashing. Olsen gestured for Rigg to get in the back of the Winthrop County car, and then got in the front beside his driver. They followed the Cook County car around the building and on to the street.

'What fire?' Rigg asked again, because he supposed he should.

'Not without recording your statement,' Olsen said.

The drive was short. They parked in back of a Cook County sheriff's branch office and went inside. One of the Cook County uniforms pointed to a door and Olsen led Rigg inside. It contained a small laminate table pushed against one wall, and three plastic chairs. Rigg took one, Olsen another, and they were alone, except for whomever was watching behind the mirrored glass on the wall.

Olsen took a small digital recorder from his pocket, identified himself, Rigg, the date and time, and began. 'Mr Milo Rigg has voluntarily agreed to be interviewed. Is that correct, Mr Rigg?'

Rigg took out his own digital recorder, switched it on and set it on the table. 'What fire?'

'Where were you last night?' Olsen asked.

'At my apartment, with a guest who will testify to that.'

'Let me be more precise. Where were you last evening, in the early evening hours before ten o'clock?'

Rigg smiled at the small camera mounted on the ceiling and turned back to Olsen. 'A muffled voice called, telling me to drive to McGarry's estate and wait. I did. I parked so I could see the ground where you couldn't find McGarry unassisted.'

'No idea who called?'

'The fire was at McGarry's, right? A fine, destructive fire?'

'You were seen at the property.'

'I saw none of your officers driving by, as you said they would, nor did I see the private security Corky Feldott hired. Whoever buried Fernandez, if indeed he remains buried on McGarry's estate, could have been working a bulldozer and your people would have missed the abduction of evidence.'

'You're not very observant. One of my deputies was pulled off, down the highway.'

'Then he can attest to my being parked along the side road for forty minutes, and that I then left without doing anything.'

'Just two outbuildings were torched,' Olsen said.

'Obviously not to destroy Richie Fernandez.'

Olsen nodded. 'No corpse was found.'

'Whoever killed Fernandez – think Lehman – wouldn't need to burn buildings to destroy the corpse. He'd already know where Fernandez's body was, there or somewhere else. There was another motive for last night, which was to get me spotted out there immediately before the fire was noticed – but you knew that, Sheriff.'

'What aren't you telling me, Rigg?'

'How to do your job, to begin with. Don't wait for the snow to melt. Find Fernandez's body or satisfy yourself that he's not there. If he's not, be on the alert for a John Doe corpse to show up somewhere. And then find proof that Lehman killed him.'

'You used to be hell-bent on getting us to dig for Fernandez at McGarry's. Now you're telling us he's not there?'

'McGarry's emergence from the ground changed my thinking. He had to be silenced. He was put where Fernandez had been, but Fernandez could be more useful if he was discovered somewhere else. His DNA will match to something placed on Bobby Stemec's foreign DNA in the Cook County medical examiner's office. Fortunately, that won't let Kevin Wilcox off the hook for the boys' murders. There's testimony that places Stemec, at least, at the stables, where he traded work for rides.'

'So Lehman wasn't your caller?'

'It was someone else, someone with different motives.'

'Who?'

'I'm getting close,' Rigg said.

'Close to what?'

'Traces.' There was no doubt: the word was growing on him.

Olsen gave it up. He and his deputy drove Rigg home in silence. As Rigg got out, Olsen powered down his passenger window. 'Keep an eye out,' he said.

Rigg nodded. 'I think the killings of the girls have stopped. They served their purpose.'

'What purpose?'

'I don't know, but I am sure their murderer wants no more risk. He wants things tidied and done.'

'That's you, Rigg. He wants you tidied and done,' Olsen said.

'Not if there are traces,' Rigg said, voicing what was growing stronger in his mind.

'What are these traces you keep mentioning?'

'Glet must have left traces of what he knew.'

Olsen signaled his deputy to pull away.

Two hours had passed. Aria was gone, but traces of her remained. She'd made his bed and tossed his old shirt in the hamper, but the shirt she'd worn so fetchingly that morning was carefully laid out on the bedspread, as if to signal that she expected to return soon.

He felt a flicker of joy, the first he'd felt since before Judith was killed. But then he felt guilty. Feeling joy was disloyalty.

The chant of an old Beatles song began playing in his head, something about life going on. Now it came mockingly, asking him to choose between memories of the past or hopes for the present. He pushed the song away.

He set water on the stove to boil and opened the cabinet for a cup. They'd bought a set of six, each in a different color, right after they married. It occurred to him now that he'd only ever used the yellow one and Judith had only ever used the green. The rest – the red, the orange, the blue and the white – had always been pushed against the back of the cabinet, unnecessary and unneeded, because they'd never had anyone over to their apartment. Always, they were each other's best company.

Aria had tidied the cups. She'd pulled them all forward, the used among the never used, and aligned them neatly in a row with their handles pointed outward. He reached up, pushed the green one, Judith's cup, to the back of the shelf where it could not be seen. The day was to be the first day of his exile from the *Examiner*, and so, perhaps, it should be a day of other new beginnings.

The kettle whistled. He reached past his usual yellow cup and took down the orange one. New beginnings. He took the coffee to the love seat to consider again what he'd hinted to Feldott, Aria and now to Olsen. Surely there must be traces – notes or documents – of what had excited Glet. Almost certainly there'd been the Richmond Labs' DNA confirmation of Wilcox as the boys' murderer. It had made Glet confident that Wilcox was the boys' killer. But if Glet had left any trace or proof of that, it had not yet surfaced.

And then Glet had brought in a soda pop can and a paper cup for later analysis. And that was what puzzled. Rigg had searched

Glet's house and his car, but found nothing, though that might have meant only that Lehman had found things and that they were now locked away. Traces of those might be impossible to find.

But nobody needed to know that.

He finished his coffee and went down to his car.

FORTY-ONE

He called the Pink before he got on the expressway.

'Milo, I . . . I . . .' Eleanor stammered.

He managed what he hoped was a reassuring laugh. The word of his exile was out, though he doubted Aria had tipped anyone that he'd been snagged for questioning that morning.

'A mere pebble on the rocky road of life,' he said, and asked to speak to Aria.

She picked up immediately. 'Arson?'

'Two of McGarry's outbuildings were torched last night.'

She inhaled sharply. 'Lehman, destroying evidence of Richie Fernandez?'

'No. Even if Richie Fernandez is still buried at McGarry's, Lehman would know exactly where and wouldn't need to torch multiple buildings to destroy the body. Plus, he wouldn't want to draw new attention to the site.'

'You still believe Lehman took Fernandez away.'

'To resurface later. His DNA can still be compared to the Stemec slide.'

'Who set the fires?'

'Somebody who panicked. I have no motive to torch anything. I got hauled in this morning only because Olsen wanted to know what I know.'

'You're sure you have no idea who called you?'

'Only that it was the girls' killer, desperate to divert attention.'

'About what?'

'Traces I'm uncovering,' Rigg said. It was not yet a lie.

'You keep saying "traces". What traces?'

'Just pass that on to Donovan,' Rigg said, shamefully sure that she had to be used like everyone else. Everyone had to be played to get one person to believe. 'Tell him I'm going to make Glet speak from the grave.'

'He won't publish you, because of the *Curious Chicagoan* photos.'

'Someone else will. Tell him that, too.'

'Damn it, Milo. What have you got?'

'Not until it's all exposed.'

'Give it up, Milo, for your own safety,' she said, her voice rising.

'It's almost over,' he said, because, for the first time, he thought he knew just how to make that happen.

He drove to the Kellington Arms, not so much because he expected to find new witnesses to the Fernandez bust, but because he wanted to kill what was left of the afternoon without thinking anymore of what he planned to do.

A new desk man was dozing at the counter, two new denizens slept upright on the two lobby chairs. Rigg headed upstairs. Just Wally was long gone, likely to another of the flops in Chicago. Rigg peeked in his room anyway, but it was empty except for the stained mattress and box spring leaned against the wall, and whatever lived within them.

He worked the floors, spent the afternoon and the first part of the evening going up and down the halls, tapping gently on doors and asking those who answered if they knew Richie Fernandez. He struck out, door after door. In the vernacular of the neighborhood, nobody knew nothing.

He hadn't eaten all day. He drove to the Rail-Vu.

'Trouble?' Blanchie asked, thirty minutes later. 'You've been frowning at your laptop the whole time.'

'Always trouble, Blanchie,' he said. He'd combed the Internet for any fresh mention of the girls' murders, but the cases had gone as cold as Fernandez. With Glet dead and Corky Feldott not yet started up, the case was in a dead zone.

She took away his untouched hamburger. There was always trouble enough to go around. He headed home.

Turning down the one-way street to come into the parking lot from behind, he caught movement on his top-floor landing. He killed his lights, pulled to the curb and leaned forward to see through the windshield. The new exterior light bulbs were too dim to illuminate much beyond creating faint, long shadows, but it was enough. One of the shadows outside his apartment door was moving.

He eased his car door open, got out and ran in a crouch to the parking lot and the car parked closest to the back of the central staircase.

Footsteps padded softly, coming down, and then they went silent. The shadow had gone through the walkway to the front and out to the sidewalk.

Rigg followed to the front and peeked out. A hunched figure was hurrying away. Rigg got to the sidewalk just as the shadow turned into the darkness of the next side street. He ran down the sidewalk, his footsteps muffled by the thin blanket of snow still covering the cement, and got to the next corner just as headlamps appeared from midway down the block. He ducked into the shadows of the building on the corner. The car came up, blew through the stop sign and drove east, toward the city. It was a dark car, a four-door Chevrolet Impala sedan. It had no markings on its doors, no extraneous trim on its side, but it was the sort of sedan that was used by Cook County officials.

Like a cop's.

Traces. Someone might already have believed.

He went back to his building and up the stairs. His door was locked, but a cop would know how to pick a lock and then to remember to reset it.

The place looked as it always did, stripped of almost everything that reminded him of Judith. It would have been easy to search without leaving a trace – search for the traces Rigg had begun saying that Glet left behind. He'd told it to Feldott, who would have passed it on to Lehman and any number of other co-workers and cops. He'd told it to Sheriff Olsen, who could have passed it along, unknowingly, as well. He'd even told it to Aria. Any number of people now knew about the traces Rigg was supposedly on the verge of discovering. It was his hope. And now someone had come, risking exposure to find out what Rigg had found. That had been his hope, too.

He hurried through his apartment to be sure. His dresser, his socks, underwear and white shirts looked undisturbed. His suit and black tie hung neatly in their usual place – orphans, not used since his wife's funeral.

The kitchen was as he'd left it. The four mugs that Aria had so neatly aligned remained as they'd been, up front, their handles in perfect symmetry. The green cup – Judith's cup – was farther back, where he'd pushed it, out of sight. The orange cup he'd used that morning was where he'd left it on the counter.

It was the living room that had changed. The top two rows of file boxes were too neatly aligned, resting too precisely on top of the ones below. They'd been searched, for traces. Nothing had been found. That did not mean that someone would not come again, someone who knew how to beat information out of people.

And there was something else. His visitor had come out just as Rigg was approaching the parking lot. Such a close escape could have been lucky timing.

Or not.

His apartment was no longer safe. He threw clothes in a duffel, drove to a Walmart that was open all night, and sat in his car in the parking lot to think, and maybe to sleep.

FORTY-TWO

Carlotta's first yellow card nagged during the night. That it listed the marks on all four girls was necessary to establish the credibility of the sender as their killer. But Anthony Henderson was from another time, another killer. His birthmark didn't belong on that list, except to link the murders of the boys to the killings of the girls. The sender had wanted credit for both sets of murders, but the sender hadn't known about Wilcox when he delivered the first card to Carlotta.

Rigg could only think that pointed to Lehman and McGarry; McGarry had had access to both the boys and the girls in the morgue. They'd set off to frame Fernandez first for the boys, and likely then for the girls.

Unless it pointed to someone who set out to frame *them*.

He worked that theory on and off during the night but could make no sense of it.

He'd thought of other things that night, too – things he could make more sense of, things he could plan. By eight o'clock the next morning, Rigg was sure there was only one next step. He called Pancho Rozakis and then he drove into the city.

He knew the war zones south of the Congress Expressway from years of reporting. He knew about the eyes beneath the hoodies on the corners and the other eyes behind the drawn curtains in the houses that still remained. He knew that all those eyes would take him for law; stupid law to be coming so early. It couldn't be helped. What he was seeking was gotten best in the dark, but that wasn't one of his options. Things had accelerated; traces were feared. What he needed, he needed fast, without paperwork, identification – and without questions.

He bought it at a corner, a kid's personal piece. A nine-millimeter Glock with two extra clips. The kid, no more than fifteen, but wiser to the ways of the neighborhood than Rigg could ever be, gave him a hard look. 'Ever shoot one of these, man?'

'Sure,' Rigg said, but it had only been once, and that was for a story. It had scared him.

'Don't make no difference,' the kid said. And that was the truth of the transaction, the way of so many such transactions in Chicago, the way so many bullets got fired so easily and so randomly, sometimes finding people merely laughing on an expressway, hundreds of yards away.

He called Greg Theodore before he walked across the street to the Dead House. 'Glet was murdered,' Rigg said.

'Who did it?'

'Not quite ready to say,' Rigg said, like he knew.

'But you know?'

'Glet was chasing something huge.'

'So he kept saying. Do you know what that was?'

'Not quite ready to say about that, either,' Rigg said.

'But bigger than Stemec Henderson, the girls, and that Richie Fernandez you've been harping about? Why are you calling me?'

'I lost my trumpet. I'm done at the *Examiner*. Donovan won't publish me.'

'Those pictures of you in this morning's *Curious Chicagoan* at the hot Mrs Henderson's? You were set up. Maybe we could give you a freelance trumpet here at the *Trib*.'

'I think McGarry had money in the *Examiner*,' Rigg said.

'I heard that,' Theodore said, sounding not surprised, 'but I can't get confirmation.'

'Not important. Glet's the story. He left traces.'

'Of his fireworks case?'

'People are already coming after me for what I know. Yours to use, Greg, just not until after noon.'

'I'm being used?' Theodore asked.

'More to follow,' Rigg said, and clicked him away. He crossed the street.

'I think Mr Feldott is in conference,' Beige Jane at the front desk said.

'Try him anyway,' he said.

She checked and told Rigg the department secretary said he could go up. Rigg moved toward the stairs, but got snagged by a thought before he got to the first step. He turned around. Jane at the desk was busy on the phone. He walked straight ahead, went through the swinging doors and took the stairs down to the basement.

He'd never been down there. The morgue was on the first floor, the offices were on the second. But the basement was reserved for storage. All sorts of storage.

A corridor ran down the center, lined on both sides by the same beige cinderblocks that lined the first floor. The doors in the basement were much more utilitarian, made of gray steel with identifications stenciled in red letters, all connoting what was being kept behind them. Most had ordinary, key-locking doorknobs, but the one marked *Specimen* had a hefty bronze keypad lock attached to it.

'Help you?' a male voice asked, irritated and sounding not at all eager to help.

Rigg turned. A short, bald man in a white lab coat, black trousers and gray athletic shoes had come up.

'Cornelius Feldott,' Rigg said.

'You're two floors too low,' the man said. 'Take the stairs you came down on. Keep going up.'

'That door marked *Specimen* – is that for DNA storage?'

'Take the stairs you shouldn't have come down on. Keep going up.'

Rigg took the stairs he came down on and kept going up.

Feldott met him at the top of the stairs. A slender, bright orange necktie descended down his blue, spread-collared shirt.

'I was getting worried, Mr Rigg,' he said. 'I was told you'd be right up.'

'Curiosity got the better of me. I went down to the basement.'

'Not very comfortable down there.'

'That door marked *Specimen* – is that where the DNA samples are kept?'

'Have I heard right, that you're done at the *Examiner*?' Feldott asked as he led them down the hall.

Word had indeed traveled. 'I'm tidying up,' Rigg said. 'That *Specimen* door?'

'Yes, yes,' Feldott said, stopping at a different door. He'd moved into McGarry's old office. Rigg had only been in the office three or four times, but what he remembered most was its barrenness. No papers had lain on the mahogany back credenza. No papers, pens or pencils lay scattered on the matching desk. It had been the office of a man with nothing to do except wait for better opportunities, and, as McGarry had undoubtedly learned, to do as he was told.

Feldott was waiting for nothing. Two leather cups held pens and pencils, four piles of papers were neatly stacked on his desk. A laptop computer was open on the back credenza, below the antique Northwestern University print.

'You cleaned him out quickly,' Rigg said.

'Sadly, there wasn't much to clean out, though I doubt we'll ever completely clean away the stain of him.' He sat behind the desk, Rigg sat opposite. 'Sheriff Olsen called me yesterday morning. Woke me up, actually. He told me about the fire at Mr McGarry's estate. He wanted to know if you were capable of such a thing, but he didn't sound serious.'

'I got an anonymous phone call to go out there. I parked, waited, and was noticed by one of Olsen's deputies staying in my car, doing nothing. The fire started right after I left.'

'By whoever called you?'

'It was a clumsy, desperate attempt to get me blamed for destroying evidence of killing Richie Fernandez, I suppose, put in play by someone who fears what I know. I didn't notice any of your security personnel.'

'There was a mix-up. They didn't work that night,' Feldott said. 'Anything new on those traces from Glet?'

'I found three pages of scribbled shorthand, torn from a wirebound notebook, taped beneath a drawer. I have to decode them.' He'd decided to keep the lie vague. Specifics might trip it up.

'What do they say?'

'As I said, they're coded – some numbers, some jumbled letters, no whole words,' Rigg said.

'Want me to have a look at it?'

'I'm headed to my dune to try to figure it all out. Glet was a simple man. It shouldn't be hard.' He paused, then said, 'I suppose you'll have to tell Lehman.'

'He's in charge. He'll want those pages.'

'I'll hand them over when I come back.' Rigg stood up, looked around the office. 'Folks wondered why a hugely wealthy fellow like McGarry would leave his money machine to become county medical examiner. I guess he was after power, aiming for a seat on the county board, and, from there, the mayor's office or the state house.'

'He thought wrong, poor fellow,' Feldott said, standing too.

'The CIB has put you in motion toward the sheriff's department, Cornelius. Be careful of Lehman.'

'I may be starting my own investigation, but he's still the sheriff. I have to tell him about those notes you found.'

Rigg wondered, now, if Corky understood. It was why he had come.

Pancho Rozakis had texted while Rigg was in Feldott's office: *Three units in the trees, motion-activated by larger, human-sized shapes. Batteries good for three days. Recorder underneath the caboose. Driving back now.*

He'd lied a little to Greg Theodore and a lot to Corky Feldott. There was one more lie to make. He called the sheriff's headquarters. 'Milo Rigg for Sheriff Lehman,' he said, not expecting to be put through, because the sheriff would already be on the phone, taking Feldott's call.

But Lehman, and perhaps Feldott, by not calling him right away, surprised him. Lehman picked up. 'Arson, these days, Rigg?'

'I'll bet Sheriff Olsen had more to say than that, Sheriff.'

'He told me you think I killed some mysterious witness—'

'Richie Fernandez, to be precise,' Rigg interrupted.

Lehman tried a laugh. 'A mysterious witness that nobody has heard of but you.'

'And everybody who's read me in the *Examiner*. And Olsen – I also told him you killed McGarry, but I'm not calling for a comment. I want to give you a heads-up for what Feldott will confirm. Glet left traces.' Rigg was beginning to love the word. It was so perfectly innocuous and vague.

'Traces of what?'

'Actually, they're more than traces. He left behind coded notes.' He hung up. Lehman would call Feldott.

And he'd hear of the dunes.

FORTY-THREE

R igg got the text message while he was still in Illinois, stuck in traffic heading eastbound on the tollway. Theodore's piece had posted on the *Trib*'s website. Rigg exited the snarl to read it.

GLET RUMBLES, RIGG TUMBLES, DONOVAN FUMBLES, EXAMINER CRUMBLES?
Greg Theodore, *Chicago Tribune*

Milo Rigg, the *Chicago Examiner*'s on-again, off-again premier crime reporter, is apparently off-again, suspended following the *Curious Chicagoan*'s publication of purportedly licentious photographs showing Rigg leaving the home of Carlotta Henderson in the wee hours of a couple of recent mornings. Mrs Henderson is the mother of brothers John and Anthony Henderson, who were found murdered, along with Bobby Stemec, in a forest preserve along the Des Plaines River fifteen months ago. Kevin Wilcox, manager of the nearby Happy Times Stables, is currently under federal arrest for gun charges, but is expected to be charged with the boys' murders soon.

Rigg, viewed by many as overzealous in his criticism of the murder investigation back then, was transferred a year ago from the *Examiner*'s downtown offices to its supplement's suburban outpost following the scandal that ensued over the *Chicagoan*'s publication of almost identical photos of him leaving the Henderson house. Rigg, very recently widowed back then, was rumored to have wasted no time in carrying on with the comely Mrs Henderson. In a brief phone interview this morning, Rigg stated that he'd never had an affair with Mrs Henderson and that now he'd been set up to be silenced about what he's learned of recently deceased Cook County Deputy Sheriff Jerome Glet's investigation into the Stemec Henderson murders and of other matters of corruption and county foul play—

His phone chirped before he was done reading. 'Greg Theodore just posted a piece on the *Trib*'s website,' Aria said.

'"Rumbles, tumbles, fumbles and crumbles"?' Rigg forced a laugh to sound unconcerned. 'I'm reading it now.'

'Theodore says you've got secret documents that will crack all sorts of things wide open.' She was in her car. He could hear traffic noise.

He held his phone out the window so she could hear his traffic noise, too.

'Cornelius Feldott said you're heading to your dune to decipher them,' she said.

'Why are you talking to Corky?'

'I'm doing a piece on him,' she said. 'Bring the notes in. We'll figure them out together.'

'I had a visitor, a surreptitious sort in the kind of car cops drive. He searched my apartment.'

'Lehman?'

'I don't think my apartment's safe,' he said.

'Bring those damn notes in, Milo. We'll decipher them and then you'll be safe.'

'Maybe tomorrow. I need to figure them out, and I need to think.'

'Think? Think about what?'

'Basement door locks,' he said.

'You're not making sense. Lehman will come for you. It will be bombs away. You understand, right? Bombs away?'

'Bombs away, indeed,' he said, for it was what he hoped, but it was to a dead phone. She'd hung up.

He pulled back on to the tollway, slogged through another forty minutes of early rush-hour congestion into Indiana, and exited on to Route 12. He and Judith had always loved the way the old, narrow, two-lane blacktop followed the curve of the dunes and the tall grass beneath the southern edge of Lake Michigan. They'd marveled at the change of colors in the trees, season to season, and laughed at how they had to dodge and weave along the ancient bumpy surface that only rarely got repaved, and then only in spots. They'd delighted in imagining the history of that long-ago bootleggers' route, the fear drivers must have felt almost a hundred years before, running hootch in the darkness from Canada into Chicago, eyes peeled for hijackers hiding in the tall grass. But, most of all, they loved the anticipation of getting to their odd little caboose some dreamer had seen fit to drag up on to a dune. It had been well over two years since Judith had been cut down by a random bullet, two years since he'd felt nothing but despair as he drove along the old route, accompanied only by memories that blurred his eyes with tears, two years of being sure he'd never feel hope again.

And then had come Aria, and now, doubts about yellow cards miraculously discovered, and basement door locks on specimen freezers, and paper coffee cups and soda pop cans left at a DNA lab. Now, he wasn't sure about anything.

He arrived while it was still light enough to see. He'd been gone just over two weeks, but January had changed the landscape as it changed into February. The dunes were thawing. The ice running inward across the frozen water of the small lake at the base of his dune still looked to be thick, but now there was a small hole in the center. And the snow that had cast a pristine blanket over the dunes was turning to heavy slush, toppling branches into tangled litters on the ground, unremoved because there was nobody left to remove them. It was what the ecologist sought when they'd scraped away the old cottages to revert the dunes to their natural marshland.

Their dune was just beyond the eastern edge of the Great Marsh Project and they'd taken comfort in that, believing that the caboose would be theirs for a long lifetime. They'd figured wrong, then. Now, as the sun was beginning to sink behind the trees, Rigg supposed he might have been figuring wrong about all sorts of things.

He left his car at the sweep-out at the base of the ancient, railroad tie stairs, where it would be easily seen, and climbed up to the caboose. He took little time inside. He wouldn't run his generator to power the lights to show that he was home. It would make too much noise and he needed to hear. He refilled their six oil lamps, lit them and placed them by windows, so they would light the ground around the caboose enough to be seen by Pancho's cameras. He only needed a snippet of video, a fast clip of breaking and entering, coming for Glet's traces.

The ramshackle woodshed was twenty feet from the door. It was small, the size of a privy, but he and Judith had spent an entire weekend strapping it together from fallen tree limbs and branches, laughing at its crooked rusticity when they were done. They filled it with more fallen wood they cut to fit the tiny pot-bellied wood-burning stove that heated the caboose. They'd joked they had enough to heat the caboose for a lifetime.

The shapes of the surrounding trees were now smudging into blackness, darkening the road below the dune into invisibility. He hurried to pull out the wood at the very back, the first that he and Judith had cut, and began restacking it toward the front. It took but a few minutes to create enough space at the back to hide. He was cold, despite the three layers of fleece beneath his down jacket. He would get colder, waiting. It was the only thing left to do.

An automobile engine sounded somewhere far off. Headlights flickered through the trees and then switched off, but the engine grew louder. The car was being run without lights – dangerous in the deserted, branch-littered roads. No benign driver would take that risk.

The engine stopped. He strained to listen, but heard no car door open and ease shut. The car was likely too far away, down by the shore of the mostly frozen lake.

He hurried to slip behind the stacks of wood, moving a few more pieces so he could see out. The glow from the oil lamps cast the ground around the caboose in light bright enough to see. Two of Pancho's three cameras were aimed at the door. With luck, the break-in would be quick, a fast look around to see that there was nothing inside, but the image would remain in Pancho's cameras, damning enough to expose.

The dune had gone silent. No bird chirped, no raccoon rustled. The creatures knew that someone was on the move at the base of the dune.

He took the Glock from his pocket and rested it in his hand on top of the wood. With luck, he would not be seen. With no luck, he would have to fire.

Footfalls began beating slowly up the slush on the railroad-tie steps. The climb was long. It took a couple of minutes. And then shadows reached into the light cast from the caboose.

They were two, both shrouded, both wearing hoodies and long coats. It was no surprise, not after seeing the solid keypad lock on the specimen-room door, not after accepting that his intruder had not been merely lucky to get out of his apartment just in time. There'd been an accomplice, a lookout who'd spotted Rigg pulling up. They'd gotten nothing from Rigg's apartment. Now they'd come to his dune.

He crouched lower behind the stacked wood. Pancho's cameras would record their faces as they tried the door, found it locked. They'd knock. There would be no answer. They'd have to break in. It would all be caught by the cameras.

They stepped farther into the light. He'd feared them for having drawn guns, but their arms were low at their sides. He sucked in his breath. Each was carrying two red plastic, five-gallon gasoline cans. Soft thuds sounded as they set them down in the snow.

Twenty gallons of gasoline would turn the caboose into a pyre that would burn to nothing in minutes. The dunes were deserted, the surrounding cottages scraped and gone. Even if somebody did spot the fire through the barren trees from a distance, it would take at least a half-hour for the fire department to respond, and that would be futile, anyway. The caboose was high up. No fire nozzle from a truck had force enough to reach the top of the dune.

The Glock shook in his hand. The caboose was Judith's, the only place where he could still smell her perfume, the only place from which he could retrace their steps to Lake Michigan to hear her laughter in the sound of the waves.

They bent to uncap the gasoline. They thought he was inside. It would go down as murder by arson, by nameless perpetrators who would never be found. They would get away long before anyone came to those deserted dunes.

They splashed the gas against the aged wood by the door, the stench fouling the air. Rigg pushed his way out of the rickety shed, aiming his gun at the taller of the two.

'Damn you!' he shouted.

They both spun to the sound of his voice. The hand of the taller reached into a coat pocket.

The other jumped in front of the taller shadow.

The taller's gun fired, and fired once more. The smaller shadow slumped.

Rigg fired once, and again, and again, each pull of the trigger kicking the Glock up wildly until the clip was empty and the night went silent.

FORTY-FOUR

The thaw had warmed much of the Midwest, from Ohio to well west of Winthrop County. Warm for late February, the weather people said.

Revealing, Sheriff Olsen hoped. He deployed a dozen of his men to McGarry's estate. Four of them had cadaver-sniffing dogs. The thaw had melted the snow, showing no place where dirt had been disturbed. Richie Fernandez was not there.

Four days later, a body was spotted caught in a dam along the Rock River, just a few miles north of McGarry's estate. The cold had preserved him. He was about five foot six and dressed in stained, worn blue work pants and a brown plaid flannel shirt with a torn chest pocket. He was unshaven. His face was black and blue and contorted. He'd been beaten. He'd died screaming.

Winthrop County's medical examiner supervised the extraction. The man's rigor had undoubtedly relaxed, but the cold kept him stiff. He was placed in a beige vinyl body bag and taken away in an ambulance.

'We can only hope his DNA is in the database. If not, he might be Richie Doe, dead at the hands of persons unknown, for forever,' Olsen had said when he called Rigg.

'You'll have an artist's sketch.'

'Of course,' Olsen said. And so it went. He let Rigg tag along when, at Rigg's insistence, he brought the sketch to the diner, though he told him to wait by the door.

'Richie Fernandez,' Gus the grill man said.

'Richie Fernandez,' Lucille agreed.

Just Wally had moved out, of course, and no one else at the Kellington Arms admitted to knowing Richie Fernandez. The woman at Apex Screw Products wouldn't look at Rigg as she swore to Olsen that she'd never seen the man in the sketch. Rocco Enrice had quit his apartment and stopped driving a cab.

Two days later, the Winthrop County medical examiner issued a finding that, although the dead man's DNA was not found in any government or ancestral databases, a sketch of him was tentatively identified as Richie Fernandez by the owners of a Chicago diner. He'd been submerged too long in the river to offer anything like foreign DNA to point to whoever had beaten him to death.

Equally disappointing, the Winthrop County M.E. had previously issued a separate statement that no usable foreign DNA had been found on the body of Charles McGarry, the Cook County medical examiner who'd been found buried on his own estate.

'And, no, although I tried,' Till said, calling Rigg a couple of days after Fernandez was discovered.

'No, what?' Rigg asked, faking dumb.

'No to Lehman's DNA being on that soda pop can or Starbucks cup Glet brought to the Richmond lab.'

'Now that you mention it . . .' Rigg said, because it was expected.

'You knew I'd check.'

'Of course,' Rigg said.

Till chuckled. 'No match to either. Glet's samples belong to two other people.'

Rigg then had to ask, 'They've not been run through any other databases?'

'No,' Till said. 'I have no authority to do so.'

'All right, then,' Rigg said, because it was quite all right.

'What are you doing these days, Rigg, now that your paper's gone down?'

'Looking for work,' Rigg lied. His apartment was paid up through the rest of February and there was still several months left of Judith's insurance money. And that was all right for the time being.

Lehman resigned, citing health issues, and said he was going to enjoy his county pension in Florida. No mention was made of prosecuting him for the murder of Richie Fernandez, since the only link between them was in the statements of a grill cook and his wife, saying only that Lehman had come around with McGarry seeking the whereabouts of Fernandez.

Similarly, the state's attorney for Winthrop County didn't bother to announce that no evidence had been found to prosecute anyone in the bludgeoning death of Charles McGarry.

As Glet had insisted, proximity continued to figure into the case against Kevin Wilcox for the murders of Bobby Stemec and John and Anthony Henderson. The Happy Times Stables where Wilcox worked was less than two miles from where the boys' bodies were discovered. But it was the depositions of several of Stemec's classmates saying they'd gone with him to the stables, and that he often brought friends there, that triggered Wilcox's indictment for the boys' murders. The state's attorney dismissed rumors of previous claims by Sheriff's Deputy Jerome Glet that DNA linked Wilcox to at least one of the boys, saying that Johnny Henderson's foreign DNA sample was missing and that the remaining sample, that taken from Bobby Stemec, had been tested previously, but had not been matched to anyone. He stated that prosecution of Wilcox for the killings would be deferred until he was tried in federal court on the charges of unlawful gun sales.

Without Lehman and Glet, the Cook County sheriff's department went rudderless. The investigations into the murders of the Graves girls, Jennifer Ann Day and Tana Damm lapsed and slipped from public notice, trumped by the fresher horrific murders that occurred most every day in Chicago.

The Acting Cook County medical examiner, Cornelius Feldott, had gotten the final word on Jerome Glet's death, writing in the case file that the gunshot residue found on Glet's sleeve and the position of the body clearly pointed to suicide. He noted, too, that a packet of yellow index cards, identical to those sent to Carlotta Henderson and the Day family, was found in Glet's bungalow, but stopped short of concluding that the packet in any way pointed to Glet's involvement in the girls' killings.

These were Feldott's last recorded words. He'd vanished. Staffers from the medical examiner's office found his condominium to be as if he'd just left it to go out. His closets were full, his official, dark county sedan was parked in its designated space. Speculation ran that he'd been killed, perhaps bludgeoned like his boss, Charles McGarry.

Rigg had written none of it. The *Examiner* tumbled after Donovan failed to meet his balloon payment, and neither of the two remaining queens had called, requesting Rigg to freelance on the boys' or the girls' murders, or the mysterious deaths of Glet, McGarry or Richie Fernandez. The photos the *Curious Chicagoan* had run looked to have rendered him permanently toxic to what remained of journalism in Chicago.

That was fine. He stayed in his apartment for the rest of February, venturing out only to take long walks in a wooded forest preserve, shop for groceries, eat occasionally at the Rail-Vu and, one time, to accompany Sheriff Olsen into the city to secure Gus and Lucille's identification of Fernandez in the police sketch.

He ventured out, too, to visit the campus of Northwestern University, where he spent parts of three days.

On the last day of February, he took his mattress down to the dumpster and threw it on top of his boxes of files, the love seat and his kitchen table and chair. He put his few clothes and the yellow coffee cup he almost always used and the green one of Judith's into his car and vacated his apartment to face, at last, the dunes that he'd fled on that horrible night.

FORTY-FIVE

Greg Theodore showed up on the second Wednesday of March. 'I never figured you for having the patience of a fisherman,' he yelled from the shore.

Rigg waved, laid the bamboo pole into the rubber dinghy and lowered his hands so that Theodore couldn't see him undo the sixty yards of weighted, marked line that he then jammed wet into the pocket of his parka. He knew this day could come if some reporter looked hard enough. And Greg Theodore was one of those that always looked hard enough.

He struggled as always to row the unwieldy dinghy toward the shore. When he got close, he threw the rope to Theodore, who by then was bent over with laughter at the sight of Rigg thrashing to keep the bobbing dinghy in a straight line.

'I never catch much, but I find the process calming,' Rigg said, as Theodore pulled him on to the muck of the shore and tied the rope to a tree.

'You don't answer your phone and your voicemail is full.'

'I'll have to fix that,' Rigg said, thinking to do no such thing. He'd put the phone into a drawer the instant he'd returned to the dunes and hadn't brought it out since.

Theodore pointed to the caboose sitting high and bright red through the trees. 'Your mansion?'

'I'll make us coffee.' Rigg led him up the railroad-tie stairs, because there was no alternative. Theodore had not come for an idle chat. He'd learned something that now needed to be deflected.

'Compact, but extremely nifty,' Theodore said, as he sat at the small banquette in the corner of the tiny galley kitchen.

Rigg added grounds and water to the coffee maker. 'The guy who dragged this thing up set it perfectly level on deep concrete piers. We fitted it with the oak cabinetry in here, the bath and the sitting area, and built the bunkbeds in the hall.'

'A flower, even,' Theodore said, pointing to the little white plastic daisy at the center of the table.

'Judith's,' Rigg lied. He'd bought the thing at a gas station – not for its plastic flower, but for its fake green grass and red plastic pot – on his way back from the jeweler in Grand Rapids the week before.

'Surprisingly roomy,' Theodore went on, still looking around, taking his time.

'It's sometimes too big,' Rigg said.

'What happened to the guy that dragged it up here?' Theodore asked.

'He died – collapsed in a food store, two miles from here. Never got to enjoy the place much.'

'And then you and Judith bought it.'

And then she died, having never gotten to enjoy the place much either, but there was no need to give that words. Rigg filled two cups and brought them to the table. 'What's up?' he asked, to spur things along.

'A former colleague at the *Trib* teaches at Medill,' Theodore said, naming Northwestern's journalism school. 'He'd heard you were interviewing professors at the college who knew Aria Gamble.'

Rigg shrugged, as he'd planned. 'The *Examiner* had shut down. She was my boss; I couldn't reach her. I figured she'd connected with someone where she went to school.'

'I found three professors you talked to. They said you also asked about Corky.'

'He's an alumnus as well. And he'd become huge news.'

'And you were investigating because, in your heart, you're still a reporter, no matter that you'd lost your trumpet even before the *Examiner* went down?' Theodore's eyes were goading.

'I told you, I was looking for Aria—'

'That's crap, Rigg. You figured they disappeared together.'

Rigg met Theodore's eyes, struggling to not grab the plastic daisy he'd so stupidly left in the middle of the table and set it out of reach. 'I admit I wondered if there was a connection.'

'The most interesting professor I found had both Corky and Aria in his undergraduate twentieth-century history class,' Theodore said. 'He said they were driven, relentless and brilliant. They paired up for their term paper.'

'Leopold and Loeb,' Rigg said, because Theodore already knew.

'Nathan Leopold and Richard Loeb. Another brilliant pair, back in the 1920s. They killed a boy, Bobby Franks, just to see if they could get away with committing the perfect crime.'

'Not so perfect,' Rigg said. 'They got caught.'

'The professor told you that Corky and Aria were particularly interested in how those two young geniuses screwed up.'

Rigg had known he'd have to give up something, if someone like Theodore came around. 'I think Feldott killed Glet,' he said.

'Corky Feldott, boy wonder, darling of the CIB, a killer?'

'I think he killed the girls, too, in one fast, vicious spurt at the end of December. It was a sick career move. I think he wanted to be seen riding in on a white horse to solve the cases.'

Theodore leaned back, unsurprised. 'Let's take this one step at a time,' he said. 'The two girls at the diner weren't the Graves sisters, right?'

Rigg shook his head. 'They were just another couple of lost girls, runaways probably. I'm pretty sure the Graves sisters and Jennifer Ann Day and Tana Damm were all snatched off sidewalks near their homes. It wouldn't have been hard to do. I saw dashboard flashers on Feldott's county car. He could have pulled up, showed his badge, and ordered them to get in on some pretext or another.'

'An ME's badge, not a cop's?'

'What teenaged girl is going to inspect a badge? They complied. They got in.'

'And were frozen to death,' Theodore said, more to himself than to Rigg.

'Or decapitated, to muddy things up,' Rigg said. 'Sick, sick bastard.'

'All so he could burnish his reputation as CIB's superstar sleuth?'

'He was a sick young man in a sick, sick hurry to show himself as solving the cases.'

'But to do that, he needed someone to pin the killings on. Enter Glet?'

'I don't think Feldott marked him as a patsy at first,' Rigg said. 'That came later, well after Glet approached Feldott for help in protecting the Stemec Henderson foreign DNA samples. Unbeknownst to anyone but ATF, Glet was working Kevin Wilcox as the boys' killer. He needed to protect the Stemec Henderson foreign DNA from Lehman and McGarry.'

'As you were inferring in your reporting of their scheme to frame Richie Fernandez for the girls' and maybe the boys' killings.'

'Glet needed access to the specimen lab at the Dead House. That room has a thick keypad lock, the kind that can't be picked. Someone had to let him in and so he approached Feldott, tipped him that he was afraid McGarry would switch Fernandez's DNA in for Wilcox's, and asked him to give him one of the boys' slides.'

'Why would Feldott do that?'

'Because, once exposed, McGarry would be out of the picture and Feldott could take over the county medical officer's job. Plus, Feldott could position himself as having helped to bust the whole enterprise. Both furthered his chief objective of catapulting his career, maybe to sheriff if Lehman was also knocked out of the picture, maybe beyond.'

'What about chain of custody of the Henderson boy's original foreign DNA?'

'I'll bet Feldott promised Glet he'd vouch for its security in being transferred to the Richmond lab.'

'Fernandez wasn't Glet's fireworks,' Theodore said.

'Feldott was, and that led to Glet's death. Glet got wise, somehow, to Feldott's being behind the girls' murders, and Feldott got wise to Glet getting wise. Maybe it was from a change in Glet's attitude, maybe it was from something Glet let slip. Whatever it was, it presented Feldott with both a chance to eliminate a threat and an opportunity. Killing Glet would get rid of the threat of exposure and give Feldott someone he could make a patsy to frame for the girls' murders.'

'What tipped you to Feldott?'

'Nothing fast and nothing for certain,' Rigg said, reminding himself to be careful to not say too much. 'The morning I discovered Glet's body, I saw Feldott leave Glet's bungalow with an evidence bag jammed very conspicuously in his coat pocket, just begging for me to question. Feldott took his time, acted appropriately reluctant, but finally he told me it was a packet of yellow index cards of the same type used to send a ransom note to the Day family and two elsewhere.'

'What do you mean, "elsewhere"?'

'Carlotta Henderson,' Rigg said. 'They were meant for me, to be photographed picking them up. I passed them on to Lehman.'

'What did they contain besides Glet's fingerprints pressed on by his dead hand?'

'A listing of body identifiers on too many of the victims.'

'What does that mean?'

'It means one of the cards listed not only identifiers for three of the four girls, but also one for Anthony Henderson, and that took me too long to understand.'

Theodore leaned back, puzzled.

'Anthony's birthmark was listed to point to the same killer for both the boys and the girls,' Rigg said.

'Or . . .?' Theodore let the question dangle unfinished.

'Or it pointed to someone who had access to the bodies of both the boys and the girls.'

'Like someone who worked at the Dead House. Like Feldott,' Theodore said.

Rigg nodded. 'It was stupid, including Anthony, but Feldott must have thought that he was invincible.'

'Superior intelligence, like Leopold and Loeb,' Theodore said.

'Furthering that, he must have thought the gods of evil were smiling down on him when McGarry was found dead and Lehman was being whispered about as being the killer.'

'With both of them gone, and Glet dead of a supposed suicide, the path was clear for the kid to become medical examiner and then, with CIB's support, perhaps the interim sheriff.' Theodore looked at Rigg. 'Catapulted, just like you said.'

'Feldott was – is – a clever fellow.' Rigg looked away, hoping Theodore had missed it. But Theodore had not.

'Was?' Theodore asked. 'Past tense?'

'Slip of the tongue,' Rigg said.

'Gutsy kid, that's for sure,' Theodore said, reaching for the plastic daisy.

Rigg got to it first, pulled it back to hold in both hands. 'Gutsy killer, you mean.'

Theodore nodded. 'Aria Gamble's admiring pieces fed Corky's

burgeoning rise . . .' he said, leaving the suggestion for Rigg to pick up.

'She's rich enough to take a little vacation, Greg. Her pearls alone were worth a fortune, maybe as much as seventy-five thousand.'

'Or?'

'Or she discovered his plan, confronted him and he killed her,' Rigg said.

'There's a third possibility, Milo. She was in on it and now she's running with him,' he said. 'Living on what they could get for her pearls.'

Rigg said nothing. He'd ventured too much already.

'It wasn't just Glet that found out Corky's plan, was it, Milo?'

'What do you mean?' Rigg asked in what he hoped was a steady voice.

'You, Milo. You found him out.'

'Not in time,' Rigg lied. 'I only guessed at most of it, and just recently. Up here, when I had time to think.'

'Something set the two of them to running,' Theodore said. 'Glet was already dead, so he was no longer a threat. I'm guessing it was you who panicked them to leaving everything behind and taking off in her car. They're together, but one thing's bothering me.'

'And that is? Rigg asked, because it was expected.

'Why didn't they come after you like they did Glet?'

'Perhaps it was too late. They had to get away fast. Her car's noticeable. Maybe it will turn up.'

Theodore leaned back, struggling to find conclusions. 'They're running together, or he killed her, as you suggested. Either way, someone's getting by just fine on what came from hocking those pearls?'

'Big bucks – seventy-five grand, she said.' Rigg turned to look out the window, down to the little lake. The surface had completely thawed; the thick ice that had run out to the hole in the center had long since melted away.

'We're left with only speculation?' Theodore asked, standing up.

'Only speculation,' Rigg said, relaxing his grip on the little plastic flower pot and standing up too.

FORTY-SIX

The *Chicago Tribune* ran Theodore's speculation on the following Sunday's front page. That was rare. Their front page was for hard news, not for something so clearly labeled as conjecture. But interest in the disappearance of the rising star of Chicago law enforcement had remained fevered; many saw young Cornelius Feldott as the only hope to rise from the muck to cleanse Cook County. Theodore's Sunday piece shattered all that.

He'd opened with the few facts:

When Cornelius Feldott, an always punctual young man, failed to show up for work or answer his phone, his staff became worried. Police were called, a wellness check was conducted. Nothing appeared to be missing from his apartment, and his county car, a black Chevrolet Impala, was parked in the complex's garage. It was as if he'd just gone out for a walk. But Cornelius Feldott was nowhere to be found.

Enter the mysterious complication of the beautiful Aria Gamble, an editor of the *Chicago Examiner*. Unnoticed in the recent collapse of that paper, when all of its employees were let go and there was no co-worker to report her missing, Miss Gamble had disappeared, too. Like Feldott, her apartment was undisturbed, appearing as though she'd stepped out for a short time. Unlike Feldott, her car, a tiny red MINI Cooper, was missing from her apartment's assigned parking space.

Intriguingly, while the two seemed to have had no visible association in their recent lives, professors at Northwestern University confirmed that they were very close as undergraduates. And Gamble's recent praise in support of Feldott is indisputable. She'd written several laudatory profiles of the rising young medical examiner, as if to help his career.

For now, these few facts are all that is known. But Milo Rigg, formerly the premier investigative reporter and crime columnist for the *Chicago Examiner*, suspects much more. He postulates a theory about the disappearances of Cornelius

Feldott and Aria Gamble, theorizing that the closeness they developed as Northwestern undergraduates led Gamble to suspect Feldott of plotting murders that would propel him into prominence in Cook County government. Rigg wonders – this is his pure speculation – if Feldott killed Beatrice and Priscilla Graves, Jennifer Ann Day and Tana Damm to set himself up to appear to solve the murders by falsely accusing Cook County Deputy Sheriff Jerome Glet of the killings after Glet was found dead, purportedly of a self-inflicted gunshot, in his Chicago home. Perhaps furthering this, alleged evidence of his involvement in the girls' murders was purportedly discovered by Feldott at Glet's home – evidence that Feldott himself may have planted, according to Rigg. Rigg believes Feldott may have had another motive for killing Glet besides needing a fall guy, namely fearing that the deputy had uncovered his scheme. Rigg believes it's possible that Gamble discovered all this and that Feldott killed Gamble when she confronted him with her suspicions.

Rigg also wonders if his relentless investigation into the disappearance of a suspect in the Graves murders, Richie Fernandez – who was later found dead in the Rock River, several miles north of Charles McGarry's Winthrop County estate – figures into the still-unsolved Stemec Henderson murders and the more recent killings of the girls. His reporting alleged that former Cook County sheriff, Joseph Lehman, had arrested Fernandez shortly before his disappearance, but no evidence has been found linking the sheriff to Fernandez's death. He also alleged that former Cook County medical examiner, Charles McGarry, later found buried on his country estate, accompanied Lehman during the Fernandez arrest.

Milo Rigg admits he is conflicted about the futures of the cases involving the recent murders of the girls and Charles McGarry, the ambiguous circumstances surrounding the deaths of Jerome Glet and Richie Fernandez, and the disappearance of his former boss, Aria Gamble. He stresses that his theories are speculative and not based upon known facts. Moreover, even if guilty of any crimes, he's not confident that Cornelius Feldott will ever face justice. 'He's cunning, clever and perhaps on the run. He'll know how to cover his tracks. He might have hidden Gamble's car after killing her and changed his appearance. Certainly, the pearl necklace she wore every day

was the real thing, likely to fetch Feldott enough money to
fund a long, long run from the law.'

Rigg closed his laptop. It was a relief. Theodore's nose was good,
but it had not been good enough.

He looked out the window, down to the small lake at the base
of the dune, recalling again that snippet of conversation from years
earlier. 'Pure silt, slushy compost if you will,' the field ecologist
had told him and Judith. 'Young bucks back in the day used to race
in circles on the ice – race, that is, until they hit a soft spot . . .
cars still sinking . . . ought to be coming out of the other side of
the world any day.'

He didn't want to remember, but he thought he might have been
screaming that as a mantra that panicked night in February, as he
crept the little car in low gear across the thick ice, until he was
close enough to put it in neutral, jump out and, with a last tug on
the transmission lever from outside, send it toward the hole in the
ice in the center of the lake.

It bobbed after it hit the water, bouncing in the splash of the
waves it had set off. Rigg stared, transfixed, at the cavorting coffin-
thing, horrified that the corpses of the shooter and the woman who,
at the last minute, had tried to stop him, would clamber out and
thrash their way to the safety of the edge of the ice. But, at last,
the tiny MINI Cooper settled as the water calmed, and then it sank.

Still, he remained immobile on the shore, weighted too heavily
by too many realizations to move. Perhaps his gut had known even
if his mind had rejected: Aria had been in it from the beginning,
conspiring with Corky to fuel his rise. She'd been too laudatory
about him and too relentlessly inquisitive about Glet's fireworks.
She'd played Luther Donovan to get assigned to the Pink, to get
too close to the *Examiner's* only reporter covering the girls' killings.
She'd played Rigg for sure, with her beauty and her wiles, to know
what he knew and what he supposed he knew, to keep tabs, to report
back to Corky. And then, when he'd tipped her offhandedly about
Glet's bringing DNA on a soda pop can and a paper coffee cup to
the Richmond lab – her DNA, Corky's DNA – they'd had to act.
They'd already gone for Glet, and when Rigg began talking about
having discovered traces Glet had left behind that pointed to the
identity of the murderer of the girls, his fireworks, she'd come with
Corky to the dune to kill again.

But in her last instant, she'd lunged to save Rigg. She'd caught Feldott's first bullets, giving Rigg time to fire back, to squeeze the trigger again and again until his clip was empty and Feldott lay dead like Aria on the ground.

He wondered then, there on that shore, if the enigma that was Aria Gamble would come for him in the nights, beckoning from behind flat bars, from a new black cage. He wondered if he'd ever understand, but there was no knowing that, not then, and so he'd gone back up the dune and torn the cameras from the trees. Then he stayed up all night, watching the lake down below shimmer in the moonlight until the dawn came, searching for any glimmer of red beneath the surface of the water in the middle of the ice. But there was none. Finally he drove back to his apartment outside Chicago.

Now, five weeks later, on a Sunday in mid-March, he dared to hope that Gregory's piece in the *Trib* might end it. The girls', Glet's, Fernandez's and McGarry's murders would never be officially solved. Lehman would bask in Florida, Aria would always be disappeared and Corky Feldott would forever be on the run. But a sort of justice for the girls and Glet had been rendered on the top of his dune – a justice rendered in a panic and only reflexively, to be sure, but it had been a justice, nonetheless.

There would be justice of a sort for the Stemec Henderson boys too, he hoped. Glet was dead and had left no usable evidence against Kevin Wilcox behind. But there would be punishment. The federal gun case against Wilcox looked solid, and would almost certainly result in a conviction and a long prison sentence.

Now there remained only the last pearl.

He reached for the little plastic flower pot he'd clutched before Theodore could touch it. Rigg had cursed himself at that moment, for, if Theodore had picked it up, however innocently, he would have wondered about the rattle in the bottom of the plastic pot. If he'd poked a finger beneath the little plastic flower to see what caused it, Rigg could have been indicted for murder.

The glint of the pearls torn from her as she fell, lying scattered down the dune, had stopped his breath when he finally returned to his caboose, late in the morning of the last day of February. Frantic, he'd scrambled down to scoop them up and jam them in his pocket. And then he drove, as he'd planned for days, to a sporting-goods store in Michigan City to buy the bamboo fishing pole for pretense, a line to weight and mark off in five-foot increments, and the rubber dinghy, for, by then, weeks had passed and the small lake had thawed. Rigg rowed his new dinghy to the center of the lake that afternoon.

'What goes to the bottom keeps descending?' Judith had asked.

'All is welcomed,' the field ecologist had said.

Rigg dropped the plastic bag of pearls and sand overboard and eased the weighted end of the marked line in after it. Anyone watching would notice the bamboo pole and think he was merely fishing. He located the metal roof – a hard spot, five feet higher than the surrounding silt. He'd paid out forty-nine feet.

He rowed out every day, after that. As the small lake warmed, the silt grew more welcoming. The hard spot at the bottom of the lake settled more. By the second Wednesday in March, when Greg Theodore came out, the top of the car was down to a depth of fifty-four feet.

Now, on Sunday, there was one thing left to do. He put the lone pearl he'd been saving, for reasons he did not quite understand, into the small jar he'd filled with sand.

'Paste, but good paste,' the jeweler in Grand Rapids had called it. Rigg had driven all the way up there to be sure no one near the dunes would know.

'The string is broken,' Rigg said, as it surely was when she lunged to stop the bullet meant for him.

'The value of a whole necklace would be a thousand dollars, no more,' the jeweler said.

Rigg thanked the jeweler, put the last pearl in his pocket and walked out into the sunshine. He'd had the thought to toss it into one of the city's garbage receptacles on the street, but it didn't seem fitting. And so he'd brought it back to the caboose, kept it safe at the bottom of the little plastic flower pot, hoping it might nudge him into understanding. The woman had schemed horribly, perhaps even helped to kill. But, in her last instant, she'd saved his life.

He supposed he'd have to add that question to the other torments he'd struggle with for the rest of his life, but that was not for now. He rowed to the center of the lake, found the hard spot. It was fifty-six feet down, that Sunday.

He eased the little jar into the water and let it go. It would drop to the car and the other pearls, and keep settling for forever beside the enigma of the woman he'd once thought he might learn to love.

For Susan

For what was,

For what is,

For what will be,

For forever.